William Phillips Tilden

William Phillips Tilden

Autobiography and Personal Tributes

William Phillips Tilden

William Phillips Tilden
Autobiography and Personal Tributes

ISBN/EAN: 9783337015145

Printed in Europe, USA, Canada, Australia, Japan

Cover: Foto ©Raphael Reischuk / pixelio.de

More available books at **www.hansebooks.com**

WILLIAM PHILLIPS TILDEN

Autobiography

AND

Personal Tributes

PRINTED, NOT PUBLISHED

BOSTON
PRESS OF GEO. H. ELLIS, 141 FRANKLIN STREET
1891

THIS VOLUME HAS BEEN PREPARED FOR THE FAMILY
AND NEAREST FRIENDS.

CONTENTS.

AUTOBIOGRAPHY

I.

ANCESTRY.

HAVING passed my seventy-seventh birth anniversary, I have thought it might be well, while enjoying a fair degree of memory and strength, to jot down some of the incidents of my long and somewhat varied life.

I do this particularly for my children and grandchildren and hoped for great-great-grandchildren, thinking it possible that many years hence, when I shall be to them only a memory or a tradition, they may like on some stormy day, when they have nothing else to do, to look it over, and possibly talk about it to their children and children's children.

First, let me say a word of the old town in which I was born, and tell you something of our ancestors as far back as we can trace them.

Scituate is one of the old towns of Plymouth County, Massachusetts. It borders on Massachusetts Bay, has a coast line of seven or eight miles, and is about halfway from Boston to Plymouth. Its aboriginal name was "Satuit," the name of a brook that empties into the harbor. It means "cold brook." That is the way the town is spelled in the earliest records. Shortly after it was written "Seteat," then "Cittewat." But about 1640 the orthography was settled as "Scituate."

The town was settled very early. It opened unusual facilities through its harbor and the North River, which formed the southern boundary line, for commerce, fishing, and ship-building. These have been its leading industries from the beginning until fifty years ago, when all three began to decline.

But, when I was a boy, the North River was lined with ship-yards, and the harbor filled with fishing vessels and coasters. The first ship that visited the Northwest coast from this country was built on the North River in 1774. She was called the "Columbia," and commanded by Captain Kendrick, who explored the river Oregon, and renamed it after his ship "Columbia." It still retains both names.

Among the earliest settlers of Scituate was Nathaniel Tilden, who came from England with his family before 1628. Just how long before is not known. But in this year the old records tell of large tracts of land sold by Henry Merritt to Nathaniel Tilden, showing that he was a man of means. He was from Tenterden in the county of Kent. Other gentlemen came with him from the same place, and they were called "the men of Kent." The first street laid out was called "Kent Street." This was near the harbor. On this street Nathaniel Tilden lived. A few years later he was chosen "Ruling Elder" of the first church in Scituate, and after that is known as Elder Nathaniel Tilden. All his children were born in England. Their names were Joseph, Thomas, Mary, Sarah, Judith, Lydia, and Stephen. He died in 1641, and his will shows that he had property,— "a stone house with lands in Tenterden, England, with large possessions, in lands, in Scituate and

Marshfield." In his inventory are "ten swarms of bees,
appraised at 10£." Rev. Samuel Deane, in his History
of Scituate, from which I have gleaned liberally, says,
" It is the earliest notice we have met with of the
keeping of bees in the Colony." So that, if any of my
children's children's children should choose commerce
in honey as a profession, they can quote their American
ancestor as a pioneer in the business.

From Elder Nathaniel's eldest son, Joseph, our branch
of the Tildens descended. He succeeded to his father's
estate on Kent Street. He was a member of the second
church, and was chosen deacon in 1655. He belonged
to the liberal or moderate class of Puritans. His father
had willed him lands in Scituate and Marshfield. He
married, and had nine children. His son Samuel, born
1660, settled on the North River in Marshfield, near
Gravelly Beach. He had a son Samuel, born 1689;
and he, living on the same homestead, had a son Samuel,
born 1718, who was the father of my grandfather Samuel, who lived to about ninety-four, occupying the same
lands which had been in the family since 1640. After
my grandfather had passed his labor, he divided his
property, mainly in land, among his children, and they
became responsible for his support,—a common thing in
those days, but very unwise, as it always proves. So
the old estate was cut into bits, and has since passed
into other hands.

And now a word of our English ancestry.

Elder Nathaniel seems to have come from good stock.
My cousin, the late Thomas Tilden, of New York, when
he was in England, visited Sir John Maxwell Tylden,
knight of Milsted, county of Kent, and learned from
manuscripts in his possession that our American ances-

tor traced his lineage in direct lines through a succession of Tyldens, among them Sir John, Sir Thomas, Sir William (who fought in the van of the English army under the Black Prince, at the battle of Poictiers), Sir Henry (time of Edward II.), to Sir Richard Tylden, who lived in the reigns of Henry II. and Richard I. of England. He was seneschal to Hugh de Lacy, constable of Chester during the reign of Henry II. He afterwards assumed the cross, accompanied Cœur de Lion to the Holy Land, and fought under him at the battle of Ascalon against Sultan Saladin.

Thus we are enabled, from reliable sources, to trace our English lineage back to the latter part of the twelfth century. In Burke's "Landed Gentry," 1858, the Tylden family is spoken of as one of great antiquity.

The Tylden coat-of-arms combines the insignia of the Church, the military, and the nobility. St. Andrew's cross on the shield denotes the Church, the battle-axe upon the crest the military, the ermine on the cross nobility. As our earliest known progenitor, Sir Richard, assumed the cross and fought under Richard the Lion-hearted for the Holy Land, we see the appropriateness of the cross on the shield and the battle-axe on the crest, while the titles to the family names, from generation to generation, abundantly justify the "ermine" as a token of nobility.

As native-born Americans, citizens of a republic whose nobility consists in noble men and noble women, we do not put a high value on titles: we prefer the real thing; and yet it is pleasant to know that our English ancestors, living in an age when titles of distinction were highly regarded, and under a government which conferred its honors on supposed real worth, were deemed not unworthy of an honored place in society. We like to feel that we have a worthy ancestry back of us; and we can freely forgive their titles in the assurance we feel that there was true nobility among them.

Should we, as the American descendants of Elder Nathaniel, our branch especially, ever devise a coat-of-arms, while we should hold on to the cross as the symbol of our Christian faith, we should want to substitute for the "battle-axe" a *"broad-axe"* crest, as more fitting. And we could do it with pride, as the battle-axe is a symbol of *de*struction, while the broad-axe is a symbol of *con*struction. But real nobility is the same celestial plant under whatever skies and whether named or nameless.

Somehow, in his emigration from the county of Kent, Nathaniel lost the "y" from his surname. Before he came he was Tylden, and after arriving he was Tilden. Perhaps it was only because "i" is more easily written than "y."

And now to return to my grandfather, Deacon Samuel Tilden, who lived near Gravelly Beach on the North River. He had ten children, nine sons and one daughter, all living to be married. My father, Luther Tilden, was the seventh son, born Jan. 2, 1777. He married Philenda Brooks, my own precious mother, born Oct. 3, 1778. They were married Sept. 18, 1800. My father was a ship-carpenter, as were most of the men living near the North River.

When I was born, May 9, 1811, father was living in a house, still standing and in good repair, about a mile and a half from the ship-yard where he carried on shipbuilding in company with his brother Jotham.

MY CHILDHOOD.

1811–1817.

Of the first three or four years of my life I remember very little; and yet all this time I was sunned beneath my mother's smile and nurtured by night and day, in sickness and health, by my mother's love,—all forgotten, but not lost. My little brain was too soft to hold the impression, but my infant nature absorbed the sweet influence all unconsciously; and these forgotten years have been woven into the texture of my long life. A mother's love is deathless, not only in itself, but in its influence.

I have been told that I was rather a sickly child at first. Fortunately, I have forgotten that, too. But I remember hearing mother say that, when she told a neighbor noted for her closeness how feeble I was and that I would eat nothing but loaf sugar, the neighbor exclaimed, "Why, can you afford it?" Mother's eyes always flashed as she told the story; for, dear as loaf sugar was in those early days, her sick baby was not to be named for value with all the sugar refineries of the country.

One of my earliest memories is of going out doors after a shower and sailing the top of a little wooden trunk in a puddle of water in the yard. This was my first nautical experience.

We lived about five miles from the seashore, and could hear the dull roar of the surf after a storm. Besides, my father built ships; and perhaps it was the two put together that led me to extemporize my first ship and launch her out upon a yard of rain-water sea. I remember, also, looking out of the front window one morning after a heavy wind, and seeing that the roof of the barn had been swept away during the night by the furious gale. I can see it now just as it looked then.

I cannot tell when I began to know father and mother and brother and sisters. I guess I always knew them, they looked so natural. There were four children in the home before I came. The oldest, Philenda, was named for her mother. She was a pretty little brunette, of slight figure. The next, Luther Albert, took his father's name, Luther, with Albert added to avoid the Jr. He was my only brother, seven years older than I. The next, Julia, with brown hair, rather delicate; and the next, Sarah, a two-year old when I came, with flaxen hair and rosy cheeks, full of romp and frolic. So, when I began to peep with the rest, we had five chicks in our home nest.

Our sweet little home is still standing, and looks just as it did when I sailed my first ship in the end yard. The barn, too, is essentially the same as when visited by the gale.

In due time I was sent to school to learn the alpha-bet. The modern method of learning letters from pict-ure-books or blocks with large letters on each square was then unknown. The art of learning made easy had not been discovered. "The hill of science" was hard to climb, and the gate that opened into the narrow way was the alphabet. So, in charge of my older sisters, I was sent a half-mile or more to learn how to open that gate. It didn't look as if it could be opened, and the teacher seemed to take the most unnatural and awkward way possible of lifting the latch.

This was the process. "The school-ma'am," as we all called her, sat in her chair, with Webster's Spelling Book opened at the alphabet in her lap. Holding the book in one hand and her open pen-knife in the other, she called the urchin to be instructed to her. He comes and stands by the teacher's side, bobs his head in token of respect, and is told to look on his book. He does so. She then, with her slender blade, points to A, and says: "That is A. Say it after me, 'A.'" He does it the first time. Then follow B, C, D, E, F, in rapid succession, till the whole column of queer-looking characters is finished. That is lesson No. 1. It wasn't so hard as the little fellow thought it would be. He could call the letters after the ma'am every time, just as easy. But the gate was just as fast as ever. This process was repeated twice a day, for what was deemed a suitable length of time, till the pupil, getting the hang of the order, and knowing just what was coming, could repeat after the ma'am with a glibness that promised well for a high literary career. Soon he could say his letters without any prompting by the teacher and without looking on the book. But, alas! a day of trial came, when the teacher began to skip. That was dreadful. Just as the pupil could say all the letters in the alphabet in regular order without missing one, to skip from A to D and from F to R was enough to break down all previous attainments, and throw the poor child back to first principles, utterly discouraged. Finally, after many days of struggle, with some boxing of ears, and tears, it begins to dawn upon the pupil that each letter has its own name, and he must learn to call it by its own name whenever and wherever he sees it, just as he calls Tom, Tom, and never Charles. The mystery is solved. He opens the gate, and walks through into pastures not always green.

My world during my early years was small, but it was right in the centre of all things; for the highest place in the great blue dome of sky was always directly overhead. Some of our neighbors were queer old people. Singularly enough, I remember them much better than the children.

One was Uncle Lazarus, as we used to call him, who with his wife lived in an old house near by. He was a farmer, and she attended to the dairy and made butter and cheese. He had a nice garden near the house, open to the spring sun. I liked to see him work in it. One day, I remember I was " helping him," when he was preparing beds for sowing. Just as he had one nicely smoothed for dropping in the seed, I carelessly stepped on it. It was too bad. The old man flared in righteous indignation, as he exclaimed: "Go home! Go home, or I'll hang you!" I was frightened, and bounded off like a rabbit with a dog at its heels. For a while I kept indoors at home; but after a time I ventured out, and saw Uncle Lazarus coming towards the house, with a rope in his hand. With his threat of hanging ringing in my scared ears, I verily thought my time had come, and dashed into the house. But my fears were assuaged when the dear old man came

in to return the rope he had borrowed, having forgotten probably all about the scolding, and little dream-
ing what a fright he had given me.

Another neighbor, in the opposite direction, was Mr.
George Cushing, a farmer with a large family of nice
children.   They had a large barn, with attractive hay-
mows for boys and hens.   One day, when I was perhaps five or six years old, Ned Damon and I strayed
into this barn-yard.   I think the cow-house door was
open, and we entered and soon began hunting for
eggs,— a very innocent and delightful thing to do in
one's own barn ; but this was in Mr. George Cushing's
barn, and that wasn't Ned's father's name nor mine.

But we didn't stop to think of that ; or, if we did,
we didn't stop hunting, and, alas ! we found.   We had
never studied history, and knew nothing of the rights
of a discoverer.   So there was no valid excuse for our
appropriating those eggs as we did, and bearing them
away to a convenient place, where we amused ourselves
with "thrashing" them, as we boys used to call it.
We would lay one down, walk off so many paces, and
then with a long switch march up, blindfold, and *thrash*.
Who hit first I don't remember.   I only remember that
some of them were defective.   But we thought them
sound when we took them.   So I don't name that to
palliate the crime.   At last the fun was over, and it was
time to go.

Ned left, and I went home alone.   But somehow I
began to feel very lonesome.   What would mother
think if she knew it ?   If it had only been in *our* barn !
But it wasn't.   If it had only been in Uncle Ledard's
barn !   But it wasn't.   The more I thought it over,

the more troubled I was. I went home ; but I couldn't
laugh, I couldn't play. Mother, with her quick eye,
saw something was the matter, and wanted in her
sweet way to know if I was sick. I told her I was, and
I told the truth. I was sick,— sick in a way I had
never been before. It wasn't the headache, it wasn't
the stomach-ache ; and yet it was some sort of an ache
that made me sick all over. Mother wondered what
could be the matter, and made me up a little bed in the
room where she was working. But the tenderer she
was, the worse I felt. At last, after rolling and toss-
ing, I could stand it no longer, and faltered out,
" Mother, what do they do to folks that steal ?" She
looked at me an instant: "Do? They put them in
prison, to be sure. Why ?" The rock was smitten,
and the waters gushed. I told her all, and went to
prison forthwith,— the prison of my mother's arms,
God's first and best reformatory institution the world
has ever known. It was my first experience of the
voice of God in my soul ; and, though I did not understand it then, I have since regarded it as one of the
truest religious experiences of my life.

Our nearest neighbor was Judge Nathan Cushing.
He lived in a fine old mansion, close to our house. He
was a distinguished man, a graduate of Harvard, a
brave patriot in the Revolution ; and in 1789 he was
appointed judge of the Supreme Court. He married
Miss Abigail Tilden, of Boston, a relative of father ;
and this may have added somewhat to the neighborhood ties, for he was a good friend. He died while I
was very young ; but his fine old home, with its pleasant
surroundings, was one of the attractions of my early

childhood. Aunt Lizzie especially, a domestic in the household, a sort of general-see-to-everything, was my special favorite. Perhaps it was her seed-cakes and other dainties which lent a charm to our intimacy that has lodged her pleasant face in my memory.

The old judge was particularly fond of my little brother Albert, and used often to take him out to ride. One day, when the time was approaching for Albert to shed his frock, the judge took him home, and, unbeknown to mother, had the frock taken off and tied up in a bundle, and the boy arrayed in a beautiful suit of velvet he had bought for him. Thus changed from petticoats to velvet pants and jerkin, proud as a peacock, he was carried home to his astonished mother. The tradition of this pleasant incident is remembered as one of the fairy stories of home life. If one wants to make himself a hero and attain to earthly immortality, let him give some boy his first suit of jacket and pants.

By and by I was old enough to go to winter as well as summer school. The winter school was taught by a "master" who could handle the big boys in case of mutiny. It was quite an experience for a child to pass from a "ma'am" to a "master." My experience was not altogether lovely. Our winter teachers were often Harvard students who were allowed a winter vacation for teaching, to eke out college expenses. One of these I have reason to remember. I remember even his steel-gray coat, trimmed with black braid, which gave him quite a military air.

If he taught me anything, I have forgotten it; but I have not forgotten a most unmerciful boxing of the ears he gave me for something,— I cannot tell what,— and how they turned blue, green, yellow, and less gorgeous colors as they passed through the various stages of convalescence. I remember, too, how I vowed, as many a whipped boy has done before me, that, if ever I got strong enough, I would "lick him." But steel-gray left us when the term was over, and my child wrath soon subsided.

That little woodshed at the end of the house was the children's play-room, where we pounded old nails and young fingers. We had a flag-pond, too, in the lower field, back of the barn, which yielded abundance of flag-root and pussy tails. A nice place for running and catching butterflies was a high sodded bank next the wall between our house and Judge Nathan's.

Our stormy-day play-room was an unfinished chamber where odds and ends of castaway things were collected. The most noteworthy of these were father's old military trappings. He had held a captain's commission; and in the war of 1812, as it was called, his regiment was called out to guard the coast. A British seventy-four lying off the harbor had sent a boat's crew ashore for fresh provisions. These the loyal farmers refused, and in retaliation they set fire to the vessels in the harbor. Ten fishing schooners and coasters were burned. A great sensation was created, and the militia was called out. I was too young to remember, but mother and the old military relics kept the story fresh. There in our rainy-day play-room were the epaulets, brass-mounted sword and scabbard, and scarlet sash father wore, and the long spontoon he carried.

When I was about six years old, father sold our snug

little home, which was all paid for, and built a new house on the North River, where he and his brother carried on ship-building. This proved an unfortunate change financially, for the new house, which father spared no pains in building, cost much more than he got for the old ; and from the debts thus incurred, followed by a decline in business, he was never able to extricate himself. I remember how mother mourned over it ; and how, in view of this experience, she used to say to me, "William, never get in debt." But, child as I was, I was delighted, as all children are, with the idea of moving ; and remember going to the place selected, close to the ship-yard, to see them break ground for the cellar with oxen and ploughs and scrapers. Our moving from the old house to the new may mark the transition from my childhood to my boyhood.

III.

MY BOYHOOD.

1817–1822.

BLOCK HOUSE BUILT.— COASTING.— SKATING.— FISHING ON
THE NORTH RIVER.— TANDEM FISHING.— OUTSIDE FISHING.

THE site of our new house was at a bend of the river,
just above Union Bridge, known from early days as the
"Block House," where there were a fort and garrison
in Philip's War. This was the dear spot where I spent
my boyhood. It is precious with a thousand memories
that can neither be told nor forgotten. The new house
was but one story, like the old one; but it was larger,
and two chambers were finished. We had a large barn,
and convenient out-buildings for pigs, hens, etc., and a
garden plot. Soon after moving, we had a "house-
warming," a large company of old and new neighbors
being invited. Father and mother loved society, and
made the company enjoy themselves. We had dancing, I remember, in the long kitchen, with yellow
painted floor. There was a colored man named John
Wood, who played the violin. He wore a tall bell-
crowned hat, and cut quite a figure. He was not
much of a musician. My Uncle Elijah used to say
that the only way he could *turn* a tune was by *bearing
on harder.* There were no pianos in our neighborhood. I doubt if there was one in town. So we all

depended on John Wood. We always gave him his
whole name. He was an important personage. Oh,
how long it did seem to us children for him to get
ready to play, to tune his fiddle! How he would resin
his bow, and screw up the strings, and scrape away till
they were almost in tune! One screw more, and *twang*
goes the string. Then a new piece of catgut is unrolled,
and fastened, and wound up. Scrape, scrape, scrape
again, till at last "all ready." "Fisher's Hornpipe" or
"Money Musk" is started, and partners balance and
twirl up and down the middle in hilarious joy. I think
there was more fun in dancing, when I was a boy,
than there is now. There is more skill at present. We
had few dancing-schools. Our young people took it
the natural way, as their fathers and mothers did; and
a jolly good time we made of it.

What a happy night that was to me! I was the
youngest, and was permitted to sit up. I think it was
my first ball. I presume I bawled the next day from
fatigue after my late hours.

We had not been long in our new home when we had
a great surprise,— a sweet little baby. I had been the
baby for seven years, and I liked it. To be sure, my
growing legs reached nearly to the floor when I sat in
mother's lap; but I liked the dear chair so well, I had
rather be laughed at than to give it up. But now a little
daughter had come, and I could play baby no longer.
She was called "Lucy Brooks," after a favorite maiden
aunt, a sister of mother. Two years later another
little sister came to keep her from being lonesome.
This was the richest furnishing we had for the new
house. Now we were a family of *seven*,— a sacred num-

ber,— and the golden chain remained intact till mother
died, seventeen years after. Mother was forty-two
years old when her youngest was born. She was called
"Caroline," and a darling child she proved. There was
so long a space between me and the two youngest that
father used to call them the children of his second wife.

My main work at first, before and after school, was
to bring chips from the ship-yard for our open fires.
We never had a stove, while I lived at home, in kitchen
or sitting-room. Everything was cooked by a large,
open fire. On one side of our wide kitchen fireplace
was a brick oven, heated once a week, for great dome-
shaped loaves of brown bread and pies, and sometimes
meat. The clean white-oak chips made splendid fuel ;
and, though there were plenty of them, it was no small
job to keep a full supply in cold weather. I did not
always go to my task willingly, I am sorry to say, and
would sometimes roar like a "bull of Bashan" when
mother sent me for chips if I was not in the mood. I
think my grandchildren are a great improvement on
their grandfather when he was a boy.

My brother Albert was seven years older than I, so
that our playfellows were not the same. He fraternized
with the big boys, I with the smaller ones. At school
they used to call us "Butt and Bill," for short. All the
boys were nicknamed. Our district school was a very
good one, care being taken to secure good teachers.
We had about four months' summer school and three
months' winter. This gave long vacations. But my
school-days were very happy, as was, indeed, my whole
boyhood. Within an eighth of a mile were two great
attractions : one, London Hill, grandly steep for slid-

ing; the other, Thatcher's Pond, a glorious place for sailing boats in summer and sliding and skating in winter. On one side of it was a high hill, slanting down to the water's edge. When sliding was good, we would start from the top of the hill, and, passing swiftly down, strike the smooth ice of the pond and shoot across it. It was real fun. We little folks had to scamper, when we saw a sled coming; and, when we got larger, other little folks had to pay their obeisance to the kings.

Fortunately for our peril and consequent enjoyment, there was a narrow cartway about half-way down the side of the hill. It made a capital "jump." We went over it with an exhilarating bound. Sometimes, on moonlight evenings, the larger boys would take Mr. Thatcher Tilden's ox-sled,—"Old Thatcher," I am sorry to say, we all called him,— they would take his ox-sled, throw the heavy tongue back on the bottom, drag it with infinite pains and by main strength to the top of the hill, and load it with boys, heaping them up into a dome of squirming and shouting life. One or two stout boys would keep off to start the loaded sled, jump on, and steer. Sometimes a good deal of pushing and shouting — especially shouting, each one giving orders as if he were skipper — was necessary to start. It was a kind of launching on a small scale. Finally, she starts, the steerers jump on, and away she goes, increasing her speed every moment with her heavy load, so that, when she goes over the "jump," she leaps clear of the ground and comes down with a whack that scatters the little fellows on top over the snowy sides of the hill, and rushes on with all who can hold their grip till she strikes the glassy pond, and slides on away, away across the pond, amid shouts such as fabled Bedlam could hardly have surpassed.

There I learned to skate ; and such a time as I had of it, and such skates ! My first were little low irons, ground down on one side,— for what I never knew, except to exercise small boys in tumbling. These were tied on with strings. In a year or two I graduated into straps and buckles. Perhaps they were an old pair that "Butt" had outgrown : I don't remember. But at last I became quite skilful, and could "cut rings" and "figure eights" and "scull backwards" as well as forwards and sidewise with any of them, though I never was an expert.

At the winter school the big boys had to cut all the wood that was burned in the school-room. The wood was dumped in the yard, and a delegation of boys was selected by the master to cut and split and pile up in the shed. To get appointed on this outdoor work was regarded as a great favor. It was such a relief from over-exacting studies ! Our chief article of luxury at school recess was molasses candy. This brought a uniform price of one cent a stick, though, when molasses was cheap and the candy merchant generous, we may have had a longer or thicker stick. At first there were a good many competitors in this line of business ; but, here as elsewhere, genius tells. There was one family that had a real genius for molasses candy. It was always nice, well pulled, of delicate straw color, cut in equal lengths, crisp, and brittle,— just the kind a boy liked, not only to eat for himself, but to give to the sweetest girl he knew.

I remember one day at recess I had a nice stick,

and a flock of not-at-all-diffident girls pressed around me with "Oh, give it to me, give it to me!" As I was holding them at bay, undecided which should have it, a little plump hand was reached out from behind the door. I knew the hand, though all else was hidden. I slipped the candy into that hand, to the great annoyance, no doubt, of the besiegers, and went my way. When I grew to manhood, I took that little hand in mine, and "vowed to love, cherish, and protect as long as we both should live." 'Tis sweet, modest diffidence that wins, if the girls only knew it.

The North River abounded in fish. Eels were caught with bobs in the spring, from the banks, with pole and line, and in winter through the ice, with spears long enough to reach the bottom and draw them out of their snug winter home. Herrings and shad were caught in abundance in seines, in the spring of the year. Perch and bass were not very plentiful, but very delicious; and the clam banks in the lower reaches of the river, near the sea, yielded an abundance of very sweet clams. These various kinds of fish, with smelts, taken by hand nets from the herring brooks, formed a large part of our food in winter-time. Taken right from the water, with mother to cook them at an open fire, they were superb.

The method of fishing for bass and perch through the ice was peculiar. A large round hole was cut over the channel, the deepest place in the river, where the current was the strongest and the fish most likely to swim. Into this hole, made very smooth at the edge, was dropped a net attached to a long pole.

The iron bow to which the net was attached was

about four feet in diameter, the hole in the ice
about five, to give it easy play. First, the net was
dropped, as fast as it would sink, and the long pole
laid flat upon the ice ; then the end of the-pole farthest
from the net lifted to an angle of about forty-five degrees, and the net run down till it touched the bottom.
Then the end with the pin was taken, breast high, and
swept round and round, the pole easily slipping round
the smooth-cut edge, the fisher making a circle at
about ten feet distance, like the path of a horse round
a cider-mill. After sweeping round about a dozen
times,— thirteen is a lucky number,— the long pole is
drawn up and laid flat on the ice, so that the bow of
the net will lie horizontal with the surface of the water
in the hole. It was fun, while the net was in this position, its contents all unknown, to go and lift a section
of the net with thumb and finger, to judge by feeling
the twitches what sort of a haul had been made. One
soon learned to tell if there was a bass in the net
by the vigorous jerk. Perch were less demonstrative,
though some of the larger ones would beguile you with
the hope of a bass. After this process of prophesying
had been duly indulged, the net was lifted and drawn
out upon the ice. Perhaps a striped bass of three or
four pounds, though this was rare, and a number of
shiny perch, which was more common, would be spilled
out upon the ice or picked out of the meshes where
they had caught. This fishing was all done by night,
and at certain times in the tide.

After I got large enough, I used to help father in
this fishing. So we made a tandem team, with the colt
ahead. Father was the fill horse, and held the pole to

his breast, pushing round and round the circle made
white by the irons attached to his boots to keep him
from slipping. But it was hard pushing against the
tide. So a rope was attached to the pole, and, taking
the end over my shoulder, I planted my little irons in
the ice and pulled away. But I confess I liked prophesying with thumb and finger better than pulling.

Living so near the river, I early became expert in
the use of boats. Father had a float, as he called it,—
a large canoe, which was very easily upset; but I soon
learned to manage it, and the first money I remember
to have earned was for paddling men, one at a time,
across the river in this float. There was a toll on the
bridge, a quarter of a mile below; and carpenters wishing to take a short cut to Marshfield would give me a
cent or two for paddling them across. So, like Vander-
bilt, I began my business career with "a ferry-boat."
But here the resemblance ends. When a little older, I
worked for the neighbors in haying-time, raking scat-
terings and stowing away on the load and haymow, at
a quarter of a dollar a day. That was good wages.
But the season for such exorbitant pay was short.

I well remember my first experience of outside fishing,— outside the beach. Father was in the habit of
going out in the bay for cod and haddock, in spring
and fall. It seemed to me very attractive, and I begged
to go out with him next time. He consented, to my
great delight. We took a large whale-boat, and, with
four or five men and stores for two days, we rowed
down the river to the beach for the night, and went up
to a barn on the cliff, a corner of which was made into
a house occupied by "old Hyland." There we ate our

supper, and bunked for the night on his soft haymow.
As soon as the day broke, we were up and off to our
boat, stowing snugly away our water-keg, lines, and
reels, and superfluous garments, shipping the oars all
ready for use. The men then seized the boat by the
gunwale on either side, and slid her down the sandy
beach to the surf.

There was no land between us and Europe, so that
an east wind set into the bay with great force, and
sometimes the breakers were so high as to make a
launch through them difficult. A sea would strike the
bow of the boat on one side and throw her round
broadside to the beach and swamp her. But this
morning the wind was inshore and the breakers moderate. Running the bow of the boat a little way into
the foamy surf, the men rested and waited for a good
time to launch. "Now is the time, boys! Let her
run!" Father jumps in and seizes the steering oar.
Then strong men on either side wade in and push the
boat till, just as she clears her keel from the beach,
they spring in, out oars, and with a few strokes there
we are, the surf in a wreath of white foam behind us,
and three thousand miles of briny deep before us.
And, though we didn't propose going so far, yet to the
little shaver cuddled down in the bow it was a memorable occasion, his first voyage to sea. Oh, how
delightfully the lapstreak boat rose and fell with rolling waves!

There were certain places two or three miles from
shore where the best fishing was supposed to be found.
These were indicated by certain objects on shore.
When old Hyland's barn was in range with some-

thing on the hills, and Scituate light-house with something else, then we could ship our oars and drop our
stone kedge. Now we are still. The boat swings to
the wind. We pack the oars close to the gunwale,
stow things snug, bait our hooks with the clams dug
the afternoon before, and throw over our leads. Away
they run, ten fathom, twenty fathom, when we feel
the lead strike the bottom. The scines attached to
the lead and holding the baited hooks are about two
feet long. So we haul up the lead about two feet, that
the bait may rest on the bottom. They don't bite at
once. So we can take a view of the shore. How
strange the cliffs look from the outside,—like a half-
loaf of brown bread with cut side to the sea, as mother
used to put it to the fire to toast for my milk! And the
beach,—how low it looked, the surf all gone! Father
sits in the stern sheets, and draws his line up and
down. Ha! a rub! a nibble! a bite! Father's face
glows, he stands up, pulls away hand over hand, till by
and by we see the fish gleaming and whirling fathoms
below; and now over the gunwale it comes,—a fine cod
right from the briny deep.

"Hurrah for the first fish!"

And now another and another. I don't remember
whether I caught any or not. I soon lost my ambition.
Somehow I grew pensive. I thought of home and
the nice shagbarks I gathered the day before under
the shady walnut-trees. I almost wished I hadn't
come. I didn't like outside fishing. I hauled in my
line: the bait was gone. I had had a bite without
knowing it. I lay back on the thwart. I looked into
the blue sky. It didn't look handsome as it used to at

home. I closed my eyes. Suddenly a peculiar sensation. I threw my head over the gunwale. My breakfast was gone: I felt better. I raised my head. Oh, how lovely the shore looked! Should I ever tread it again? And again the beauty faded from shore and sky. Again to the gunwale, and whatever was left of breakfast was given without a murmur to old Neptune. But how could I stand it? It was only nine o'clock in the morning, and we should not go in till the afternoon. Could I live? It didn't seem to me that I could. So I begged father to set me ashore, and I would stay on the beach till they came. The indulgent man consented; and, the other men being sympathetic, they hauled up our kedge, rowed in, and landed me on the beach.

Oh, what a happy creature was I when my feet touched the golden sand! The boat pushed off again, and left me there to roam up and down the surf-smoothed, sandy floor, to gather shells and kelp and bits of driftwood tossed ashore from the vasty deep. At last, as the sun began to cast a longer shadow eastward, I saw the little speck of a boat, away off yonder, moving toward me. Now I could see the fleck of the oars, now see the men, now see father at the helm, now hear their voices. Now I was bold as a lion. I could rush into the surf to help haul the boat ashore, and hurrah with the loudest over the fine fare of fish *we* had caught. But I didn't ask to go the next time.

IV

BOYHOOD.

1822–1824.

My Father.— Madame Cushing.— Death of Playfellow. — Grandfather Tilden.— Old Church.— Grist-mill.— Grandfather Brooks.

Though we had but little land, we kept a cow and hired her pastured. I was cow-boy, and responsible for finding and bringing her home at night. One after-noon, I remember, a tempest came up. I went for the cow, found her; and, as I was driving her home, the chain lightning ran in brilliant crinkles along the ground, so close as nearly to touch my feet. I do not remember to have seen the phenomenon since.

Every autumn father laid in his winter store,— pota-toes, beef, and pork enough for the year. When he killed his beef and pork, I remember how he always selected some nice pieces for certain neighbors, not very well off, and sent them around. Dear man, his heart was always larger than his means. He was a great gunner, a fine shot; but, while he generally brought home a good lot of birds, he derived more pleasure than profit from his gunning.

One of the fine old places in Scituate was Madame Cushing's, in the centre of the town. Her husband, Judge William Cushing, was a relative of Judge Nathan

Cushing, who gave my brother his suit of velvet. He was quite distinguished in his day,—the friend of Washington, and selected by him for one of the Justices of the Supreme Court of the United States at the organization of the government. He died before I was born, but his widow continued to live on the place. She was a lady of the old school, who had been accustomed to the best society. She was known always as "Madame Cushing"; and her fine old mansion and beautiful grounds were a delight to my boyish eyes. There was no place like it in town. Then, too, she was generous to us boys, and at cherry time would invite us into her beautiful garden, and give us the free range of her magnificent "black-heart" cherry-trees, the largest and finest I ever saw. But a boy's stomach, though capacious, has its natural limits; and I remember with shame how, on one of these generous treats, I overstepped those limits, and lost my relish ever after for that most delicious fruit.

When eleven or twelve, I met with my first great sorrow in the death of a dear playfellow,—Harry Cushing. He was a little older than I ; but we were neighbors, went to the same school, joined in the same plays, and he was very dear to me. Indeed, he was dear to all his playfellows,—a general favorite. He got accidentally injured, and died of lockjaw. His death made a great impression upon me. It waked my better nature, and started deep resolves for a new life. Our minister was deeply moved at the funeral; and I remember to this day some of the things he said in his prayer.

It was customary to select pall-bearers from among

those near the same age. I was one of them. Before starting in the funeral procession, we boys were invited into a small room to take something to drink. It was the custom of the time, and we thought nothing of it. Its omission would have been regarded as a lack of courtesy. But Harry, dear Harry! How truly we mourned for him! I think his going was an epoch in my religious life. It made me thoughtful,— the first step in the upward path.

Soon after we moved to the new house, father and his brother — Uncle Jotham — built a fishing schooner for Captain Josiah Ryder, of Chatham. The captain stayed at our house some time while the vessel was being finished. He was the tallest man I had ever seen. Indeed, I don't know as I ever saw a taller man out of "Barnum's Greatest Show on Earth." He was six feet and — I don't know how many inches. His long boots, worn over his pants and coming up to his knees, were enormous. I used sometimes to try one on before he was up in the morning.

The captain was as good as he was tall. He was a fervent Methodist, and used to sing with enthusiasm the Methodist tunes then current. The chorus of one of them became quite popular with us children, and ran thus : —

> "Through grace, *free* grace,
> Through grace, *free* grace,
> To all the Jews and Gentile race."

We had little idea then of the Methodist devotion to "free" grace; but the tune sung itself, and we liked it.

At that time my oldest sister was a pretty black-eyed girl of about sweet sixteen, and the schooner was named for her, " Philenda."

A young sailor captain came to take charge of her, by the name of Godfrey,— Captain George Godfrey. He was a fine young man, handsome, good, promising in every respect. Dear fellow, he was lost soon after. He was coming in to Chatham with a full freight, and foundered on Polluck Rip. All perished. But he left a sweet, sad memory in our home.

My grandfather, Deacon Samuel Tilden, lived in Marshfield, near Gravelly Beach, about a mile above the Block House. He was a direct descendant from Elder Nathaniel, and inherited land held in the family since 1640. The situation of the old house was beautiful, with hills on the east and the winding river and fertile meadows on the west. My grandfather was a very old man when I was a boy. He was nearly blind for many of the latter years of his life. I used frequently to be sent over the river and through the pastures to his house, on an errand. He was a dear, good old man whom everybody loved. How plainly I can see him, in a woollen cap to cover his bald head, and green •baize dressing-gown! He was a small man, with a kindly face and large, full eye. He had no stoop in his old age, but was straight as an arrow. He was slow of speech ; and his voice was thin, but tender and loving. When I went in, he would call me to him, and, laying his hand on my head, would say : "Who's this? 'Tain't William, is it?" He always guessed right, blind as he was ; for he knew the voices of his grandchildren. He lived to be about ninety-four, and died universally es-teemed. He had ten children, nine sons and one daughter. My father was the seventh son.

My uncle Jotham,. father's partner in ship-building, lived just over the river on a hill a quarter of a mile away. He had a family of four sons and two daughters. They attended church with us at Scituate. And it was a pretty sight to my young eyes to see them winding along, in their best attire, down the hill to the river, on a Sunday morning, and across in the large, flat-bottomed boat made for the occasion. Landing on our side, they would come up by our house, where we would join them, and all walk up through the pastures to the main road together, and then a third of a mile further, to the old church on the hill, the sweet-toned bell all the time calling: "Come! Come! Come!"

On the roadside the sweet fern grew in great abundance. I used to pluck it and chew it, as the disciples did the ears of corn on the Sabbath day. Even now, whenever I taste in the country that fragrant shrub, I am carried back to those Sunday mornings when I plucked it on my way to church.

In the church we had the old-fashioned square pews of the period, with high backs to break the draught, hiding the inmates from the view of all but the minister, who could look down from his lofty pulpit, and see if all his sheep and lambs were in their pens. Round the tops of these high-backed pews there was a sort of frieze of open work, four or six inches wide, divided into narrow spaces by turned pieces of hard wood held by a rail above and below. This seemed made for the children to peep through, the little turned uprights offering a great temptation to try to see how far they could be twisted round without squeaking. Of course, we could not tell till they did squeak ; and then — well,

we mustn't do it again. But, then, how *could* we keep
our hands off? The little rollers seemed to have been
made to turn and to squeak. The seats all round the
four-sided pews were without cushions, and hung on
hinges, so as to turn up and make easy standing during
prayers, when every one stood up. Such an indecency
as sitting during prayer had not then been heard of.
When at last the long prayer was over, along with and
drowning the "Amen" of the minister, slam, bang, slam,
bang, went the seats all round the church, up and down
the long aisles and across the short ones, like the sharp
report of a platoon of soldiers on muster-day trying to
fire all together, but missing it. We had no stove in
church, even in coldest weather. Mother used to
bring with her a little foot-stove, with hard-wood coals
taken from the home fireplace.

Right under the pulpit there was a long, narrow pew
where the two deacons sat. They were literally under
the droppings of the sanctuary. The communion table
was a wide shelf, or leaf, hung on hinges to the front of
this pew, being lifted only when the table was spread.

Near the pulpit, on the right of the broad aisle, were
a few long pews, with oak backs and seats, for such old
men as were too poor to hire seats ; and on the left-hand
side the same provision was made for poor old women.
There was a wide gallery on three sides of the church,
where the seats were free; and above that, in the
farthest corner, a little box, a sort of crow's nest for
the colored people, of whom there were several families
in our part of the town.

The bell was rung on a floor high up in the tower,
and from that floor there was a single square of glass

away up close to the ceiling of the church through which the sexton could look and see when the minister was in the pulpit. Then, with three strokes of the bell, all was silent, or supposed to be; for the people kept coming in for some time after the minister was ready to begin. The fashion was to stay round the church door, outside or inside, talking of national or neighborhood matters, the vessels on the stocks, the condition of the crops, etc., till the minister was in his place. And it was not all irreverence. Sunday was the only day in the week they met, and the meeting-house the only place of *rendezvous;* and, as theology was never a subject of much contention in our parish, they talked on the subjects of most pressing interest.

The choir occupied seats right in front of the pulpit; and, as the pulpit was on the side of the church, not the end, as is now the fashion, the singers and the preacher were not far apart. Of course, we had no organ or melodeon. The time for such instruments in country churches had not yet come. But we had a bass-viol and a double-bass, a flute, a clarinet, and some other instruments. For the rest we depended on human voices. And fine voices some of them were. My aunt Lucy Brooks sang very sweetly. And one man by the name of Oldham, who stuttered most distressingly in common conversation, had a splendid tenor voice, and sang like an angel.

Our minister, too, Rev. Samuel Deane, was a superb singer. On one of the Forefathers' celebrations at Plymouth, he was selected to sing "The breaking waves dashed high." That he did it grandly all who had heard him sing in his own church will easily believe.

He knew so much of music that he was independent of the choir, and would strike in in unexpected places and sing round them, always in perfect harmony. The choir, half through a line, would hear his voice, clear and musical, begin at the beginning, give each syllable in distinct enunciation, and, bounding over the spaces, come out with them on the last word in time and tune as perfect as if he had been with them from the beginning. It was a sort of musical sleight-of-hand that I never fully understood, but greatly enjoyed.

A word more of the old bell that hung in the open belfry, with wheel and rope exposed to all weather. I hardly know why I loved that bell so well, for its tones were not all happy. It sometimes had a "sweetly solemn sound," especially on week-days. On Sundays it sent forth a joyous call for worship "over the hills and far away," as if there were an angel in the belfry singing "Praise God from whom all blessings flow," "I was glad when they said unto me, Come, let us go up to the house of the Lord." But, whenever we heard it on a week-day, it startled us. We knew it meant that somebody had died. It was the custom in early morning, after a death, to give the sad intelligence by the bell. It was the quickest and the most fitting way to do it. Whether it was a child or man or woman was indicated by certain strokes of the bell. Then, after a short pause, if it was an adult, the age would be tolled, giving as many strokes as the person had lived years. As soon as the solemn sounds had ceased, began the subdued inquiry, "Who can it be?" On the streets, in the stores, in the fields, in the ship-yards, in the home, "Who can it be?" I remember being out in the pasture one morning,— perhaps I had been to drive the cow,— when the bell began to strike the age. I started to run home, counting as I ran, to be the first to tell, and join the wonder, "Who can it be?" Precious old bell! I remember how tame and flat other bells in the towns around seemed when I first heard them.

In front of the old church, not far from the door, was a horse-block for those who rode to meeting horseback, on pillions behind their husbands. But most came in open wagons or walked. There were but few chaises in town. One second-hand barouche, I remember, created quite a sensation.

The old grist-mill was one of the institutions of my boyhood. It was a shackly old mill, with a small pond, dry a part of the year; but it did most of the grinding of corn and rye in our neighborhood. It was not far from father's, across lots; and I was frequently sent with a half-bushel on my back to get it ground. The rocks in the pond served as a gauge of its capacity. If the "bushel rock" was just in sight, the old miller could grind a bushel; and so down to the "peck rock." When that showed its brown head, only a peck could be ground. Below the "peck rock," there was nothing to do but leave your grist and wait for a shower. The old, dark flume, the rickety old gate, lifted by a lever, the black wheel whirling around in a tub away down below, were all deep mysteries to my boyhood. What if I should fall into the flume, go through the gate, round the wheel in the tub,— how much of me would there be left? The hopper-room, where the grists were left to wait their turn, was on a

level with the dam, over which the cart-path passed.
In the next room below was a long wooden trough,
breast high, into which the meal came down. There
the old miller, "Uncle Tom," used to stand, letting the
meal pass through his fingers to test its fineness. If
too coarse, he would turn a screw over the trough and
let the stones come closer together. If too fine, the
screw would lift the upper stone. How often have I
stood and watched and wondered! There were generally a number of bags in the hopper-room waiting their
turn, "first come, first served," being the rule. This
story used to be told of a little grandson of Uncle
Tom. The child's father loved a joke, and, when he
sent his boy to mill for the first time, he told him he
was sorry to say that his grandpa needed watching,—
that he had been known to take a small portion of corn
out of the hopper while it was being ground, and put
it aside for himself. The little boy thus set to watch,
and knowing nothing of toll, kept his eye closely on
his grandpa. When he got home with his grist, his
father said, with a twinkle in his eye, "Well, sonny,
did grandpa take any of it?" "Yes, he did; but, when
he went below, I put it right back again." I don't
know whether grandpa ever knew that he ground that
grist without compensation. Sometimes, in long
droughts, we had to go to the harbor, four miles away,
to get our grain ground at the tide-mill that never
failed.

In going to the harbor, we passed the post-office
near the centre of the town. It was kept at this time
by a respectable old farmer, on the upper shelf of his
kitchen closet, in a box about large enough to hold

seven pounds of sugar. The mail came once a week, I think; and the letters were safely boxed till called for, when the postage must be paid. Neither envelopes nor stamps were then known. Nothing was prepaid, and the postage was high, depending on the distance. Twenty-five cents was often paid for letters. Many curious and ingenious methods were adopted for folding letters so as to give space for the largest amount of writing without a word showing on the outside. All this ingenuity lost its stimulus when the envelope came into use.

In 1822 my sister Philenda, then twenty, was married to a young man,— Joseph Bond,— a druggist from Boston, who had come to Scituate to visit a relative. He saw Philenda, and fell in love with her, as well he might; for she was very handsome, and as smart as she was good-looking. She did not care for him at first, and once, I remember, when she saw him coming, ran away from him, jumped over a gap in the wall, and went into the school she was then teaching, some distance away. Perhaps he didn't know why the bird had flown. But he believed "faint heart never won fair lady," and persevered till he won. And as kind and pure and noble husband he made as ever a woman had. He settled as a druggist in Waltham, Mass.; and the visits I used to make to their new home, so tasteful and neat, are among the pleasant memories of my boyhood.

I have told you of Grandpa Tilden: let me tell you also of Grandpa Brooks, mother's father. Captain William Brooks, as he was called, lived nearly opposite Grandpa Tilden, on the Scituate side of the North River. His children were: William, Sally, Seth, Philenda,—that was mother,— Temperance, Elijah, Lucy, and Nathan. All married but Lucy. She was a favorite maiden aunt, the one who sang in the choir so sweetly. Mother used frequently to take me with her when she went to see her father; and it was a charming place to visit. There was a sweet and never-failing well on the hillside near the house, and the water was brought down in an open wooden spout. I loved especially to go there in the autumn, for there were two immense peartrees whose fruit was delicious. The apples were good, but the pears were the never-to-be-forgotten luxury. My mouth waters at the remembrance of them. Grandpa Brooks was a ship-carpenter, as nearly all were,— a large, rosy-cheeked man, of an English build. He owned a large farm, and worked on the land as well as in the ship-yard. I was a small boy when he died.

V

BOYHOOD.

FIRST LEAVING HOME — SCHOONER "HOPE." — GREAT STORM. — "RISING MIDDLE." — SOUTH-WEST HARBOR, MT. DESERT.— ROXANNA.— HIGH LINE. — MACKEREL FISHING, SEINES, TRAILING, JIGGERING, DRESSING AND SALTING THE MACKEREL.— COOKING.— STORES.— PRESERVED BLOATERS. — PACKING DAY.— LEARNING TRADE.—TWENTY-ONE.

THE summer I was thirteen was eventful to me, as it was that summer I first left home,— not for a long season, but long enough to be an event in my home life.

Mackerel fishing at that time was a great source of revenue among the coast towns, from Portland on the North shore to Plymouth and Provincetown on the South. Scituate Harbor, Cohasset, and Hingham Cove, each fitted out a large fleet. It was an honorable and, at times, quite lucrative calling,— not quite equal in dignity to "going to sea," but a step in a nautical direction. As I had picked chips for years from the yard where father had built fishing vessels, I seemed foreordained to the calling.

A favorite skipper, sober and kind, in whom mother had confidence, lived in the neighborhood. I wanted to go with him, and she consented. So I shipped as

"monkey." The smallest boy on board had the poor-
est place to fish assigned to him, and was called "monkey." It was an appropriate name.

When it was decided that I was to go, then came the
fitting out. I must have a pea-jacket, with pants to
match, red flannel shirts, cowhide boots, and a tarpaulin hat.

All but the boots mother made with her own hands.
If I was a little proud in my new rig, it was only
because I was human and susceptible to human ambi-
tions. We sailed from Hingham in the schooner
"Beaver," owned by Thomas Loring, Esq.,— "Old Tom"
we irreverently called him,— a fine-looking old man,
wearing short-clothes, and plated buckles on knees and
shoes. Hingham Cove was about eight or nine miles
from our house, but we used to walk back and forth, carrying our bundles. We went over the mountain road,
as it was called. On the highest point there was a
large beech-tree we used to call the "Half-way Tree,"
where we could rest awhile in its welcome shade.
After the "Beaver" was fitted out, we sailed first for
Boston to "take in salt." This was my first visit to
the new city. It received its city charter only two
years before, and then had a population of about forty-
five thousand. But it was the biggest place I had ever
seen, and seemed to me very wonderful. We were
rather unfortunate in our fishing that summer, and I
had nothing coming in the autumn, but it was a memorable experience; and, when we "cleared out," I considered myself a regular "Old Tar." If I "rolled" in
walking like a sailor, and "trimmed ship" and went
"in stays" and "let go jib sheets," and cried, "Helms

alee!" and "Land ho!" when there seemed to be no occasion, it was only as a Freshman in college talks of Virgil and the classics to his mother, on his first home vacation.

The next season I went with another neighborhood skipper in an old schooner called "Hope." If I had known as much about vessels then as I did afterwards, I should have thought "Fear" a more appropriate name; for she was a rickety old craft, scarcely seaworthy, and the wonder was that she did not spill us all out before the season was over. She was a long, low-decked vessel; and, standing on the quarter, in a heavy sea we could see her bend and twist like an old basket to adjust herself to the waves. And yet she carried us safely through one of the severest gales I ever experienced. We were off Sandy Hook as the storm began to brew, and our mate was very anxious to run in for the night. But the skipper was opposed, and laid her head off shore, into the gathering storm. Oh, how homelike the houses looked on the shore as we left them behind! Soon it blew a gale, so that we had to take in all sail save a close-reefed foresail, and lay to. Under this sail, we made little headway, but drifted almost dead to leeward. This drift was nearly in a line with the coast, and along the coast lay the dangerous Barnegat Shoals. We could not tell whether we should clear them or not. But on the other tack, we should be sure to be wrecked; so there was nothing to do but to keep on, and take whatever might come. I rather think the skipper wished now he had taken counsel and gone in to Sandy Hook. But, of course, he didn't say it. As the darkness deepened, the gale increased, and the sea swept over our main deck so that no watch could stand against it. Indeed, watch was useless, for nothing could be seen in the pitchy darkness. Every now and then a heavy sea would break upon the quarter-deck and pour down the gangway. The skipper saw we were entirely helpless. The helm was lashed hard down. If we came in contact with a vessel, there was no help, for we could do nothing. If we struck on the reef we knew we were near, there was nothing to be done but to go down. So at last the skipper had the companion way closed and fastened, and we were all shut in below, leaving the crazy old basket to the mercy of the winds and waves. It was a terrible night. Few words were spoken. We all knew the danger. The sea swept over us as over a log. Hour after hour passed, and still we did not strike. The old hull bent and twisted, but did not break. The short hours came, and we still lived. At last there was a lull. We opened the companion doors, and the day had broken, the wind was going down, the sea was easier. We crawled out, one after another, on deck, holding on for fear of being wrecked or blown off. The wind was down, the danger was over. Dear old " Hope,"— she was well named after all. She had brought us safely through the gale, and we would never call her bad names again,— never, no, never !

Soon there was a dead calm, the clouds lifted, and, when the next breeze sprung up, it was from the opposite point of the compass, and we saw a ship coming toward us under full sail, studding sails all set, as if she had been running all night with a fair wind over smooth seas, as she probably had, our north-east gale having spent itself before it reached her. How beautiful that ship looked, — a white-winged angel coming with a message of joy and gladness from "Him who holdeth the waters in the hollow of his hand"!

When we had caught our fare of fish, we went into New York and sold them, packing them in Brooklyn. This was the first time I was ever in New York. It was in the summer of 1825, and I was fourteen years old. Immense as the city then seemed, it extended only from the Battery back as far as the City Hall. Brooklyn was a quiet suburb of summer residences, with extensive and beautiful gardens. The ferryboats, I remember, were side-wheelers, driven by treadmill horse-power. But it was the same beautiful harbor as now, and even then alive with shipping.

When I began mackerel fishing at thirteen, I had, of course, to give up my summer school. So all the schooling I had after that was about three months in the winter. The early mackerel fishing off Block Island and the Jersey Coast, was not profitable, as the fish were lean and brought only a low price. So, on my third summer, I waited till the mackerel were fatter. I then shipped with a smart young skipper in a vessel named "Rising Sun." She, too, was old and crippled. She had been aground in early life and got badly hogged. We used to call her the "Rising Middle." In this humpbacked craft with a beautiful name, my fisherman's luck began to rise. We had a smart young crew to match our skipper. It was his first season as captain. He was ambitious, he was a driver, he made good trips, and we made a good summer's work.

We caught most of our fish wide off Mt. Desert ; and once, I remember, we went in to the South West Harbor, so noted now as a watering-place, for potatoes. It is one of the finest harbors on the coast. There were only a few huts on the shore then, and no one on land or sea dreamed of the beautiful place it was destined to become. Blueberries were in their prime, and the burned fields with a fresh growth of low bushes were literally covered with them. But in substantial deliciousness they were cast into the shade by the potatoes. Growing on new soil, recently burned over, they were superb,— especially to us hungry fishermen. We had some finely cured salt cod on board. Boiled cod, with *such* potatoes, was a luxury beyond description. No circle of aldermen ever sat down to a Parker House dinner with such gustatory satisfaction. Those new potatoes went with us all through the trip, and were an ever new source of pleasure till the last one was gone.

The next summer I went with the same skipper. He had proved himself so smart that the same owners gave him a larger vessel. "Roxanna" was her name. She, too, was venerable in years, but stanch and sound. The "Rising Sun," crooked as she was, was fleet of foot. Few went by us, with a good breeze ; and she would ride the sea as easily and gracefully as a gull. But poor old "Roxy" was long past her prime, and from never being swift had become so slow that everything went by us, so that we needed a watch set over taffrail instead of the bows, as the danger was not in running over anybody, but in being run over. In beating to windward when we tried to go in stays, "she would bob three times to a sea, and then go round it."

It was her courteous way of doing it. There was little difference between her bow and stern. They were both modelled for repose, not motion, suggesting the fabled method of building ships by the mile, and sawing off any required length, to suit the purchasers. And yet in that clumsy old tub we were high line in Scituate that summer, packing over a thousand barrels. This was my most fortunate season.

The next year I went with a brother of the smart skipper in a new schooner built at the Block House, on which I had worked. She was called the " Rival," and rivalled, by many a league, all the vessels I had thus far sailed in. I continued this summer fishing till I was about twenty, giving the rest of the year to my trade after I was sixteen.

But I will not follow this farther, but tell you a little more in detail of the mackerel fishing. Mackerel have been found on our coast from its first discovery. There is probably some food of which they are fond in our bays and on our banks. They migrate in schools, and it is not till midsummer and autumn that they are taken in any great numbers on our coast. The aborigines called this famous fish " Wawunneke-seag," a big word, meaning " fatness," — an appropriate name, for in its prime it is one of the fattest and most delicious of fish.

There have been various methods of taking mackerel. At first they were taken moonlight nights, with seines. The schools rise to the surface, and, as they break the water with their back fins, may easily be seen. In the night they often show, also, a phosphorescent gleam. Skilful fishermen, taking out their nets in small boats, run them under the schools, and then, gathering in the edges of the net, bag them, and scoop them out with hand nets. This method was given up long before my day, though our fishermen have returned to it again of late years.

After this method came what was called "trailing." The vessel was put under easy sail, and the fishermen ranged themselves on the weather side and let their hooks, with light sinkers, trail out astern.

But trailing had its day, and was succeeded by jiggering, which was the uniform method during my fishing experience. In this method the vessel is so laid to the wind as to have *no* headway and drift square off to leeward. The fishermen were arranged, as in trailing, on the weather side, their small jigs thrown square out from the vessel's side. The drift dead to leeward tends to keep them out. Still, they need to be drawn in and thrown out often, to keep them near the surface. The skipper's place was the first abaft the main shrouds ; and the "second hand," or mate, was the next, forward. The one farthest aft was the "monkey." Aside from these, the crew shipped for particular places, those of largest experience getting the best, which were considered the nearest midships.

Mackerel are generally dainty and shy. A stamp on the deck will make a whole school dart like a flash. But they soon return. They seem to be very sensitive to sound. Sometimes, when there are thousands alongside, they will not touch a hook ; and then they will bite so ravenously that every line will be straightened at once, and the one most skilful in hauling in, striking off, and throwing out the jig, will get the most. There

comes in the skill. There is a special knack in striking off the fish into a deep tub and throwing out the
jig as a part of the same motion. It is only by experience this can be acquired, though natural gifts come
in play here, as in preaching. Long arms are important, and to know how to use them still more so.

There are few things more delightfully exciting than
a hungry school of mackerel hanging round the vessel
for a quarter of an hour, seizing the hook as soon as
it touches the water, bare or baited, and giving to each
man on the vessel's gleaming side a chance to show
his skill. Seen from a little distance, when the strike
is on the side of the schooner, it seems all alive
with gleaming flecks of silver. Then in an instant
the strike is off, and the school sweeps on. Then the
fishermen leave their lines and go round looking into
each other's tubs, to see who has caught the most.
Though, after a few years' experience, I was generally
pretty well up with the best, yet many and many a
time after a smart spirt, I have felt, when looking into
other tubs, like a defeated politician after election,—
I had had a bad run. Perhaps a dog-fish took my jig
right in the midst, and I had to haul him in, throw him
on deck, put my cowhide heel on his horned back, and
cut the hook from his sharklike mouth. All that took
time, and never is it more true that time is money than
when mackerel are on a rampage. We usually baited
our jigs with a bit of uncooked salt pork rind, because
it was tough and wore longer than anything else. But,
when they were in dainty mood, we would coax them
with a thin slice from one of their own or their fellows' tails. That would sometimes take them, when
they would turn like a Jew from swine skin.

A skilful fisherman was allowed three lines, if he could use them and not tangle his neighbors'. The third line was called a fly,—a very light jig, just weight enough to be thrown out with skill. It would float near the surface on the outer rim of the school, and now and then pick off a noble fellow, to the great annoyance of such as twitched their lines in vain for a bite. Then we had gaffs, with long slender wire running down two or three feet below the wooden handle, so as to pass easily through the water. When the fish refused the hook, and would swim round the vessel's side in a most provoking way, we would run our gaff below them, and with the hook in the end take in the most aristocratic among them in a most ungentlemanly way. It wasn't fair. It was a shabby way of doing it. It might do for a clumsy lobster under a rock ; but, for a genuine *wawunnekeseag* of the shining ancient race, it was a method of gouging that should not have been tolerated.

Dressing and salting the fish were just as necessary as catching them, but not so pleasant. To do this, we divided in pairs. One split, the other "gipped," the fish. To split, the mackerel is laid on a splitting board about waist-band high, and a sharp, thin blade run the entire length from nose to tail, with one drawing stroke shaving close the upper side of the backbone. The facility and ease and accuracy with which this is done by a workman is quite wonderful. The fish thus split is thrown with the same hand that held it in place into a "cover," a shallow tub set on two wash-barrels, where the gipper seizes it and with just three motions takes out the entrails and gills, and, breaking the belly to show the depth of the fat, throws it, flesh side down, into a barrel with two buckets of pure ocean brine at the bottom. The rapidity with which a wash-barrel of fish may be dressed in this way would astonish one who witnessed it for the first time. When the fish are all dressed, the barrels are filled with salt water and left to soak for half a day or so. Then the water is turned off, the fish thumbed and changed to another barrel, which is again filled with fresh sea-water.

"Thumbing" is rubbing the thumb over the break of the fat, to make the fish look fatter than it is; for it is the fat that decides whether the fish is No. 1, 2, or 3, the fattest being No. 1 and bringing the best price. It is to mackerel what "deaconing" is to a barrel of apples. The deception is so universal that it doesn't deceive. After remaining awhile in the changed water, they are poured out on deck, washed clean, and thrown down the hatchway for salting. After a heavy day's work, it would take a large part, at times the whole, of the night to dress and soak and salt the catch. Then there was no need of calling all hands in the morning. We were all up to see the day break, but so hungry and tired we hoped no one would feel a nibble when the lines were flung out. But ordinarily there was plenty of time, as there would sometimes be days and even weeks that we would not take a fish. Then we would strike large schools with a good appetite, and take a full fare in a week. When every available barrel and tub and bucket were salted full, we would salt as many in the bait shovel as it would hold, hoist our colors, make all sail, and head for home. That was the happiest part of the trip,—homeward bound with a full fare.

I must tell you about our arrangements for cooking.
We carried no cook, as they do now ; but each man
had to take his cook-day in turn. The duty of the
cook was to make tea or chocolate for breakfast or
supper, and get dinner for all hands. The dinners
were usually fish, salt junk, or stewed beans, each one
finding his own hard tack. Whatever each one wanted
for breakfast or supper, aside from the common tea or
chocolate, he must cook for himself. In this private
cooking, as in carrying a grist to mill, "first come, first
served." We had no stove, but a brick fireplace, with
a barricade round the hearth to prevent things "fetch-
ing away." The funnel above the deck was of wood,
lashed firmly to the deck, with a cleated board we
could change round on the top to prevent the wind
from blowing down.

Our fuel was wood, stowed away in the forepeak,
where it was kept nice and *damp* for ready use. As
friction matches had not been invented, the vessel was
provided with tinder-box, steel, and flint. But, in the
dampness of a fisherman's cabin, it is not easy to keep
tinder dry. So it was often no small job to make the
spark catch and hold long enough to ignite the brim-
stone match applied. But the fire once built could be
kept along through the day, especially as there were so
many to use it,— some for frying fish, some for cooking
bloaters, or stir puddings or shortcakes.

We ate our meals in a very independent way. We
did not stand for ceremony. The skipper and second
hand usually sat at a movable shelf, called, from home
association, a table. The rest of us took it standing
or sitting, as was most convenient. As somebody

must always be on deck, the hatches or weather side of the quarter-deck where the spray didn't wet was a good place for a mug of chocolate and a tin dish of beans. It was not deemed important to wash our private dishes as long as we could remember what we used in them last.

We had to be very sparing of fresh water. A barrel was always on top, lashed firmly beside the gangway; but we were allowed to use it for drink only, never for washing face and hands or any article of clothing. We carried about a dozen barrels for a four weeks' cruise. They were always stored directly under the main hatches, easy of access; and one of the first things to be done after getting fairly out to sea was to visit the water barrels with a gimlet, and bore a hole through every barrel near the bung. Without this ventilation the water would become stagnant and ropy, — unfit to drink.

As only the dinner was in common, each one carried his own stores. Mine, as I remember, were generally flour, meal, sugar, molasses, butter, eggs, pork, and rum. This last was to treat with; for fresh hands, "monkeys" included, were liable to a call to "treat all hands," when a cape or light-house not before seen was made. However, as each one carried his gallon keg, it wasn't so much the drink as the fun that demanded the payment of "duties." Still, we generally had some hard drinkers; but the harder they drank, the sooner the keg was empty, and the sooner Dick was himself again.

As I have recalled my fisherman days and the moral as well as other atmosphere of my fisherman life, I have thought that nothing could tempt me to permit a child of mine to be exposed to such influences. But a boy of thirteen who has had a good home can generally be trusted. Somehow, the wool grows on the naked back of a spring lamb, so that, when the October winds come, he has a nice warm coat to protect him from cold. "In heaven their angels do always behold the face of my Father." The angel on earth that waved her mystic wand over my exposed head was my mother, whose last words to me always were, "William, be a good boy." If I wasn't always good, I never was as bad as I should have been without those precious words.

Passing from exposed boys to preserved bloaters, let me tell you what a *bloater* is, and how it is made. The finest and fattest mackerel are selected, and, after being dressed as described, the backbone is taken out and the head and tail cut off. Then they are salted a couple of hours, just to harden the flesh. Then the salt is washed off carefully, and the fish laid, flesh side up, in the sun and wind to dry and ripen. After they are "done brown," they are ready for use ; and, when cooked before an open fire, set up on skewers made for the purpose, they are delicious.

We generally managed to have a few ready to take home when we arrived. Sometimes, when we got into the harbor in the night, and I walked home with a happy heart under the stars, I would hang a nice bloater on the front-door handle of a certain house where a certain sweet girl lived,— the very one whose little hand took the candy from behind the school-room door,— to let her know as she swept off the doorstep in the morning that somebody got home from fishing in the night. Who said she expected me the next evening? I didn't. It was your guess.

Packing day was a great occasion, especially when we brought in a full fare. Our colors were run up, and snapped joyfully in the breeze, and sometimes a long pennon would float out gracefully over the water. The skipper was happy, the crew was happy, the inspectors were happy, the packers were happy, and the owners were happy; for a full fare meant a full purse all round.

Then on that day it would be decided, with government sealed scales, who was high line. Generally, it was the skipper,— he prided himself on that; but the summer I was sixteen *I was high line,*— not for a single trip only, but for the season, taking with my own hands a hundred and thirty-four barrels. I think I must have grown an inch that year. But this promise of my boyhood was not fulfilled, I regret to say, in after life. I never have been high line in anything else that I have undertaken.

On packing day the owners gave the whole crew a dinner at the hotel on shore. And such a dinner! Roast! boiled! baked! with all the richest vegetables and fruits from garden and field, finishing up with plum pudding rich enough for Thanksgiving. It was a dinner to tempt the appetite even of a well-fed landsman; but for a dozen hungry fishermen who had lived on hard tack and beans for a month, without the smell of a fresh vegetable, it was simply *celestial.* We could go another whole trip on the memory of it. I feel like thanking those owners, long since in heaven or somewhere, for their superb packing dinners. I can smell and taste them even now, though more than sixty-five years have passed since we feasted upon them.

But I must leave my fishing experience, though it continued, for a part of the summer, till I was twenty. But, when about sixteen, I graduated from the district school, and began learning the trade of a ship-carpenter with my father, as my brother Albert had done before me.

Just before this father had given up building for himself, and was taking jobs of work from other builders, sometimes "timbering and planking," sometimes "putting in a deck," and the like. He took me with him. I began work on the North River, which at that time was dotted with ship-yards all along its serpentine course. It was one of the earliest industries of that region. A large part of the young men became ship-carpenters.

In the early days the forests around yielded an abundance of white oak, the best material for ships, if we except the live oak, which is found only in the South. These forests of white oak, however, were not inexhaustible; and before my day they began to fail, and building on the river to decline. Besides, the shifting sand-bars at the mouth of the river, and shoals inside, became more and more troublesome, so that it was with difficulty a large ship could be got down the river and out to sea. At first many Nantucket whaling ships were built here; but the shallowness of the river and the growing scarcity of old-growth timber at last drove the business into deeper water, where timber from abroad was more accessible, and Medford, Chelsea, and East Boston became the great places for ship-

building on our Massachusetts coast. I had not worked
long for father before he took jobs of work in other
places ; and, being ambitious, I soon earned for father,
who needed my aid, a man's wages. We used to work
in those days from sun to sun, even in the long days of
summer. The halcyon days of "eight hours" or even
"ten" had not then dawned.

At one time, when we worked at Braintree and went
home Saturday nights, mother would get breakfast
for us Monday morning by about three o'clock. Then
we would start off, and, walking twelve miles, often
be the first in the yard. After that a long day's work.
As I look back on those days, I don't see how we
stood it ; but we did, and I don't remember ever to
have thought that I had a hard time.

In the ship-yard as well as on board the fishing
vessel, rum was a common beverage in those days. All
hands were called at eleven o'clock and at four for
grog. Besides this, many kept a private bottle in their
tool-chests ; and it was interesting to see how often
such men would want a particular tool in that safely
locked chest.

In those days fathers claimed the wages of their
sons till they were twenty-one, clothing and feeding
them, of course, in the mean time. I was glad to give
father my wages, for I knew he needed them ; but,
when I was twenty, I told him I would like to buy my
time for the remaining year. I would give him one
hundred dollars, as I could earn it, to let me off, and
begin the world for myself. He knew I was worth
more to him than that ; but he was a dear, generous
father, and to my great delight accepted my pro-

posal. I was a fair workman, took jobs of work, so making more than day wages, and at the end of the year paid over the hundred and had more than another hundred, if I remember rightly, in the locker. Now I was free. Now I was twenty-one, that goal to which my boyhood had looked with longing eyes.

VI.

YOUNG MANHOOD.

1832–1834.

FEVER IN MEDFORD.— BROTHERS AND SISTERS.— MARRIAGE.—
HOUSEKEEPING.— GUNNING.

ANDREW JACKSON was President. I name this, not
because I was interested in politics, but to let you know
how long ago it was.

Soon after I was free, I had a fresh experience of the
power and blessedness of a mother's love. I was at
work on a lower deck, in company with others, in Medford, in the hot month of August, and was suddenly
smitten down with what threatened to be brain fever.
The doctor was sent for, and gave transient relief to
my bursting brain by bleeding. In my boarding-house
my fellow-workmen were ready to watch, and kind as
they could be, and as clumsy as they were kind. I
grew worse so rapidly that, becoming alarmed, my
dear good Uncle Elijah Brooks, a brother of my
mother, took a private team and drove to Scituate to
bring mother, all unbeknown to me. He went with
speed, returning in the night. I felt a gentle hand on
my pained head. From that hour I began to grow better. Never was such medicine as I found in mother's
face, and mother's hand, and mother's love. It acted
like magic. In ten days I was up, and resumed my

work, though pale and weak enough to make my fellow-
workmen exclaim, as they saw me take up my tools to
help them finish the job. I should not have gone to
work again so soon ; but it was the first year of my manhood, and I was ambitious to do the best I could.

The older children at the Block House home were
scattered by this time. Philenda, the black-eyed fairy,
had been married to Joseph Bond, Jr., of Waltham, for
ten years. My only brother, " Butt," had married Sarah
Foster— Sarah Albert, as we have always called her —
four years before. Sarah, the rosy-cheeked blonde, had
married William Turner, of Scituate. One year later,
and the year I was twenty-one, Julia married Captain
James Southworth, of Scituate. So only Lucy and
Caroline, fifteen and thirteen, were now left in the old
home with father and mother. I never want to forget
what a pleasure it gave me to use some of my first earned
money for my young sisters, who had few ways of earning money for themselves. They were lovely girls. I
shall tell you more about them by and by.

When I had laid up a few hundred dollars, I began,
as young men do, to think about a home for myself.
But one cannot make a home alone, any more than a
single bird can make a nest. Only mates build nests
or make homes. Did I think of anybody in particular ?
Well, maybe so.

Her name was Mary Jacobs Foster, and she was then
living with her sister, Aunt Tempie,* at Brookline,
where Turner and Magoun were building ships.

We were married on the 15th of May, 1834.

I was twenty-three six days before, and Mary was

* Mrs. Francis Turner.

twenty-three the 6th of the next October. When
any one inquires of me the proper age to marry, I
say promptly, twenty-three. On the morning of that
eventful 15th I was at South Boston. I had just finished a job of work there. I took the stage for South
Scituate as it came out of the city, and at about four
in the afternoon we passed through the door of the
venerable old house where I left my cod on the handle
when I was a fisher-boy, and, taking a country chaise,
we rode to the residence of the minister of the First
Parish,— our parish was then without a pastor,— and
were married by Rev. Edmund Q. Sewall. Mary's
sister Hannah, and a dear playmate of my boyhood,
Tom Southworth, went with us as bridesmaid and
groomsman. I thought it a beautiful service, though
I am not sure that I could tell a word of it the next
day, or even that afternoon. But it was beautiful, very
beautiful,— I know it was ; for then we were joined
in a holy wedlock, which was the joy and blessing of
my life for over forty years.

After remaining a few weeks with father and mother
at the Block House as boarders, I took a job of work
at Commercial Point. Having finished that in August,
I went mackerel fishing for old associations sake. But
I had lost my luck, and left before the season was
over. In November I found work in Medford, took
Mary with me, and there, in a part of a new house built
and occupied by my uncle, Gilbert Brooks, we first
went to housekeeping. We had the upper part of the
house, and furnished it as neatly as good taste — of
course we had that — and a reasonable amount of hard-
earned money could do. Oh, it was a charming, cosey

little place for a young mechanic to start out with! It was near where I worked; and it was so nice, when the day's work was over, to go *home*, and feel that it was my home. No, *our* home; for there was Mary at the window to greet me.

One day, having worked steadily for a long time, I concluded to take a half-day's recreation. Meadow-birds sometimes came up on the banks of the Mystic; and, being used to gunning on the North River, I thought I would recreate that way. But I had neither gun nor ammunition. So I borrowed the first, and went up town and bought the second, and started out for birds enough for a pot-pie, such as mother used to make from the gray-backs and plovers father brought home.

It was a beautiful morning, and I went out with high hopes, leaving Mary to make ready for the pot-pie, telling her how mother did it, and making both our mouths water in anticipation of the rich dish that would carry us back to the days of our youth; for by this time we began to feel quite old.

But, alas! the fondest hopes are liable to disappointment. The birds that morning were scarce,— not a yellow-leg or a gray-back on the meadows. How far and long I wandered in vain search, through how many muddy swales I waded, over or into how many ditches I jumped, how often I left a shoe in the mud, and lost the other in trying to recover it, I will not attempt to tell; for it was a good while ago, and memory is treacherous, like the salt marsh.

But this is clear. The peeps were few and shy, as if they had a suspicion that my father was a good shot;

though, if they had known his son, they need not have
been afraid. At last the sun grew hot, and I grew
tired ; and, knowing that Mary was waiting with all the
anxiety of a new housekeeper for the birds, I sighted
a lonely, melancholy-looking flock, and brought down
two,— two peeps, about as large as English sparrows.

I took them home in crestfallen sadness, feeling
much as I have often done after making a very poor
speech. Mary was lenient. She knew it wasn't a good
day for birds, and that I hadn't used a gun for years.
Indeed, she was probably so glad to see me home again
with that gun, alive, and with none of my fingers missing, that she was more disposed to rejoice than to rebuke or make fun of me. So she set herself to work to
do the best she could for the pot-pie with the material
she had. The birds were small, to begin with ; but,
after they were picked and dressed, they were smaller
still,— scarcely discernible with the naked eye. But
I assured her mother had made good pot-pies out of
peeps, and it was true. I think I didn't name the
quantity. Of course, it was natural for a young housekeeper to think that what was lacking in bird-flesh
could be made up, in a measure, in seasoning. So a
liberal use was made of salt and pepper. It didn't
take long for the frail creatures to cook.

So the table was spread with a dainty white cloth,
our new plates and new knives and forks were laid in
order, and the smoking and savory pie brought on. We
tasted, prepared to exclaim, and we did ; but it was not
with gastric joy. Salt ! salt ! salt ! Pepper ! pepper ! pepper ! It was seasoned with a vengeance. We could not
eat a mouthful. The invisibility of the birds deceived

us both. We were willing to share the mistake. But it was a memorable experience. I had lost a half-day's work, clean cash, lost the price of my powder and shot, we had both lost our dinner; but it may have proved, after all, the best half-day's work I ever made, for it was the last of my gunning, and the fun we both got out of it was seasoning for many a jolly reminiscence.

VII

CRISIS.

1834-1837.

RELIGIOUS EXPERIENCE.— LONGING TO PREACH.— STUDY.—
MOVING TO SCITUATE.— VISIT TO CAMBRIDGE.— REV.
S. J. MAY.— SCHOOL-TEACHING.

I NOW approached what proved the great crisis of my
life,— a crisis that changed radically its whole course,
and opened to me a field of labor entirely different
from what I had regarded as my life-work.

As the change in all my plans and purposes was so
sudden and so great, I must try to tell you a little
about it, though in doing it I shall have to speak of my
religious experience,— a subject on which reticence is a
virtue ; for too much handling rubs the bloom from the
most delicate fruit.

But you are my own dear children and grandchildren ;
and, as I love you, I want you to know about these deeper
experiences in life, which made a new man of me and
led me into the Christian ministry.

I was never an entirely thoughtless boy. Though
full of fun and jollity, I had, like most other boys,
seasons of serious thought. I was brought up to go to
church, and soon came to love it. I even remember
just where I sat in the old church, when I first began
to listen to the sermon and to understand that it had

something for me, child as I was. It was an epoch in my child-life when I learned that the sermon was for me. It led to the habit of *listening,*— a habit that has clung to me through life ; for, however limited my power to *instruct* has been, I have always been a good listener, and owe as much to that, perhaps, as to good reading.

Conscience began to speak to me early. I have told you how it thrashed me after I "thrashed" those eggs. I have told you of the impression the death of a dear playfellow made upon me. But I was a rubber ball, and easily bounded out the impression made. The old parish where I was brought up was "Arminian," so called, at the beginning, but had gradually grown into the first type of Unitarianism. It was anti-Calvinistic, very decidedly, though the main stress was always laid not on doctrine, but a good life. Good, wholesome doctrine was preached, but it did not move me much. It did not rouse and stimulate me. When I left home, I still held to my church-going and enjoyed good preaching. But by and by I had an inward awakening. I cannot tell what started it. Maybe it was the same voice that spake to me when a small boy. But it said to me : "Be a man. Live a truer and nobler life." I knew what it meant, for I had some intimate associates whose influence was not good. Not that they were bad. They were very fair, average young men, with no very bad habits. I liked them, enjoyed their companionship, and we spent many happy evenings together. But I wasn't satisfied with them or myself. I wanted other associates, to talk of other things ; and so, when the voice came, saying, "Come up higher," I resolved I would quietly break away from this sort of

companionship. To do this, I saw I must change my
boarding-place. I had an uncle and aunt in the town,
who were good, earnest Baptists; and, although I had
no liking for the sect, I liked them, and thought I
would be glad to board in their quiet home.

So one evening I stood alone at their front door, in
the moonlight, ready to lift the latch. But, after all,
was I ready to take the step? What would my companions say? I couldn't tell them why I left. They
would think it very strange in me. Should I go in or
should I go back? I thought of a good many things as
I stood there under the light of the serene heavens. I
thought of mother. At last I think some good angel
decided it for me; and I lifted the latch, and was cordially welcomed, engaged board with them, and became
an inmate of their family. It broke an entangling spell,
and I was happy.

As I had no place in particular to go to church, I
went with them. The preaching was very different from what I had been accustomed to. I didn't
like it. But gradually it took hold of me. My soul
was already awake before I heard it. I was receptive;
and, although my intellect rebelled against the harsh
doctrine, my conscience was moved, my moral and
spiritual nature was quickened. I was overwhelmed
with a sense of sin ; and, after some weeks of great spiritual agony, a sweet peace stole into my soul.

I had passed through what was regarded as a real
evangelical conversion. Oh how kind the friends all
were ! how they rejoiced that I had passed from death
unto life ! Soon I felt a strong desire to join the church
and take up the cross of duty, which seemed no cross

now, but a crown. But I soon found that it was only my heart that had been converted, not my head.

When the doctrinal statements were given to me, I found I could not subscribe to them. I was Unitarian still. My friends labored with me to show me my error. They gave me a copy of their articles of faith, with reference to the passages of Scripture where they were *proved* true added to each one. I seized on this with avidity, for I wanted to satisfy my mind. But, after turning to the passages, I could not find the proof. I was told it was because I was totally depraved, that I must not trust my reason, but accept the creed on faith. But this, strange as it may seem, did not convince me. This was before I was married. Had I been married, Mary would have helped me out. As it was, I struggled on with a converted heart and an heretical head. Had the new school of Orthodoxy, that puts Christ above creed, been in existence then, I should undoubtedly have joined them. But something better than that was in store for me. After I married and moved to Medford, Mary not enjoying the Baptist preaching, we went one Sunday to the First Parish Church, Rev. Caleb Stetson, pastor. We were both pleased. We went again. We were still more pleased. He was a Unitarian, but not of the old kind. It was such Unitarianism as I had never heard before. It was transcendental Unitarianism. He preached the immanence of God in nature and in the soul of man. He emphasized the divine *fatherhood* and human *brotherhood*, sin its own sorrow, and goodness its own eternal reward. Orthodoxy had given me the doctrine of the Holy Spirit, which old-fashioned Unitarianism said little about; but it was linked with a

trinity I could not understand. The doctrine of the
" Immanence of God " gave the Holy Spirit to me in
sweeter, tenderer, more rational form,— an ever present
holy influence from God, not going and coming like a
revival preacher, but a perpetual, indwelling presence.

My head and heart were satisfied. I could still hold
on to my "new birth" as a divine reality, for which I
have always devoutly thanked God, and hold on to my
reason, too, as equally divine with conscience and the
moral sense.

Through all my religious interest and experience
thus far I had never had the most distant thought of
preaching. Indeed, I think my whole nature, intellectual and spiritual, had never been in complete harmony
before. But now the gospel of Christ shone with new
beauty, and came over me with new power, as a fresh
revelation from on high. Now a longing such as I had
never felt before came over me to preach. Oh, I
thought, if I could only fit myself for the humblest pulpit, in the humblest parish, to preach this gospel of the
immanent God and the Eternal Life, here and now, it
would be the greatest joy of my life. But could this
ever be ? Did not my lack of early culture forbid ? It
would indeed seem so. But the vision haunted me. I
could not order it away. So I wrote a letter to the
dear minister whose preaching had, under God, waked
this longing and inspired the vision, and told him all.
He kindly encouraged me. Mary encouraged me, too.
Without that encouragement I should have been helpless. But even with it there were most serious difficulties.

Since leaving the winter district school at fifteen or

sixteen, I had paid no attention whatever to study. I had liked to read, but only read what I liked, with no method. Indeed, I had found little time for reading of any kind. The old romances of that day, "Robinson Crusoe," "Arabian Nights," "Thaddeus of Warsaw," "Children of the Abbey," and later Scott's "Waverley Novels" had their charm for me as for most young people. But I had given little attention to history, natural or national, and none at all to literature. This seemed a poor and weak foundation to build on. But my soul was alive with a great purpose, and I resolved, God helping, to try. Mary was a better scholar than I, and we two started a little school together in our cosey sitting-room. We began at the beginning, English grammar and the common branches. I kept at work in the yard a part of the time, to pay our way, and studied the rest. The flame of interest burned, blazed, and every fresh sermon I heard added fuel. Mr. Joseph Angier taught a private academy in Medford at that time; and I engaged Mr. John Buttrick, his assistant, to hear me recite at certain odd hours. He helped me greatly. He entered at once into all my fond hopes and aspirations; and, seeing I was in real live earnest, he offered me every facility in his power. I made rapid progress during the three months I recited to him.

In the spring of 1836 we decided to leave Medford and return to Scituate, where we could live at less expense while I continued my studies. It would have been very hard, giving up our dear little home, but for the end we had in view. That made it easy. A fellow-workman was about being married, and he took our house with all its furnishing, except the beds and bedding, just as it stood, paying us nearly the cost ; for it was all new and fresh.

Soon after going to Scituate, I learned of a house to be sold very cheap, near my father's ; and I bought it, putting into it all the money I had. It was a good investment. We began keeping house again, with spare furnishing, but luxurious hopes. Here I renewed my studies.

The Rev. E. Q. Sewall, who married us, became interested in my purpose, and heard me recite in Whately's "Logic and Rhetoric." Here, too, I began the study of Latin and Greek; for my purpose then was to enter the Theological School at Cambridge as soon as I became qualified. I still had to work with my hands a part of the time, to keep along. I undertook to make shoe-boxes in my father's barn. This was while I was learning the Greek alphabet ; and I chalked the letters on the collar beam before me to jog my memory.

But my shoe-box enterprise yielded small profit, and I gave it up. Once in a while I could get a small job at my trade. At last I thought I would go to Cambridge and see just what the requirements were, and what aid, if any, I could get. I went and had an interview with one of the professors. No doubt my general appearance — a countryman, a mechanic with hard hands — was against me. Besides, I was married ; and, although I brought a letter from Rev. E. Q. Sewall, it might have been written out of the kindness of his heart rather than his good judgment. I never blamed the professor that he didn't "thuse"

over me. There was small reason that he should.
His remarks were cool and judicious. He was evidently not inclined to raise any false hopes. He was
kind, but cautious. He told me the qualifications required, and the aid I might expect if I proved worthy
of it. It was probably just the thing to say to me.
But I was expecting something different, and left disappointed. I saw the few hundred dollars I had would
soon be gone, and I should leave the school heavily
in debt ; and mother's warning, " William, never get in
debt," rung in my ears.

I went home feeling as if I had been wrapped in a
wet sheet. It took long and patient rubbing to get up
a reaction. I even thought of giving the whole thing
up. Of course, I never could have given it up ; but for
the time I was utterly discouraged.

I returned, not to study, but to work. I took a
windlass to make at Scituate Harbor for thirty dollars.
I needed the money to live upon. But I did not give
up my hope. It was waiting for a providential breath
to kindle it to a flame.

Our parish had been, since the death of Mr. Deane,
without a pastor. We had had many candidates, to
whom I had listened with great interest. At last the
Rev. Samuel Joseph May, who had served for a year
as the agent of the Massachusetts Anti-slavery Society,
came as a candidate ; and, although there was not much
anti-slavery among us, we were all delighted. While
he was perfectly outspoken on the great questions dear
to his heart, he was so genial, so kind, that he won us
all, and disarmed prejudices so completely that he received a unanimous invitation to become our pastor,
which he at once accepted.

I was strongly drawn to him from the first. I could not keep my secret from him. I soon told him all,— my fond hopes, and my disappointment at not being able to go to Cambridge. He took my hand in his, that warm, loving hand so full of blessing, and told me not to be discouraged. Cambridge, good as it was,— and he knew how good, for he graduated from the University and the Theological School,— was not absolutely necessary to a useful ministry. Frederick T. Gray, educated in mercantile life, had studied with him. He would help me, and I could help him in many ways. It was the old method of studying for the ministry, and most gladly I accepted the proposal.

He soon put me on a course of preparatory reading, opened his large library and his great, loving heart to me, and I began again, with a new hope of fitting myself for some humble field of labor in the Christian ministry.

The following winter I taught the district school, where I used to attend, for thirty-two dollars a month.

VIII

PREPARATION FOR THE MINISTRY.

1837–1840.

MOTHER'S DEATH.— REFORMS AND REFORMERS.— OUR FIRST-
BORN.— DR. WALKER'S CHURCH,—CHARLESTOWN.—" UNTO
US A SON IS GIVEN."— SUPPLYING MR. MAY'S PULPIT.—
FIRST SERMON.— TEACHING.— APPROBATION TO PREACH.—
LABORS OF LOVE.

THE next spring, March 7, 1837, my dear mother
died. It was our first great family sorrow. But it did
not come suddenly. She had been slowly declining for
two or three years. But, oh, she was so good and true,
so unselfish and loving, it was hard to let her go even
to heaven! She knew, of course, all my fond hopes of
entering the ministry, and rejoiced in them. I used
sometimes to bring with me a little poem I had written,
and read it to her, as if from a newspaper. After getting her approval, I would tell her of the innocent cheat,
which she enjoyed as well as I. She was a sweet
soul,— everything to father, everything to her children. She died before the Daguerrian art was discovered, so that we have no picture of her. This I
deeply regret. But I suppose no picture, could we
have it, would equal the one she left on our hearts. In
her days of health, she was bright, full of humor and
Brooks wit, the life of company, and making all around

her happy. Her religion was of the quiet and unobtru-
sive kind. She said little about it, but let it run into
her daily life. Her "William, be a good boy," was
Bible plenarily inspired with human and divine love.
She was patient and trustful, and willing to go, if it was
the Father's will; but she knew, as every true wife and
mother knows, how much she was needed, and longed
to stay. She had suffered so much and so long that the
suffering had impressed itself upon her face. She had
grown old fast, though she was only fifty-eight. But
when the angel of death had gently taken the spirit out
of the sick form, and touched the wan cheeks with his
celestial fingers, the old sweet look came back again.
She was young and fair once more, and a sweet smile
as if from visions of peace and beauty rested on the
dear face. It was a real comfort to look upon her. It
was not death. It was rest in a higher life.

I have spoken of Philenda's marriage. Luther
Albert and Sarah and Julia had also married and made
homes for themselves, so that dear father was left alone
with Lucy and Caroline for his housekeepers. But
they were noble girls, and did all they could to make
his home comfortable.

When I began my studies under Mr. May, I dropped
my Latin and Greek; but, as I had not given much
attention to either, they had not far to fall. I enjoyed
my winter school-teaching, and think I was successful.
It was a great advantage to me, as it enabled me to
make up the deficiency of my early education, and lay
a good foundation for English study in all depart-
ments open to me. But my best text-book, intellectual,
moral, and religious, was Mr. May. He set me at

work ; made me superintendent of his Sunday-school ;
took me with him to school-house meetings, educational,
temperance, anti-slavery, and religious.

Mr. May had a wide acquaintance with the leading
reformers ; and they all came from time to time to Scituate to confer with him, to enjoy his fellowship, or to
lecture, so that I was privileged to see and hear the
foremost reformers of the day. He believed that
women who felt they had a word to say for "truth and
right and suffering man" should be encouraged to say
it. The first woman I ever heard speak from the pulpit
was Miss Angelina Grimké, afterwards Mrs. Theodore
D. Weld, whom Mr. May invited to speak in his church.
She was very eloquent and persuasive, and proved her
right to speak to be divine.

Garrison was one of Mr. May's intimate friends, and
A. Bronson Alcott, his brother-in-law, used to spend his
summers there with his family, so that I probably had
a richer variety of all sorts of opinions than I should
have got at Cambridge, had I entered. Transcenden-
talism, non-resistance, anti-slavery, woman's rights,
teetotalism, Emerson, Carlyle, Theodore Parker, were
my daily meat and drink. And it was good, nourishing
food, especially as served up by Mr. May on Sundays.
He was always most eloquent on these matters. On
ordinary Christian themes he was sometimes dull. But
on the great reforms dear to his heart he would blaze
and burn with an interest that would set the congregation aglow.

In the summer of this year I opened a private school
to eke out our living. I had nineteen scholars at three
dollars a quarter. I did not bear well the confinement
in hot weather, and continued only three months.

On the 30th of June this year, only a few months
after mother's death, a great event transpired in our
little home. A sweet child was given us, our first-born,
a daughter. We had been married over three years,
but had only a house. Now we had a household; and
how fondly we did hold the new treasure, and how earnestly we prayed for grace to train the little one to
nobleness of life!

After I had closed my private school, not feeling very
strong, I went for a few months mackerel fishing, as
that had always benefited me. My health was improved, but my purse only slightly replenished. I had
lost my luck. It was my last fishing voyage.

The winter following I kept school again in my
native district. This brought me in $120, but hardly
sufficed for the year, as we had now a family of three.
So in the following April I went to Charlestown and
took a job of work of Magoun & Turner, which lasted
two months. During this time I attended Dr. Walker's
church (Unitarian), took a class in his Sunday-school,
and attended his Bible class meetings. It was a rare
privilege to sit under his preaching, and come into close
contact with him. While there, I gave a lecture in
a Methodist chapel, I think on anti-slavery, and kept
my mind active as well as my hands.

Returning to Scituate in July, I took work, to the
amount of $26, on a schooner built on the North River.

Giving what time I could to reading and study in the
autumn, I again, for the third time, took charge of the
same winter school, for the same compensation. About
this time Horace Mann, as Secretary of the Board of
Education in Massachusetts, had worked a real revival

in common-school education, and the interest spread all
through the State. Educational conventions were held
all round, to which Mr. May, with his family carriage,
an omnibus which would always hold one more, would
carry all who wished to go. Our little district school
caught the awakening, and I would sometimes wonder
whether, after all, teaching were not quite as high a
calling as preaching.

After closing my school, I set myself to the study of
Norton on the " Evidences of the Genuineness of the
Gospels," and became deeply interested. I doubt if any
student at Cambridge studied it with any greater interest. Mr. May's large library, and his larger wisdom and
experience, were my constant counsellors.

On May 25 of this year, 1839, the heavens were
again opened in benediction on our little home, and
"unto us a son was given." Now we had a pair in the
home nest. We called him Joseph. It was the name
of the eldest son of Elder Nathaniel from whom our
branch of the Tildens descended. He was a lovely
boy ; and our hearts were happy, never for a moment
doubting that means would come to meet our growing
needs.

I continued my study of the Bible, Old Testament and
New, critical and exegetical, read Paley, Verplanck,
Whately, the German theology, and Professor Norton's
criticism of it, the best published sermons and essays
in Christian literature and doctrine,— in short, did what
I could, with the best of teachers, to make myself acquainted with the best thought going. I did not aspire
to be a scholar, only, if possible, a useful Christian
minister.

Mr. May had told me, when he first spoke his great
word of encouragement, that the way to learn to preach
was to preach. But so far I had not attempted to conduct a public service of worship. I had spoken with
Mr. May at school-house and town-house, and given a
lyceum lecture, but had never attempted a Sunday service.

This summer Mr. May decided to visit his old society
at Brooklyn, Conn. He was to be gone two Sundays.
I was already the superintendent of his Sunday-school;
and he said to me, " Mr. Tilden, you must supply the
pulpit while I am gone." I saw there was nothing to
do but attempt it. But I had never written a sermon,
and could not do it on so short notice. So I read a
printed sermon each Sunday, and conducted the other
services as best I could. It was a hard thing to do in
the parish where I was brought up. It seemed to me
I could have done it more easily anywhere else. But
I saw I must, or give up all idea of ever preaching;
and the kindly feelings of the people, especially the
encouraging words of Mrs. May, cheered me greatly.
When Mr. May returned, he was so pleased with the
result that he gave me out of his library Horne's " In-
troduction to the Old and New Testaments " in four vol-
umes,— a very valuable work in its day, and one which
proved of great service to me in the earlier years of my
ministry. Soon after this I wrote a sermon, that I
might have something of my own to say in case I should
have another invitation.

But I still had to work occasionally at my trade to
" keep the pot boiling." As I was working on a job on
the North River one Saturday afternoon, the Rev.

George Leonard, of Marshfield, came into the ship-yard. I dropped my broad-axe to greet him, for I knew him well. After the usual salutation, he told me he had come to ask me to give him a labor of love the next day. I felt a little queer about my left breast, and I presume looked warm; but I wiped my sweaty brow, and told him I would come. My hands had clasped the broad-axe handle for so many years that I could not possibly straighten them so as to touch my palms, but the Bible requirement was for "clean hands," not straight ones; and, having now a sermon, I promptly consented. I went, and in Mr. Leonard's church, at East Marshfield, in June, 1839, preached my first ser- mon. I have it now,— not for inspection, but as a relic which I highly prize. I find, on looking on the back of it, that I gave it twice the next month, once at Pem- broke and once at Scituate. It contains no evidence of ever having been preached since.

The next winter I taught our district school for the fourth and last time. These winter schools of boys and girls of all ages, from six to twenty, I greatly enjoyed. I look back upon my work as a teacher with great pleas- ure. The minister of my boyhood, Rev. Samuel Deane, used to say of a certain teacher that "he could really teach more than he knew." I don't know as I ever quite came up to that, but I did have the gift of teach- ing *all* I knew, and of greatly interesting the pupils in their studies. My youngest sister, Caroline, who was afterwards distinguished as teacher in one of our State normal schools, was my pupil. There was great pleasure in starting her in her brilliant career, though she soon left me far behind.

At this time the schools were not graded, save as I graded them naturally into classes. One of these, in which I took great delight, I named "my class without books." I called them into the floor, and asked them questions in geography, beginning with the geography of South Scituate, and widening out to all the towns in the county, all the counties in the State, all the States and Territories in the United States, capitals, chief mountains, rivers, etc., the class answering in concert. So with other branches, together with questions "on common things" not in the books. This was a new thing at that time, and as richly enjoyed by the children as by myself. All the common-school studies were fresh in my mind from recent attention to them, and the new methods of teaching waked new interest in the school.

But, much as I had come to love teaching, the old call which first lured me from the ship-yard still sounded in my ears, and drew me on in my ministerial studies.

In the summer of 1840 I read a sermon before the Plymouth and Bay Association of Ministers, at one of their regular meetings. In the kindness of their hearts, the brethren were pleased to consider it satisfactory, and they gave me what was called an "Approbation to Preach." As it is my only "theological diploma," I here give it in full: —

[COPY.]

This may certify that Mr. William P. Tilden has been approbated as a preacher of the Gospel of Christ, by the Plymouth and Bay Association of Ministers, and is hereby recommended to the

churches and societies that may wish his services as a man, in the
estimation of the members, well qualified, intellectually and morally,
to advance the interests of the Redeemer's Kingdom.

Attest: JOSIAH MOORE.

COHASSET, Aug. 12, 1840.

During the spring, summer, and autumn of this year
I wrote a few sermons and gave labors of love to nearly
all the ministers in the Association. I was everywhere
kindly received. But, while words of encouragement
were sweet, my diffidence made my early efforts very
embarrassing. I was not trustful enough to be calm
and self-possessed. I was afraid, of what, I conld not
tell. I used to run away before service, and try to
walk and whip myself into courage. This held on so
long that I began to fear it would conquer me, and that
I should have to give up my chosen life-work. But I
kept on fighting against it, till by and by the natural
diffidence began to yield, and I became more trustful.
One sharp experience helped me. I was conducting
the Sunday service in Hingham for Rev. Mr. Stearns
(afterwards D.D.). I was offering prayer, when all at
once my thoughts failed me. My mind was a blank;
not a word could I speak; I was dumb; I seemed suspended in mid-air. How long I was in this condition I
could not tell. At last it came to me, "Pray for a
thought." I did pray, silently; and the answer came.
Thoughts and words came, and I went on with the service under a sweet sense of relief and assistance. It
was a lesson of trust, and it gave me confidence in the
divine aid.

Late in the autumn of 1840 I went to West Bridgewater, to spend a Sunday with the Rev. R. Stone, the

pastor of the Unitarian church, and give him a labor of love. Mr. Stone had a charming wife and a large family of promising children. He was very cordial, and seemed so well pleased with the ship-carpenter minister that he recommended me to the Unitarian parish at Norton, whose minister, Rev. Asarelah Bridge, was about leaving.

IX.

EARLY MINISTRY.

1840.

INVITATION TO PREACH IN NORTON AS CANDIDATE.— DRUNK-
ARD'S FUNERAL.—UNANIMOUS CALL.—ORDINATION.--WINE
AT COMMUNION.— ADIN BALLOU.

SOON after this, as Mary and I were sitting in our
quiet little dining-room and kitchen, both in one, we received a letter postmarked Norton, Mass. We knew
not a soul in that town.

We broke the seal, and, lo ! it was a letter from Mr.
Leonard Hodges, asking me to supply the Unitarian
pulpit four Sundays, *as a candidate.* This was my first
invitation to preach as a candidate or for pay. It was
what we had been looking for and hoping for from
some source before long ; but this came so unexpectedly
that it set our hearts beating and our tongues flying.
What sort of a place was it? What sort of people?
Would they listen to me when they learned that I had
no diploma from college or divinity school? All was
uncertain. But we were full of gratitude and hope.
The invitation had come without our seeking it. It did
seem as if " He who feeds the ravens when they cry "
had something to do with it. I was to begin the next
Sunday. We could think and talk of nothing else.
Mary packed my carpet-bag with unspoken prayers for

my success, and on Friday, Nov. 6, 1840, I left home, arriving in Norton that evening. I was to board with Captain Dauphin King, and went directly to his house, where I was kindly received. He had married for his second wife the daughter of Rev. Dr. Allen, of Pembroke, one of the Association that approbated me, so that I found myself, though among entire strangers, not utterly unknown.

The next day I looked round and took account of stock. I found a pleasant village, with a broad, shaded street, with two churches, small, but neat, and nearly new. The old parish church was still standing, used for a town house, in which a political meeting was held that very afternoon. An attractive feature of the village was the Wheaton Seminary, established a few years before by Judge Laban Wheaton, the oldest and richest man in the village.

Sunday came, my first Sunday as a candidate. Only the week before Mr. Bridge had preached his farewell. So I was their first candidate. I felt awkward and constrained. Had a hard day of it, in which the people doubtless shared. I made a melancholy record in my journal. I could not call my début a success.

The week following I went round among the people. I found them mostly farmers and mechanics, plain, kind-hearted people, in moderate circumstances. I liked them, and as they said nothing disparaging of my service, I plucked up new courage, and perhaps did a little better the next Sunday.

Half of my engagement was now out, and it might seem to some folks that I should have stayed the other two Sundays before going home. But I couldn't do it, with Mary and the children within thirty miles, and so much to tell them. I was homesick, and so started for home early Monday morning. Oh, what a delightful week that was with my family, and how we canvassed the Norton parish and speculated of coming events! The next Sunday I was in the pulpit again, and did decidedly better, so that I wrote in my journal, "I have had a very happy day."

Between this and the next Sunday came Thanksgiving, and I wrote and preached my first Thanksgiving sermon, which proved so satisfactory that I repeated it in the evening in the neighboring church at Mansfield.

The next Sunday I finished my engagement and held my breath. I was the first candidate. Would they hear others before deciding? It was the common course. It seemed reasonable. But the parish invited me to continue with them till the 1st of April.

This was a great encouragement. Here was a four months' engagement, which I accepted at once. I thought that, whatever might be the result of this further candidating, I could not be separated from my family through the winter. So I engaged board with one of my parishioners, James O. Messenger, who with his wife became fast friends, and whom we have always held in high esteem.

I returned to Scituate, we packed up such things as we needed, and, taking a good, full draught of Mr. May's spiritual "Elixir of Life," we came to Norton early in December, 1840.

As I had but few sermons to begin with, and had already used nearly all that were worth preaching, I saw hard work before me. I had few books, and my mate-

rials for sermons were scanty ; but I loved the religion
of Jesus as I apprehended it, and felt a reasonable assurance that, if I was loyal to Christ, it would "be given
me what I should speak."

Four years' study and labor with Rev. S. J. May, four
years' fellowship with his great-hearted, philanthropic
spirit, had imbued me thoroughly with the reforms of
that period.   The trinity of public evils against which
I felt called to wage unceasing warfare were *war, intemperance,* and *slavery.*   Against all war, offensive and
defensive, I took the ultra, and, as it seemed to me,
Christian ground.

The New England Non-resistance Society, formed
while I was studying, adopted literally the words of
Jesus : " Resist not evil.   Render not evil for evil, but
overcome evil with good."   Quite a large number of the
early anti-slavery advocates joined this society, and came
out from all participation in the national government
because it was based, as a *dernier ressort,* on the right
to take human life.   William Lloyd Garrison, Edmund
Quincy, Adin Ballou, Samuel J. May, and many others,
became Christian non-resistants.   Others withdrew from
all participation in the government because the Constitution was interpreted so as to sanction human slavery,
that crime of crimes against God and humanity,— that
" sum of all villanies," as Wesley had called it.

The temperance reform was waking the people to a
solemn sense of the sin of intemperance, such as was
never so widely felt before or since.   We were in the
midst of the great Washingtonian movement, as it was
called, whose only method was moral suasion, which
proved more effectual in winning inebriates from their

cups and in stopping the sale of intoxicating drink than any of the methods since adopted. Not only the adult portion of the community became deeply interested, but "Cold Water Armies" for the children, with badges and banners and music, became so popular that it did seem as if the next generation would grow up free from the temptations of this appalling evil.

As I entered the ministry breathing this moral atmosphere, I counted it joy to make my voice heard and my influence felt against this devil's trinity of evils.

Fully recognizing the necessity of the gospel for individual regeneration of heart and life, I felt that a testimony must also be borne against these wide-spread national and social evils, clear and unmistakable. So I was carefully and prayerfully watchful over myself lest, through that "fear of man which bringeth a snare," I should fail to declare the whole counsel of God against these sins.

This winter opened to me the real work of the ministry. I had had no experience in pastoral duties. I had attended one or two funerals while I was at Scituate, and visited a few sick people, but only as a lay acquaintance, not as a pastor. Now my visits to the sick and bereaved assumed a more intimate and responsible character. There was only the usual amount of sickness and death in the parish. But the ministry to sorrow these experiences involved, becoming a personal matter, bore heavily upon me. One death especially, in the course of the winter, was most painful, not only to the friends of the deceased, but to myself, as the officiating minister.

A middle-aged man, of intemperate habits, was

missed from his home in cold weather. Several days
passed with no tidings. At last he was found in a by-
path near the woods, frozen to death, with an empty
bottle by his side. This termination of his intemperate career was a dreadful blow to his family and a great
shock to the community. The funeral at his father's
house was very largely attended. Some came from
real sympathy, and others from curiosity to know what
that young carpenter-minister could say. It was a trying service for me. There sat father and mother,
brothers and sisters, in heart-breaking grief. Sympathy with them whispered, " Oh, do not say one word
to lacerate their stricken hearts !" But the neighbors,
friends, and townsmen filling the rooms, and grouped
in the yard around the door,— some of them, I feared,
still tampering with the seductive foe,—how could I
be true to my conscience without trying to voice the
solemn warning to them ? I was in "a strait betwixt
two." Sympathy pleading for silence as to the cause
of the sad event, and conscience calling, as by a voice
from heaven, to interpret truthfully this solemn warning, I felt the full force of Pierpont's lines, written
under similar circumstances : —

> " But oh !
> If thou'st a heart that pity e'er hath touched,
> Pity him who sacrifice of prayer must offer at a drunkard's
> funeral."

I spoke as it was given me, in heartfelt sympathy and
faithful warning, and I believe no offence was given. I
seemed to be swept through the strait by the force of
the current, rather than by good steering, so that I
escaped being wrecked on either Scylla or Charybdis.

As the winter wore away, I tried to give full and free expression to all my reform views, so that the people might fully understand my position before the time came for them to say whether or not they would call me to be their pastor. As I had not been ordained, I could not legalize a marriage. But some of the young people, being more sure of my remaining than I was, were willing to wait.

Finally, on the 15th of March, two weeks before the expiration of my engagement, the parish held a meeting, and I was invited, by a very large vote,—fifty-nine yeas, two nays,—to become their pastor for two years. The limit to two years was at my own request. My salary was fixed at six hundred dollars per year, one hundred more than they had given their former minister.

Having already become attached to the people, and highly gratified with the unanimity of the call, I readily and gladly accepted.

The time for my ordination was fixed for April 14th, 1840. On the 12th we began keeping house in the parsonage, built by Madame Bowen, who permitted the parish to use it without rent. On the 13th we had a violent snow-storm, which so completely blocked the ways as to render passing next to impossible. This, for the middle of April, was very unusual. The next day, the day set apart for my ordination, was bright and clear, the snow-drifts wreathed with diamonds shining in the sunlight like gems of the first water. But only three ministers and one delegate put in an appearance from the thirteen churches invited.

But the day was so delightful overhead that our parishioners broke through the snow, and made a fair show in the church. So, while the ordination was postponed for one week, it was decided to hold a service, and the Rev. Mr. Arnold, of Fall River, one of the three present, gave an admirable sermon. When the day to which the ordination was adjourned came, April 21, it proved about as copious a rain-storm as the snow-storm of the 13th. But, as some of the pastors and delegates came the day before, we had enough to form the council.

Among those who took part in my ordination were my dear Mr. May, who preached the sermon, my kind neighbor, Dr. Bigelow, who offered the ordaining prayer, and my true friend, Mr. Samuel Sewall, who gave me the charge. My sister Lucy wrote two beautiful hymns for the occasion, and it was a happy day.

So I was launched into the ministry, after having been on the stocks four or five years, giving time for the green timber to season, but with an outfit of spare sails and rigging too limited to justify any ministerial " insurance company " in taking the risk.

I preached the next Sunday morning from the text, " Do the work of an evangelist " ; and, in looking it over the other day, I could but wonder that I did so well. It was a broad, earnest statement of the work of an evangelist, as I apprehended it, a fervent plea for a higher life in the individual and in the church, a life more conformed to the teaching and life of Christ.

The second Sunday after I was ordained I performed my first marriage service by joining two of our young people, who afterwards became members of the church,

Earl C. White and Elizabeth A. Sweet. They are still living, — 1888,— with children and grandchildren to " rise up and call them blessed." Several others, as if waiting for the opportunity, followed before long. I soon began to preach on the proper way of bringing up children, the common theme for young ministers. As they grow older and gain a larger experience, the con- fident tone of these juvenile efforts is usually quite sen- sibly modified.

I was made a member of the school committee, in the duties of which my four years' experience in teaching made me feel at home.

Soon the wave of temperance interest, sweeping over the eastern part of Massachusetts, broke in refreshing on our village. Pierpont, Dr. Jewett, and others from abroad, visited us ; and, with the cordial co-operation of ministers and laymen, there was a wide-spread awaken- ing, in which many, young and old, signed the pledge, among whom were some hard drinkers.

The use of alcoholic wine at the communion had long troubled me ; and for some time I had refused the cup when it was presented to me, feeling that the cause of the Master was better served in the breach than in the observance. I could not deem it right to com- memorate the world's Redeemer by the use of an in- toxicating beverage which was deluging the world with woe. Knowing that my own hands must soon present the symbols, I was greatly anxious to substitute some- thing else for the deleterious compounds often sold for wine. I laid the matter before the church with great solicitude, for I knew the power of old custom and the difficulty of breaking away from old usage. I presented the case to them as it lay in my mind, and, to my great joy, there was not one dissenting voice to the proposal to substitute the pure juice of the grape from bloom raisins for alcoholic wine. So that at the first communion administered by myself I had the great satisfaction of using the fruit of the vine, free from all intoxicating elements.

The national Fourth of July came on Sunday this year. It was my first *Fourth* as an ordained minister, and the way I improved the occasion is indicated by this brief note in my journal : —

Sunday, July 4, 1841. — Have celebrated Independence by preaching all day upon the heaven-daring sins our country is committing by continuing to make merchandise of the image of God. I pray that I may not have spoken in vain.

This was in the early stages of the anti-slavery movement, when Church and State were united to hold the slave in his chains, and put down the incendiary fanatics who believed in a "higher law" than that on the statute book.

This summer I exchanged with Rev. Adin Ballou, of Mendon, and became acquainted with this remarkable man. He belonged to what was then called the "Restorationists," a branch of Universalists who believed, as all Unitarians do now, that all God's children will finally be restored to holiness in this world or the next. He was the finest Scriptural interpreter I have ever met. He knew the Bible by heart, and in textual criticism was a "well-instructed scribe." He often encountered Orthodox believers in public debate, and both on account of his rational views and his intellectual power was a formidable opponent. He was an uncompromising non-resistant, deeply interested in all reforms. He and a small company of kindred spirits started a " Practical Christian Community " at Milford, in which they hoped to realize a higher and purer type of Christian life. I visited with him the lovely spot where they endeavored to found the new kingdom, and rejoiced with them in the experiment of faith. But, alas ! like most other attempts made at that time to lift human life by association and withdrawal from the world, it failed, and in a few years the community was dissolved, giving place to a rapidly growing and very beautiful village.

It was a great grief to Mr. Ballou, who, in giving up the "community " on which he had set his heart, still retained, and holds to this day, in serene old age, his loyalty to non-resistance as the clear doctrine of Christ. He is the American Tolstoï, with as deep a conviction as his Russian fellow-believer that evil can be overcome only by good.

X

EARLY MINISTRY (*continued*).

1840-44.

DEATH OF LITTLE JOSEPH.— COLLINS AND DOUGLASS.— LATI-
MER.— RELIGIOUS AWAKENING.— DEATH OF MR. BOND.
— BIRTH OF WILLIAM PHILLIPS TILDEN, JR.— DEATH OF
MRS. TURNER.— ILL HEALTH.

THE weeks swept on, and I was happy in my work.
But a cloud was gathering in our clear home sky that
we wot not of. On the morning of September 6 we
perceived that our darling Joseph was ill. He had
always been a very healthy child, full of overflowing life,
just beginning "to talk in broken words, which were
music to a mother's ear," and father's, too. He was not
very sick at first, but on the third day he suddenly left
us. Even on the morning of that day he did not seem
dangerously ill. When the doctor came, he said he
could check the disease soon. He gave medicine, and
in a few hours little Joseph died in convulsions. It
was so sudden it seemed unreal. But we found it
a dreadful reality. It was our first household sorrow.
To add to our grief was the haunting fear that there
had been a misjudgment in regard to the medicine, the
darling went so soon after taking it. With some other
treatment might not his sweet life have been spared?
The idea was anguish. We found relief at last in the

thought that, supposing our dreadful fears to be true, we could not help it. We had done what we thought was right in committing him to the doctor's care. He had done what he thought was right, and there can be no higher rule of action for us than to do what seems right at the time. More light may show us a better way; but, when we do what seems right with the light we have, it is right, whatever the result. The lesson so painfully learned has been a comfort through life. But the sorrow was great. The dear God only knew how sick our hearts were. Oh, how sweetly he looked in his little casket! It was a comfort to sit with him alone. It did not seem like death, but an angel asleep. Sometimes, as I thought of him in heaven, a sweet peace would come; and I would feel as if I should never be so wretched again; and then, even as the peace was upon me, my great sorrow would roll back like a wave, and I could only bow my head and let it break, till the sunlight again appeared through the blinding spray.

He was indeed a precious boy, so intelligent, so affectionate, so full of life and joy and gladness. He was so handsome, too. His large, full eyes were open windows for his soul, and his smile and rollicking laugh were enchanting. Dear angel boy, you did not leave us utterly. You rose out of our sight, but still remained in our hearts to make real the unseen and eternal. We had much still to be thankful for. One was taken, but the other was left; and dear Laura became, if possible, still more precious, now her little brother had gone to "join the choir invisible."

The ladies of the parish united in the erection of a

chaste marble shaft over his grave, on which are in-
scribed only the two words

LITTLE JOSEPH.

It was enclosed with a circular wooden fence, which has
been kept by fresh painting from the wear and tear of
time by our good friend James O. Messenger for now
forty-seven years.

Up to this time I had often been called to sympathize
with such sorrows as ours, and thought I did so.   But
this experience was a new revelation to me of the depths
of such sorrow, and I think my ministry ever after took
on a new tenderness born of this great experience.

About a month after this we were glad to receive a
visit from my father and his new wife.   After remaining a widower more than four years, he married Mrs.
Benson of Scituate, a widow with two children.   I was
glad to have father marry again, for he was a dear
lover of home.

Caroline had been preparing for a teacher at the
Bridgewater Normal School, and Lucy felt the need of
doing something for herself.

Father's visit was brief,—he never could bear to be
away from home more than one night ; but it cheered
our hearts to know that henceforth he would have a
companion for his old age.   After we left South Scituate, I invited father to take my house, which was
more convenient and comfortable.

Not long after this the old house took fire from
some unknown cause one night, and was burned to
ashes.   Now there is nothing left but the old cellar,
well, and enclosed walls to tell of the dear spot where
the most of my boyhood and early manhood was spent.

A few Sundays later, as I was speaking to our Sunday-school, a gentleman came in whom I knew as the agent of the Massachusetts Anti-slavery Society,— John A. Collins. He came to say that he and Fred Douglass, a man just escaped from slavery, would hold an anti-slavery meeting on Wednesday evening next in our church. I was glad of the announcement, and due notice was given.

The time came, and the meeting was a grand one. Collins was a man of marked ability, but the fugitive slave Douglass was the great attraction. He was just out of slavery. He had spoken at an anti-slavery meeting a little while before at New Bedford, where he was working, and the friends of the cause were so impressed by his spirit that they engaged him at once to speak at their meetings. We saw he was no ordinary man. Though born and bred in slavery, he had the manners and speech of a gentleman. There was no lingering of negro dialect. He spoke good, honest, trenchant Saxon, with great calmness and self-possession. The leading characteristics which have since distinguished him as a debater and orator were manifest then. He was born to them. His pose and power were Websterian, and, although we little dreamed then that he would one day be Chief Marshal of the city of Washington, still we saw that he was a man of unusual power and promise. They spent the night with us, and we found Douglass as charming in the home as on the platform. He was a lover of children. Laura was then a little girl of four. I remember how he swung her on to his shoulder, and marched round with her as a conquering hero.

I had a nice parsonage garden. As the soil was

light and the hoeing easy, I kept it quite free from
weeds. But on another part of the acre lot, where the
soil was heavier and the weeds more persistent, the
appearance was not so pleasant to the eye of a careful
farmer. When my brother Albert, who always loved
a joke, came to see me, he said he knew when he got
to my house by the weeds in the garden.

I must confess to my grandchildren that I was never
much of a farmer, and that I grow no better as I grow
older. The part of gardening I like best is *laying
down to grass.* That requires no hoeing.

In the spring-time of this year I bought a little
black pacer at auction for twenty dollars, and my friend
Mr. Messenger, who was a painter, fitted up a light
covered carryall. We put the two together, and used
them in common. The team was not gay, but very
convenient for parish calls, visiting schools, and making
exchanges.

Another Thanksgiving came and found us well, but
lonely. We missed little Joseph so much all the time,
but especially at the dear old home festival. My duties
as school committee, occasional lectures on temperance,
and other reforms out of town, in connection with my
ordinary parish work, kept me constantly occupied.
But I was well, and enjoyed my labors. Occasional
letters from dear Mr. May, and one good visit from
him and sister Caroline, were a real refreshment. We
talked over the new thought of the times, criticised
everybody but ourselves, and set the wayward world to
rights with great satisfaction.

The next year, 1842, Mr. May received and accepted
an earnest invitation, made well-nigh imperative

through the entreaty of the Secretary of the Board of Education, Hon. Horace Mann, to become the principal of the Normal School at Lexington. He insisted that my sister Caroline, who had been educated at the Bridgewater Normal School, and had proved herself a promising and competent teacher, should go with him and take the charge of mathematics, in which she excelled. After this I saw little of Mr. May, and even his letters were infrequent from his arduous duties.

During this year my labors were unremitting. I don't remember whether I had ever heard of "a summer vacation" at that time ; but I am sure I had none, nor for many years after.

A deepening religious interest began to show itself in the parish generally this year. We held social religious meetings at the parsonage and private houses, and the Sunday attendance was cheering in numbers and interest.

The year 1842 opened auspiciously, and I worked on in faith and hope. I began to get accustomed to my changed life, and the professional harness came to set easier and chafe less.

The anniversary meetings in Boston were occasions of great interest to me. The anti-slavery movement, growing stronger every day, made them lively occasions. Only a small number of Unitarian ministers had then espoused the cause,— S. J. May, John Pierpont, Caleb Stetson, and a few others of less note. The opposition to these men and the cause they represented was bitter and strong. There was a determination not to hear them. Even Mr. May, honored as he was, was not allowed to speak through the pages of our only monthly, the *Christian Examiner.* But the fierce opposition made the annual meetings all the more exciting; and they became to me, secluded from my brethren all the rest of the year by constant home work, seasons of great interest and quickening.

In the autumn of 1842 George Latimer, a fugitive slave, was caught and thrown into jail in Boston, for safe keeping, by his master. From the jail he sent a petition to the churches "for their prayers." It was a spark that caught wherever there was enough tinder of human sympathy to hold it. The flame was seen and felt in many churches where sincere prayers were offered for the restoration of the imprisoned fugitive. On the Sunday the request for prayer was read and answered in our church I took occasion to preach from the words of Jesus, "Inasmuch as ye have done it unto one of the least of these, my brethren, ye have done it unto me."

When the two years for which I was settled had expired, I was promptly and unanimously invited to continue my ministry, with no limitation of time.

I accepted; for there was entire harmony of feeling, and the religious interest seemed to be steadily deepening. Many, both young and old, were waked to newness of life. Among them was an old man whose experience was deeply interesting. He must have been near seventy, and for many years had led a very intemperate life. Sometimes in his crazy, drunken fits we could hear his wild cries in the night, though he lived far away. He had probably not been inside a meeting house for years. But one Sunday he came, to the surprise of everybody. Whether from anything he heard

or from the spiritual atmosphere of the place I know
not, but he came again. He was deeply thoughtful.
He gave fixed attention; and soon he accepted the invitation to stop after the morning service to the Bible
class. His soul was melted into contrition for his past
life. He said little at first, but the tears streaming
down his cheeks told of the inward struggle his soul
was passing through. Finally, as he began to speak
more freely, he told us how hard it was for him to believe that he could be forgiven. He had sinned so
long, sinned so deeply, it did not seem to him that
Divine Love itself could forgive him. At last the light
of a sweet peace shone through his tears, and the morning of a new life broke upon the old man's soul.
Awhile after, when we saw the change was real, he
was welcomed to the church, and remained to his
death, years after, a worthy member of the church and
a respectable citizen. It was one of the best possible
answers to Nicodemus: "How can a man be born
when he is old?"

In the spring of 1843 the husband of my eldest sister, Philenda, died quite suddenly, leaving her with
three children. He was a strong, healthy man, and a
very true and noble character. I loved him as an own
brother. His father and mother and sister were of the
old Puritan school in theology, but he was an earnest
Unitarian, and was deeply interested in my studying
for the ministry. He gave me Clarke's "Commentary
on the New Testament," which at that time, when I
had but few books, was of great assistance to me.

Passing over the ordinary experiences and labors of
parish work, I come to a white day in our parsonage

home. Aug. 23, 1843,—on this day another sweet boy was given us. At first he looked like our little Joseph; but after a week or two the likeness faded. We did not regret this; for we were glad to keep the image of that angel boy fresh in our remembrance, not absorbed by or blended with any other. We wished to remember Joseph as our own dear boy, still a member of our little family, though unseen. So we did not name our new gift from heaven after him, as is so often done. That would seem as if we regarded Joseph as lost to us, and sought to fill his place with another. Mary said, " We will call the little one William Phillips," and it was done. Since he has grown up, he may not thank us for making him a Jr.; but it was with the hope and prayer that he would prove senior in nobleness of life.

In January, 1844, my dear sister Sarah, Mrs. William Turner, died. She had been sick for many months of consumption, and left a husband and five beautiful children, three sons and two daughters. She was a true wife and mother, a sweet sister, a noble woman.

I visited her at her home in South Scituate a little while before she died. I found her calm and trustful. She knew she could not stay long, but, strong as her love was for her family, she was willing to go, seeing it was the Father's will. She was the first of the children to go after dear mother. She was married when about twenty, and died at thirty-five,— a life crowded with household duties, which she performed with marked ability, finding her highest joy in her home.

Early in 1844, as the winter broke up, my health broke down. It was not strange, for the change in the habits of my life since becoming a minister was great,

and the duties of the last year, especially, had been
very arduous and constant. The break-down was quite
sudden. It was a general collapse. It would now be
called nervous prostration. It had no name then, but
it was the same dread reality. I could not read, I
could not write, I could not work: even a paragraph
in a newspaper upset me. I saw I must quit for a
season, and asked release from duty for two months.
I supplied the pulpit largely by exchanges. Mary and
the children went to our old, sweet refuge, where we
always found a welcome, Aunt Tempie's in Charlestown; and I became a circulating medium, managing
to pass without challenge, though conscious of much
alloy in my constitution. I gave myself, as far as I
could, to recreation. The gate of thinking and writing
had been shut down for me, and I had no desire to lift
it. I simply rested, using old sermons on Sunday.

XI

CONCORD MINISTRY.

1844-1848.

VISIT TO CONCORD.— STEPHEN S. FOSTER.— INVITATION TO
REMAIN.— FAREWELL TO NORTON.— BIRTH OF GEORGE.
— CHRISTENING.— INVITATION TO REMAIN ANOTHER YEAR.
— DEATH OF MRS. LEWIS.— FIRST PUBLISHED SERMON.—
MEXICAN WAR.— MILITARY CONVENTION.— WHITE MOUN-
TAINS.— SECOND PUBLISHED SERMON.— THIRD PUBLISHED
SERMON. — FAREWELL TO CONCORD. — DOVER. — CARO-
LINE'S DEATH.

DURING my rest I was invited to supply the pulpit
at Concord, N.H., one Sunday, and, engaging a supply
for my own pulpit, I went. I had never before been
to this beautiful inland city on the Merrimack, the capital of New Hampshire. I was delighted with the
place. The Rev. M. G. Thomas, who was their first
minister, and had been with them fifteen years, had
just resigned, but still lived in a beautiful house on
a swell of land just on the fringe of the city. I found
a pleasant church, a good congregation, and had a delightful time.

I was the guest of Brother and Sister Thomas. I
found them charming people. Then began a friendship which proved life-long.

The parishioners were very kind in their expressions
of interest in my services; and I left them feeling that

I had enjoyed a delightful season, in a delightful place, with a delightful people.

The Concord people were anxious to hear me again, and soon after they sent one of their leading men, Col. William Kent, to Norton to talk with me about coming to Concord, at least for the season. He knew I had been off duty from illness ; and so he urged the healthiness of the place, as well as the desire of the people, with most persuasive eloquence. I yielded so far as to say I would come again for two Sundays.

Being anxious to have them understand my reform views, I took sermons which clearly expressed my ideas in relation to the disturbing topics of the day. I would have them fully understand what they were doing in giving me a call.

One interesting circumstance gave me a fine opportunity for testing them. There had just been a great excitement in town, and especially in the churches, on the anti-slavery question. Stephen S. Foster, a young man who had studied for an Orthodox minister, but, becoming interested in anti-slavery, left the ministry and the Church because of their opposition to the movement for the slave, had felt it to be his duty to go into one of the large Orthodox churches in Concord and bear his testimony against the heaven-daring evil. He did this without permission, in the midst of the service. It was a most unwarrantable thing to do. But the society met it in an unfortunate way. Certain of their number, indignant at such disturbance of their service, rose and dragged him out of the church.

As he was a non-resistant, he just "decomposed" his muscles and left them to do it all, without any of

his assistance. It imposed a hard task on four men.
But they at last landed him on the outer steps. Of
course, it was town's talk; and, though few justified
Foster, many saw that the church method of dealing
with him could hardly be justified on Christian grounds.
Foster soon after married Miss Abby Kelly, another
come-outer. They were lecturing at this time together.
Hearing, probably, that I was anti-slavery in my sentiment, they both came one Sunday to our church. I
saw them in the congregation. As I closed my sermon, I said, "I see we have with us to-day friends who
are giving themselves to the cause of the slave, and
who always count it a privilege to speak in behalf of
the bondman. And I venture to do here what I should
do in my own church, and to invite them cordially to
say anything which their hearts prompt."

Foster rose, and said, very modestly, "that he had
nothing special to say. He had listened to a sermon
that had interested him, and he hoped that the time was
not far distant when such sentiments would be heard
from all the pulpits in the land."

I thought that, if the people invited me to become
their minister after this, they would do it with their
eyes open, at their own risk. And they did. The
treatment was in such contrast to the "dragging out"
that the parishioners, instead of being disturbed by it,
were highly gratified, and gave me a cordial invitation
to remain with them.

I could not say certainly till I returned to Norton. I found my dear people very unwilling I should
leave. It was a severe struggle to decide to do so;
but, as my health was so poor, and the change of cli-

mate and scene was so desirable, we thought it best, on the whole, to go for one year on trial.

They offered me seven hundred a year; but it was not the difference in salary, but the hope of regaining my health, that influenced my decision.

But it was hard going. I had become strongly attached to my people, and they to me. They were my first love. I had been with them in sorrow and joy nearly four years from the time of my first supply of their pulpit. I was a member of the school committee ever after I was ordained. This had made me interested in the children of the town. My interest in temperance and other social reforms had given me a wide-spread acquaintance; and it was a real trial to break all these ties.

The first Sunday in June we carried our dear little William Phillips to the baptismal font, and consecrated him in love and faith to the service of the heavenly Father. The last Sunday of the same month (1844) I preached my farewell.

My engagement at Concord was for one year only, beginning with July. At first we boarded, but soon found a cottage on the hill near Brother Thomas where we went to keeping house. Our nearness to our friends drew closer the ties of our friendship.

Here I found a field of labor very different from Norton. There they were steady-going farmers, of small means, living in a quiet way, with few things to disturb the monotony of daily toil. Here was a growing city, full of business, enterprise, push, excitement, the hot-bed of politics, the seething-pot of all sorts of speculations. I was surprised by the liberality with

which young men, clerks and mechanics, contributed
to the support of the church, some of them paying as
much voluntarily as the richest men were taxed in my
Norton parish.

They were noble men and women, of various opinions, religious and political, but kindly, and tolerant
generally of opinions they did not accept. They bade
us a cordial welcome to their homes and hearts.

I seemed to be in a new world, alive with fresh
thought, calling upon me for the best I could give
every Sunday. But the change gave me more time for
study, and I soon grew stronger, away from the east
wind, and breathing the soft summer air coming from
the "dark plains" of pitch pine across the river.

On the 19th of March, 1845, a new gift of Heaven
descended on our little cottage on the hill in the form
of another lovely boy. We hailed him with gratitude
and joy. Willie was only nineteen months old then, so
that we almost felt we had twin boys, and indeed they
were often taken for twins as they grew up together.

We had formed so pleasant a friendship with the
Thomases that we thought we would commemorate it
by the name of our new child. Mr. Thomas's name
was Moses George, so, dropping the Moses, we called
our boy George Thomas.

While they remained in Concord, they were not only
our nearest neighbors, but our most intimate friends, in
full sympathy with the general aim of my preaching. They left for South Boston in October. The
night before they went away they spent with us.
Late in the evening of October 7 our baby George
awoke. The sudden thought came to us, Why not

have him baptized now that Brother Thomas is with us to administer the rite? Water was brought, and there around the social hearth, in the enjoyment of that friendship his name was given to commemorate, the sacred and beautiful rite was administered. It was a sweet season. We felt none of the anxious care attendant on infant baptism at church. There were none to comment on the child's dress or behavior. Just as we took him from the cradle in his little flannel night-gown, we presented him. In his mother's lap, that sweet resting-place for the little nestling, he received the pure drops upon his brow. Then, as we sat together with clasped hands, the fervent prayer of our brother went up to Heaven for us all.

I was engaged only for one year; but, when the time expired, they invited me to continue and voted my salary for another year. The society was harmonious, and I did not permit my interest in reforms to interfere with my earnest efforts to promote personal piety. We had some very interesting cases of the awakening of souls to the higher life.

In the autumn of 1845 my sister Lucy, seven years younger than I, who had been married only a little more than a year, died, leaving an infant,— Helen. I went to see her just before she left, and received into my heart the benediction of her sweet trusting spirit. She talked freely of her leaving; said, " I have more than everything to live for,— so good a husband, so sweet an infant." She had, indeed ; but her trust in the Father's love was unfaltering, and the breathing of her soul was, "Not my will, but thine, be done." She had been expecting me, and expressed the wish that, when I came, the babe might be baptized. The little one was brought to the bedside of its calm and prayerful mother, and there in its father's arms, with a few friends standing round, Helen received the baptismal waters on her innocent brow. After the service was over, Lucy's husband went to her and said, "You feel happy now?" "Yes," she replied, "very, very happy." The second day after she was with the angels.

Lucy — Lucy Brooks — was not only a very lovely woman, but one of rare gifts. She had a highly poetical and deeply religious nature. The collection of poems made by her husband after her death, gleaned mainly from the *Christian Register* where they were first published, shows how natural was her power of sacred song. They are nearly all of a religious character, breathing a sweet spirit of trusting faith. She was a fine housekeeper, and had the rare art of thinking her best thoughts at her work. Very often, after a morning at the wash-tub, she would hang out her clothes,— and they were always white,—wipe her hands, take pencil and paper and write out the poem she had composed over the suds. She was as lovely in character as sweet in song, deeply interested in anti-slavery, human brotherhood, and all the reforms of the day. In this, as in love of home, she found a congenial spirit in her faithful and devoted husband.

In 1846 I preached a sermon on "The Evangelical Alliance," then recently formed in England for the promotion of Christian union. Its limitations of fellowship were so inconsistent with *union*, in any true Christian sense, that I felt it my duty to expose its narrowness and show a more excellent way. It was "published by request." This was my first published sermon.

Then the Mexican war clouds began to send forth lightning and thunder. The annexation of Texas the year before, had given rise to various disputes with Mexico as to boundaries and border regions, and in April a conflict of arms took place between Mexican and United States troops on the Rio Grande. War was at once declared by the President "As existing by the act of Mexico." The bugle blast calling for volunteers was heard all over the land. In Concord there was great excitement. Not only the peace men, but the anti-slavery men, regarded the war as unjust, and waged in the interests of slavery.

I could not be silent. One Sunday, as I was giving my view of the war, a prominent member, one Colonel ——, rose, and, wrapping "his martial cloak around him," marched down the aisle and out of the church. Of course, it made a sensation, and the timid ones were scared.

The anniversary meetings in Boston this year gave me new courage and inspiration. They were full of fervor. George S. Hillard and William H. Channing, especially, spoke at the meeting of the American Unitarian Association with clarion tongues in behalf of pure Christianity. I returned from these meetings with a song of joy in my heart.

I had told the society at the end of the second year that I thought I had better go away, as some were leaving the church, but they would not hear to it, and voted my salary for another year.

But the Mexican war *furor* deepened the excitement and intensified the feelings on both sides. The newspapers were ablaze with it. My ultra-peace principles made me, not a "target" merely, but a live pigeon or "goose" for them to shoot at.

There was a great military convention held in Concord early in June, to enkindle patriotic zeal and enlist recruits for the war. Several Independent Companies came from a distance, in full uniform,— one from Vermont. The old North Church was crowded to overflowing, and flaming speeches were made in behalf of the war and in eulogy of the military. A prominent lawyer of the place, a pro-slavery democrat, Mr. Franklin Pierce, was the presiding genius of the occasion.

I was present to hear what was said, with many other anti-slavery and anti-war friends. Mr. Pierce, in the course of his speech, said, looking directly at me and shaking his finger as he spoke, that he saw some present who sought to bring the military into contempt. He then went on in mingled sarcasm and scorn of those who opposed the war on principles of peace. There was great applause and excitement. I was near the front; and, as he closed, I pressed through the crowd, and, stepping to the platform, asked the privilege of a word. When I began, I was hailed with hisses, but after a few words they were still and attentive. I never knew just what I said. I was too excited to remember. I only know that I attempted to show how inconsistent this war spirit they had been lauding was with the genius and spirit of Christianity. I believe my word was not in vain. It gave them something to think of besides fighting to enlarge our slave territory. Soon as I closed, the large concourse of people dispersed quietly, with no hisses or groans for the peace minister.

On the two following days the friends of peace held meetings, and noble and truthful words were spoken for "peace on earth and good will to men." Adin Ballou and Samuel E. Coues were present from abroad, and added much to the interest of the meetings. Brother Ballou stayed over Sunday with me, and preached gloriously all day of the real kingdom of God.

The next month Brother and Sister Thomas came up from South Boston, where he was then settled; and, taking a four-seated carriage with a span of horses, we went together, himself and wife, myself and wife, to the White Mountains. We were gone about two weeks, leaving the children in good hands, and had a most delightful journey. Brother Thomas was a dear lover of the mountains, knew them by heart. We could not have had a better guide or more charming companions.

We spent many vacations among the mountains afterwards, but the first view of their grandeur and sublimity has never been surpassed, hardly equalled. No scream of the steam whistle had then been heard among these fastnesses of nature. We ascended Mt. Washington on horseback, by a bridle-path from Old Crawford's, going over all the interesting mountains in the long range from Webster to the summit of Washington. We went with a company of travellers : Theodore Parker and wife were of the number. We spent Sunday at Crawford's, and Mr. Parker preached an excellent sermon. Brother Thomas offered prayer, and Mary and I *led the choir*. The music was not artistic, but well meant. As we were not paid save in intrinsic satisfaction, and that could be expressed by the small-est known coin, we were not criticised.

In the autumn of this year a young man, Lieutenant Edward Eastman, who once belonged to our society, but left some years before for the West, enlisted as a volunteer in the Mexican War, and died at Camargo, taking care of the sick soldiers. His brother in Concord wished me to preach a sermon on the occasion, which I did,—a thorough peace sermon in commemoration of a soldier! To my great surprise, the friends wished to publish it. This was my second published sermon.

During the latter part of 1846, the Mexican war fever was at its height. I was often attacked in the papers. Party feeling ran high, and disaffection increased. Some left and others were frightened lest the society should be broken up. To brace up the courage of the society and make clear my own conviction, I preached " A New Year's Sermon," January, 1847, from a text in Paul's letter to the Philippians : " Stand fast, in nothing terrified by your adversaries." As I was preparing this sermon, one of my right-hand supporters called. I told him what I was doing, and read extracts from what I had written. He, too, was afraid, and thought I had better not preach it. But I had made up my mind, and gave it.

If you will read that sermon, you will get a better idea than I can give you of the nature of the opposition and the way I endeavored to make plain what seemed to me my Christian position.

To my surprise, this sermon was so well received by a large majority of those who heard it that they requested that it might be " Printed for the Use of the Society." This was my third printed sermon.

Still, the opposition was so strong that, taking all things into consideration, I thought it would be better not to remain another year. I had been the first to break the ice in preaching against war and slavery, and I thought that a new man might come and preach the same truth with less opposition. Those who had committed themselves against *me* might listen to another complacently, even though he held the same views. Still, I concluded not to resign till the annual meeting should decide whether the majority wished me to stay. The meeting was fully attended. There was free talk, as I learned, for and against my remaining, but no vote was taken.

At the adjourned meeting it was voted — 17 to 9, several not voting — that I should be invited to remain another year, provided my usual salary could be raised. By this time some of my friends, seeing the strength of the opposition and fearing the result, concluded it would be unwise for me to continue longer than the expiration of my third year, and the salary was not raised. This relieved me from the necessity of resigning. Cordially agreeing with them in their decision, I told them I thought it would be wiser not to serve out the year, but leave at once, as they would wish to be hearing candidates and I should wish to be looking for some other field of labor.

So on the 9th of May — my birthday — I preached my farewell. I left without regret, as they did not think it prudent to keep me longer, but with no ill will, and for the over forty years that have intervened since then I have nowhere found a more cordial welcome, whether in their pulpit or their homes, than among this charming people.

My successor proved, as I had hoped, a stanch anti-slavery man; and, when the vote for his settlement was pending, I was told that the very colonel who walked out of church when I was preaching on the Mexican War said that, as they had got to have a d—d abolitionist or a d—d fool, he should vote for him.

Still making my home in Concord, I was for the first time without a parish, and went forth to find a field of labor where I could be free and yet wanted.

I preached at Woburn, Wayland, and Ware, finding pleasant people and a kindly hearing everywhere.

The anniversary meetings of this year were very quickening. The League of Brotherhood, then recently organized, whose vignette was a white hand clasping a black one, was particularly inspiring. Elihu Burritt, the learned blacksmith, was deeply interested in this movement, and labored earnestly in England to advance its principles. The signers of its pledge against all war and the manifestation of the war spirit already, on both sides the Atlantic, were near thirty thousand. Hopes for permanent peace on earth were so bright we could almost hear the angels sing again the advent song.

While I was wandering, I preached two Sundays in Brooklyn, Conn., where Mr. May began his ministry, and had a delightful time with his old people, still full of love for their never-to-be-forgotten minister; also, I preached one Sunday in Lowell.

In August Mary and I visited Norton, and spent a charming Sunday with our dear old friends there. The reunion after three years' separation was a spiritual refreshment.

A little later I received an invitation to supply the pulpit in Dover, N.H., for one year, during the absence of its minister, Rev. John Parkman, in Europe. Though the society in Wayland wished me to remain with them as their pastor, I thought it best to go to Dover for one year, as it would give me rest and time for study.

Just before leaving Concord, some of our dear friends there paid us a brief visit, leaving us a gift of silver for the table, which we are still enjoying.

On Tuesday morning, August 31, having put our household goods on board the cars, we started by rail for Dover. On the way we heard of an alarming epidemic among the children of that town. We had with us three as precious ones as any beneath the stars, but we could not turn back. "Remember Lot's wife." We went on, and, although many children were sick, our dear ones were spared. We spent the first night at the American House, and the next day moved into "our own hired house," as Paul did, and I began my year's work.

My stay at Dover was one of the white years of my ministry. Knowing that I could remain only a year, I felt at liberty to select my best sermons, and write only when I felt like it, giving the remainder of the time to rest and study. The people were very kind, even cordial.

There was a strong anti-slavery feeling in the society, and my best words on the reforms of the day were welcome. Here I became acquainted with Hon. John P. Hale, the stanch anti-slavery man. He was then a Senator in the National Congress, where his voice for freedom gave no uncertain sound. He was a member of the Unitarian church, and on his home vacations was most constant in his attendance on public worship, and took a class in Sunday-school. I honored and loved him as a true and noble man.

While at Dover, I gave a lecture on Peace, at the town hall, which was published. We formed many sweet friendships here, and look back upon the "white year" with unalloyed satisfaction. It was while here that Will went into jacket and pants. His little plump form looked so portly in tights, and he strutted round with such an air that one of my neighbors used to call him "Major Bagstock."

In May, 1848, my youngest sister, Caroline, only two and a half years after Lucy left us, was called up higher. She was not only the youngest, and so the pet, but the flower of our family. She and Lucy were brought up together from their cradles, and were everything to their mother while she stayed, and to their father when she went. They lived in each other's love. Yet they were quite unlike. Caroline had none of Lucy's poetic gifts. I don't know as she ever attempted a rhyme in her life. Yet she was full of poetic sentiment. Her nature was as sensitive to her surroundings as an Æolian harp to the breeze. She was a born teacher; and the fine education she received at the Normal School developed those natural gifts, and fitted her in a remarkable degree for her life-work. She had already won success in teaching, when Mr. May, who was largely instrumental in raising the means for her education, took her with him to the Lexington Normal School, and put her in charge of the mathematical department. Here her real genius for teaching was shown. Here she won her laurels, and hosts of friends among her pupils, who have never forgotten her, but still "rise up to call her blessed."

I have often met with entire strangers who, on learning that I was her brother, have greeted me with hearty cordiality, and told me with faces full of deep feeling how dear she was to them, and what an inspiration she had been in their studies.

Governor Briggs, who was present at a Teachers' Institute when she gave a series of lectures on mathematics, remarked that she had the most brilliant mind he ever saw. Horace Mann, visiting the school and listening to one of her recitations, said he had never anywhere in the Old World witnessed anything superior to it. She gave her whole soul to her work. She was a devotee. She lived for it, she died for it. Her frail body, always frail from a child, was not strong enough to bear the high pressure of her intensely active brain. She was obliged to give up her school two years before she died, but the Board of Education, unwilling she should resign, continued her salary, hoping that entire freedom from care might give her strength to resume. But she had labored too long. Her overtaxed powers were not restored by rest. She even failed more rapidly now that the excitement of teaching was over, and after a lingering illness, sweetly borne, rose out of the body, worn out at twenty-seven, into other mansions of our Father's house.

XII

WALPOLE MINISTRY.

1848–1855.

Leaving Dover.— Settlement at Walpole.— Death of Mrs. Bond.— Dr. Bellows.— Farewell to Walpole.

IN leaving Dover, as we did in the early summer of 1848, we were cheered in knowing that we left many friends. Pleasant tokens of good will from the society and the Sunday-school made our hearts glad for the year we had been permitted to be with them. Brother Parkman having safely returned with his family, there was no need of our remaining longer; and I gave my farewell sermon June 4, and was again afloat.

Leaving my family at Dover, I preached at several places,— Wayland, where the people were anxious I should continue with them; New Bedford, to a new society; New North, Boston; and Framingham, Mass. Here the committee wished to engage me further; but I had promised to preach at Walpole, N.H., where, after three Sundays, I received a unanimous invitation to settle.

It was during this season of transient preaching that I received a most kindly and persuasive invitation from my old parishioners in Norton to return to them as their pastor. They offered me a higher salary than before, and accompanied the offer with expressions of earnest hope that I might accede to the wishes of the society. My old affection for this church of my first love drew me strongly; but Mary and I both thought that, taking all things into consideration, we had better decline the kind proposal, generous as it was.

In accepting the call to Walpole rather than any other near the coast, we were influenced largely by the hope that the inland air would be more favorable to my health, which proved to be true.

In September we left with all our goods for Walpole. We spent two nights with our dear friends at Charlestown on the way, where we always found a cordial welcome.

On our arrival at Walpole we went directly to the hospitable home of Mr. and Mrs. T. G. Wells, where we were made welcome for three weeks, till we were ready for housekeeping. Mrs. Wells was a niece of my dear Mr. May. I had made her acquaintance on my first visit. She was a member of the Church of the Disciples in Boston, whose pastor, James Freeman Clarke, was my favorite minister. Her pleasant acquaintance had its influence in my acceptance of Walpole.

I was installed as pastor of the church Sept. 27, 1848, Rev. A. A. Livermore, of Keene, preaching the sermon.

Here we spent nearly seven very happy years. The situation of the town on a beautiful terrace overlooking the Connecticut River, and commanding a fine view of the mountains of Vermont, was delightful. The air was sweet and pure in summer; and even in winter the steady cold, giving us six months' constant sleighing, was more healthy and enjoyable than the broken winters of

the coast. We were seldom visited by high winds ; and
when the thermometer fell, as it sometimes did, to thirty
or forty degrees below zero, it did not seem so cold as it
did in a high wind on the coast at ten degrees above.   In
this pure, bracing atmosphere, free from the east winds,
which had always been my bane, I began slowly, but
steadily, to improve in health.   The people were kind
and social, the pretty little church was well filled with
interested worshippers, our children were growing up
as " olive plants around our table," and the years swept
on with much general sunshine and few clouds.   There
seemed little call in this quiet, retired parish for the
kind of preaching which the time and the place demanded in Concord.   So my preaching was mainly on
personal religion and the need of a divine life to each
individual soul.   A number joined the church during
these years, and among the young people our own dear
Laura.   That was a happy day to us.

I was early chosen to serve the town as school committee, and continued in that service while I remained.
This made me acquainted with the children, and
opened to me a wide field for sowing such seed as I
chanced to have in my bin.

One difficulty was to find a suitable house to live in.
We had occupied three different ones, when the society
decided to build a parsonage on a lot adjoining the
church, which they owned.   There was not only a home,
but a parish rejoicing when we moved into it, and the
jubilee gatherings we received from parents and children testified to the joy all felt in having, at last, a
home for their pastor and his family.

It was while we were at Walpole that my eldest

sister, Philenda,— Mrs. Bond,— died at Waltham, where
she had lived, wife and widow, twenty-nine years.
After her husband died, she took charge of his drug-
store, and supported her family from it as long as she
lived. She was fifty-one when called away, honored
and beloved. She was a ministering angel to dear
Caroline in her last sickness. She had three children,
Philenda, Sarah, and Josephine. Only Josephine now
remains.

There was a beautiful and touching coincidence, as
we stood near sister's open grave, that seemed like a
voice from heaven to our hearts. There had been a
slight shower as the procession passed into the cemetery, and just as the open casket stood waiting for its
last resting-place there appeared in the east a brilliant
rainbow, looking with its divine message of hope upon
her calm face. The place, the circumstances, gave it
almost articulate voice. The orphan children, as they
looked up from their dear mother's face, saw it through
their tears. Four out of our sacred seven had now
risen to the other mansion. Only three of us remained.

At the annual parish meeting in 1854 a good, hopeful, and generous spirit prevailed. The pews rented
for more than usual, and they raised my salary to $700.
This was most welcome, as I did not meet my expenses
the year before by more than a hundred dollars.

It was here in Walpole I first met Dr. Bellows and
listened to his eloquent preaching. Here, in his ances-
tral home, he had a summer residence where he spent
his vacation. He kindly offered to preach for me occasionally. It was a great treat to me and to the people.
The only drawback was the contrast between his ser-

vice and mine. When he gave one of his magnificent sermons in the morning, and I had to follow him in the afternoon, it required an amount of grace such as seldom comes to ordinary mortals. But I stood it for the love I bore him, for he was a very lovable man. Here began a friendship with him, and a delightful correspondence, which continued till his death. He was a rare man. We had no one, when he rose, to fill his place either in the pulpit or in social life.

Could I have lived on beautiful scenery and pleasant surroundings, I might have been content; but with a growing family, and salary barely sufficient to make two ends meet, I began to feel, during my seventh year, that I must change.

In February, 1855, I preached two Sundays in Jersey City, N.Y. But the society had already decided to give a call to Rev. O. B. Frothingham, of Salem. In March I preached two Sundays in Portland. Rev. Alfred P. Putnam had also been there as candidate. At the parish meeting held after my service the votes for each of us were so near a tie it was decided, and no doubt wisely, to drop us both.

In April I preached two Sundays in Fitchburg. Directly after, I preached one Sunday in Haverhill, and at the close of the sermon received a most cordial and unanimous call from the parish to become its minister.

While considering this, I received one from Fitchburg. It was not so unanimous or cordial as the one from Haverhill, though I was told that only one voted against me. But the society was much larger, they offered more salary, I liked the location better, it being more sheltered from the east wind, and, having a comfortable hope that the missing cordiality would come with acquaintance, I accepted.

Then came the trial of leaving Walpole, and it was a trial indeed. Never did the dear old parsonage home which I had planned, superintended in building, watched over and cared for, the trees I had planted, the grounds I had graded and beautified — never did it all seem so beautiful as when I felt that I must leave it forever. And friends, too, grew nearer and dearer as the time drew nigh that I must bid them farewell.

XIII.

FITCHBURG MINISTRY.

1855-1862.

SETTLEMENT AT FITCHBURG.— DEATH OF LUTHER TILDEN.— CALL TO JERSEY CITY.— PURCHASE OF A COTTAGE.—CIN- CINNATI, SARATOGA, NIAGARA, FORT SUMTER.—MENTAL CONFLICT.—JAMES S. GREENE.—END OF FITCHBURG MIN- ISTRY.

SUNDAY, June 3, 1855, I was inducted to my Fitch- burg ministry, Dr. Bellows preaching the sermon. The next morning I had a delightful walk and talk with him, which cheered and strengthened me.

Fitchburg I found an industrious, wide-awake place, with large manufacturing interests, several newspapers, and churches enough to meet the wants of a wide diversity of religious beliefs. It was a very different place from Walpole. There were rural peace and quiet, here the clatter of machinery and the push of enter- prise. The new conditions called for a new ministra- tion of Christian truth. It was more like Concord, N. H. National affairs came again into prominence, and I felt obliged to run up the flag of liberty, temper- ance, peace, and brotherhood. The response was not altogether harmonious, but the general tone of feeling was kindly. As we became acquainted with the peo- ple, we found in them much to respect and honor. Soon we began to feel at home, and to enjoy the new field of labor. Here again I became a member of the school committee, and continued in the service I always loved as long as I remained in Fitchburg. I gave lyceum temperance and peace lectures outside my regular work, and inside tried as I best could to build up the inward kingdom in the hearts of my people. The First Parish was large, covering a wide territory. Visiting my scattered parishioners and the schools kept me busy. I lived on good terms with the other ministers of the place, exchanged with the Universalist, Methodist, and Trinitarian, or "Black Orthodox," as the last was called, on account of the strong and earnest anti-slavery position taken by the society. The Rev. Elnathan Davis, pastor of this church, was my true and intimate friend, as was Rev. Kendall Brooks, pastor of the Baptist church, with whom I was associated on the school committee. His house was on my way to the post-office, and I often ran in to his study to see what kind of a sermon he was writing, and compare notes. Our fellowship was delightful.

I adopted one new custom at Fitchburg which proved very successful. It was giving an occasional sermon to the Sunday-school, letting it take the place of the afternoon service. The school occupied the body pews, and the members of the congregation sat where they could. These addresses were given without notes,— plain talks with the children,— and proved as interesting to the old as the young.*

---

* No mention is made in this Autobiography of a small book entitled " Buds for the Bridal Wreath," which he published in 1856. It contained wise and loving advice to those just entered on the holy estate of marriage.

In a letter to his friend Mr. May at this time, he says : " It has at least one virtue : it

March 6, 1857, my father died at South Scituate. He was eighty years old the January before. He was a good father, a kind husband, a dear lover of his home. He was industrious and hard-working, but never fore-handed, though always generous beyond his means. In early life he and his brother Jotham were partners in ship-building at the Block House. After they dis-solved, he took contracts in Medford and Braintree and other places; but, save a short residence in Boston when he was first married, he made his home in Scitu-ate, within a few miles of the place where he was born.

Dear, precious father, peace to thy risen spirit!

I think I never quite fitted the Fitchburg parish. There was more or less friction, mainly on account of my anti-slavery views. Threatening clouds began to loom up in our political sky, and I had to speak again and again. The majority was with me, but a few prominent members were greatly disturbed. Finally, in the fourth year of my ministry, I thought I would leave the first good opportunity.

Mr. Frothingham having left the young society at Jersey City, where I preached about the time he was settled, I was invited to supply the pulpit two Sundays in January, 1860. They at once gave me a unanimous call at fifteen hundred dollars a year.

The next month I took Mary with me to Jersey City, and preached two Sundays. The people were so kind

is small. It has also one other: it omits the *wise counsels* upon the *vast importance* of making a right choice, which is common to such books. It seems to me rather late in the day to talk to those already married of the importance of choosing wisely; and yet how often this is done !

"You see I have not given a separate chapter to religion, because I have wished to infuse the religious spirit into every chapter, and thus show that piety belongs, not to a *single* chapter of human life alone, but to every paragraph, line, and word of life's sacred volume."

and cordial and really anxious for us to come that we decided in the affirmative. When we returned, I sent in my resignation. To my surprise, they voted not to accept it, fifty-four to nine. A committee waited upon me to report the vote, and see if they could not prevail upon me to remain. But I had gone so far I thought I had better not recall my resignation, and sent them a letter to that effect. Many were greatly disappointed. I was told that one man, when the note was read; laid his face in his hands and burst into tears. The meeting adjourned without taking any action on the letter. Soon after friends came to me, saying they would canvass the parish and get the express wish of every legal voter. The result was one hundred and seven wished me to remain, eight would like to have me go, and some five or six chose not to express an opinion on paper, though some of these wished me to stay.

I yielded to the wishes of this large majority and the earnest personal entreaty of individual friends, and consented to remain.

It was a great disappointment to the little church at Jersey City and to Mary, who thought it wiser to go. We had formed delightful acquaintances there, especially with the Armstrong family, to whom we had become much attached. On the day I had intended to give my farewell I preached instead my inaugural of the new dispensation.

After deciding to remain, we moved from the house we had lived in for nearly five years to a cottage on the hill, which I bought.

It was delightful to have a home of our own. We had a large garden, good light soil, and many young fruit-trees in the prime of bearing. It was a little paradise, till the glittering sword of a destiny always loving drew us out into broader, if not greener, pastures.

In the autumn of this year, 1860, I was invited to preach four Sundays at Cincinnati, Ohio. One of my Walpole parishioners, Mr. William Bellows, had gone there to reside ; and, as one of the Unitarian churches was without a pastor, he was anxious to have me come for a few Sundays. I had never been West, and was glad to go. I went alone. It seemed best for very obvious reasons, but it was a great drawback to the pleasure of the trip. I had never been to Saratoga or Niagara, and so arranged to take them on the way. Spent the first night at Saratoga, drank of its medicinal waters, and ate for supper the famous Saratoga biscuits, made light as a clear conscience with water only for yeast.

The next night I was at Niagara. The Falls filled me with wonder and awe. It takes time to get adjusted to them. How I did long for Mary and the children to share the grandeur with me! It was too much for one. I could only drink a drop of the ceaseless pouring, resistless flood. Oh, I thought, if the sick ones of my parish could but look upon the sight, it would give them strength to bear pain or die, as the Father of this infinite majesty might choose.

Over an evergreen arch, thirty or forty feet high, near Table Rock, was an inscription, " Welcome to nature's grandest sight." It was designed to welcome the Prince of Wales on his then recent visit. That was well; but every soul God has made capable of enjoying this grandeur is a prince, and to him also the invisible Spirit of the ceaseless wonder says, "Welcome to nature's grandest view!"

Going on by the way of Buffalo, Cleveland, and Columbus, I arrived at Cincinnati Saturday, October 27, and went directly to the house of Mr. Kepler, where I was to make my home; and it *was* a home, made pleasant to me by generous hospitality. I soon met my friends from Walpole, N.H., whose familiar faces and cordial greetings swept away the homesickness beginning to gather, and made me feel that I was not among entire strangers. Here I spent four Sundays, and formed many pleasant acquaintances. Politics ran high. Abraham Lincoln was the Republican nominee for President. Slave-holding Kentucky was separated from Cincinnati only by the muddy Ohio stream. But politics ran muddier than the river. A man said to me one day on the ferry-boat that he thought it very wrong to nominate a man for the Presidency who could not safely cross that river. It was but a straw, but i told the course of the stream, as events proved.

The two banks of the river told the stories of liberty and bondage in large type that the dimmest eyes could read. The slave bank was a century behind the free in thrift and civilization. No threats of peril in crossing the stream could intimidate loyal hearts. There were noble anti-slavery men in Cincinnati. I was introduced to one,— Hon. Salmon P. Chase, "the founder and leader of the Liberty, afterwards Free Soil, Party." He was a fine speciman of manhood, physically and intellectually. He was then in his prime, —about fifty,— had been Governor of Ohio and United

States Senator, and was widely known and honored by all who believed with him that "slavery was sectional, freedom national."

I enjoyed preaching to the "little flock," and en-joyed the outing, but was glad to make a bee-line for home when my engagement closed.

Immediately after Mr. Lincoln's election the slave-holding States began the execution of their long-stand-ing threat of secession. South Carolina took the lead, passing the ordinance of secession in December, 1860. This action was rapidly followed in turn by Mississippi, Florida, Alabama, Georgia, Louisiana, and Texas. Be-fore Mr. Lincoln was inaugurated, the Southern Con-federacy was organized, with Jefferson Davis president. They had seized forts, arsenals, and other United States property within their reach, together with large quantities of arms, ammunition, and other military stores, much of which had previously been removed from the North. Up to this time anti-slavery people did not believe that the seceders would make war with the government so sure to liberate their slaves. But on the 12th of April, 1861, the United States flag float-ing over a small garrison on Fort Sumter was shot down by a Confederate force, and the bloody war com-menced.

Never can I forget the intense excitement and deep solemnity of the day when the news of the attack on Fort Sumter first reached us. It was as if a wayward child had smitten its own mother on the cheek,— nay, fired a bullet in her heart. Each felt the death-dealing missile as aimed at him. "Then you and I and all of us fell down, and bloody treason flourished over us."

Over Main Street the stars and stripes waved slowly
and solemnly as if heavy with the tears of a nation's
grief. It seemed to me as if I never saw "our flag" till
then. The insult offered to it gave it a new meaning
and preciousness. As a disciple of Jesus, I had felt
myself forbidden to fight even in self-defence. But
here something far higher and greater than *self* was in
peril. Not I, but my country, was assailed. I would
not fight for my own life, for I would sooner lose that
than take another's; but how about our national, or
common mother's, life? That was the question now. I
could not answer it at once. I had been a non-resistant
for years. I could not change in a day. I must be
silent, I must think, I must pray. I must go up into
the mount alone, and ask counsel of Him who guides
nations as well as individuals in paths they know not.
All the week I was in mental agony. What should I
say to my parishioners on the coming Sunday? The
question was yet unanswered when I went into my pulpit, worn with anxious thought, and told them all my
struggles. I just opened my heart to them, and let
them see how it was torn by conflicting ideas and emo-
tions. My anti-slavery convictions had not been
deeper than my anti-war convictions; but here was no
question of self-defence, but the defence of great
national principles, involving the liberty and highest
welfare of millions of people. I must wait till I could
adjust myself to the new conditions.

The people received the sermon kindly, for they
knew I was honest; and I think they respected me
none the less for not being hasty in changing the conviction of years. I did not have to wait long. A

new sense of the value and necessity of a just government broke upon me, until I saw clearly that, when our
national life was assailed with brutal violence, and
especially for the purpose of perpetuating sectional
slavery and making it national, violence must be met
by violence, or the republic would fall, and Senator
Toombs would carry out his threat of "calling the
roll of his slaves in the shadow of Bunker Hill monument"

I came to this conviction, which seems so plain
to those who had never thought otherwise, only
through great tribulation and anguish of spirit. It
seemed like going down from some serene mountain
height into the valley of the shadow of death. But it
was there the great and final battle with slavery was
to be fought; and as I heard the bugle-call, and saw our
truest and bravest men fall into line, and leave all for
the great conflict, not in defence of self, but in defence
of national honor and life, I felt that it was right, and
that a God of justice would not suffer our cause to
fail.

But I was spoiled for the war. I could not enter
into it with any heart. I had served too many years
under another banner to become enthusiastic. I
bowed to the stern necessity, and read the lesson so
difficult to learn,— that God has many ways of accom-
plishing his purposes, and may in great national crises
be as truly served on the battle-field as in the house of
prayer.

Since then I have had no trouble about voting, save
that of knowing whom to vote for. I learned by experience what most others take intuitively, that human

government is a necessity, and that as a *dernier* resort it must have the right of resistance to the powers of darkness and wrong.

Still, I believe in the divineness of overcoming evil with good, and think that the less the government governs, and the more the Christ spirit pervades the hearts of the people, the better it will be for all. Hon. Charles Sumner's strong and brave discourse on the "True Grandeur of Nations" presents the highest ideal for national ambition.

Seven days after the attack on Fort Sumter President Lincoln issued his first proclamation, calling for seventy-five thousand militia for three months' service. It was then believed that the rebellion could soon be put down. Volunteers readily enlisted, and among them a young man in our parish, who was studying medicine in the Cambridge Medical School. His name was James Sumner Greene; and we had reason for regarding him with special interest, as he was engaged to be married to our own precious Laura. They were married August 21; and he immediately left for the seat of war, taking Laura with him as far as Fortress Monroe.

Willie and Georgie were both at school, too young to enlist. I was glad of it; for the shock of war was still upon me, and I could not look upon it with enthusiasm, but only as a dark and terrible necessity.

It was a summer of great military disasters to our small army. We were all unused to war, and many a noble life had to be laid on the altar of liberty before we were able to cope successfully with our formidable foe.

But I am not writing the history of the war, only naming such incidents as touched my ministry and colored its character. Though I saw the war must be prosecuted to the bitter end, yet I should have made a poor recruiting officer. The sermons most popular then were those charged to the muzzle with powder and shell. Mine were not of that character. No doubt they seemed tame to those who had fathers, sons, brothers, and husbands in the service.

Gradually, the impressions which led me to resign the year before returned; and I felt that, whether yielding to the earnest request for me to remain were a mistake or not, it was clear that the time had come for me to go.

But the attendance at church morning and afternoon— for we always had two services — was large, and apparently interested; and I was reluctant to go. I have never, in any part of my long ministry, preached to so many people continuously. I only wish I could have more fully met their needs.

At the annual meeting in 1862 my salary was not voted in full. I knew this was not owing to pecuniary inability; and so, taking the gentle hint as kindly as it was given, on the last Sunday in May, 1862, having served them as their minister just seven years, I preached my farewell.

Though my Fitchburg ministry had some inevitable trials, it had many blessings; and the friendships formed there are still fragrant with pleasant memories. But I fell so far short of my hopes that I felt somewhat as Jacob must have done, when, after serving seven years for Rachel, he got Leah. But even Leah, though "tender-eyed," was richly worth the seven years' service of light and shade.

Now we were afloat again on the wide, wide sea. But we did not forget who "holds the waters in the hollow of His hand." Laura had returned to us, leaving her husband in the service, in the medical department. We still occupied the little cottage on the hill, while I went out as a rover.

XIV.

CHURCH GREEN MINISTRY.

1862.

THE next two Sundays after my farewell I preached
at Exeter, N.H. Then one Sunday at Church Green,
Boston. The two following Sundays again at Exeter.
Here there was a movement to give me a call; but my
last sermon, on "The Refining Power of Christianity,"
so disturbed a certain few that the call was not given.
The next Sunday I conducted the service again at
Church Green, and administered the communion. The
Sunday after that I went to Norton, and had a delightful season with old friends there. The next two Sundays I preached at Jersey City, and stopped with our
good friends, the Armstrongs.

Returning to Fitchburg for a few Sundays' rest, I received an invitation to supply the pulpit at Church
Green for four Sundays. I greatly enjoyed preaching in
this old, octagonal stone church. The place seemed
made for worship. The people were reverential, devout,
and the singing was exquisite. I was pleased, therefore, when I heard they were thinking of giving me a
call, though their numbers were few, and everybody
seemed to think that the old society was going to slow
but sure decay.

Warehouses were beginning to encroach more and more upon that part of the city, and the days of the venerable church seemed numbered. Dr. Dewey had been with them for two years. Though he was an old man, his preaching was grand as ever ; and it was hoped that that would arrest, at least, the steadily waning congregation. But, when he left, the church was still declining. Still I hoped they would invite me to become their pastor ; for I thought it possible for them to gather strength enough to move and locate elsewhere, when the absolute necessity for change came.

On the day when the pew-holders were to decide on giving me a call, an incident occurred which I feared would turn the tide against me. It was early in the war, and, although I had not spoken on national matters, I had prayed each Sunday in a way that had disturbed some of the congregation, and confirmed the impression otherwise received, that I was a political radical.

On the morning of my last Sunday's engagement I found in my little room below the pulpit a note from one of my best friends, one whom I knew was most anxious for my settlement, expressing the hope that I would be careful in what I said concerning the country, as some of the people were sensitive on that subject, and it was especially desirable that nothing should occur to disturb the harmonious action of the society. I was greatly pained and deeply embarrassed. To yield to the suggestion would be time-serving and cowardly. To disregard it would seem like wantonly slighting the counsels of a friend. What should I do ? In my perplexity the thought came, "Do this: go on with your service as if nothing had happened, and then, after you have read the notice of the meeting to be held directly after the service, stop yourself, and tell the people openly and honestly just what your position is." I accepted the suggestion as from above, and went on with my ministrations with peace of heart.

After reading the notice, I remained in the church; and, when the meeting had been called to order, I rose, and told them why I had remained. I alluded to the pleasure I had taken in preaching to them, and the satisfaction I should feel in serving them in the ministry if they should desire it, but from a note received that morning, informing me of the feelings of some of the society concerning matters of vital importance to me, I feared there might be some reason for not giving the call. At all events, I thought it was right that they should all understand my position, and so had stopped to make a clean breast, and let them know just where I stood.

I then told them that my convictions on the great questions of freedom and equal rights now agitating the country were not of recent origin,— they were the growth of years, they were a part of my religion,— and that, wherever I ministered, I must be free in prayer and sermon to give expression to my convictions in such a way as my own judgment dictated. If, with this frank statement, they felt they were willing to trust me, and desired my services, I should be most happy to serve them according to my ability.

I then left the church, and, meeting Mary outside, we walked away, silent and sad, thinking, most likely, that the call would not be given. We had both become so attached to the church and the people it was painful to think that this was the last time we should meet with them. But I knew I had done right. There was comfort in that, come what might.

Soon, however, we were met in the street by a member of the society, who told us, with evident pleasure, that the call had been unanimously extended to me to become their pastor.

I accepted, and preached my inaugural at Church Green Oct. 12, 1862. We sold our cottage at Fitchburg, packed and stored our household goods, and came to Charlestown to board with Aunt Tempie, where we had spent so many happy days.*

The children now were scattered. Laura was with her husband at East Boston, who was continuing his course at the Harvard Medical School, having returned sick, and obtained an honorable discharge. Willie was left in a store in Fitchburg, where he was bravely earning his living; and Georgie had gone to Exeter to prepare for Harvard, so Mary and I were left alone again.

The next spring we moved to Boston, taking a house close to our church, 79 Bedford Street. Our parishioners were very generous in helping to furnish the home.

---

* In a letter written about this time to his friend Mr. J. B. Smead, of Fitchburg, he says : —

"We brought with us enough to furnish one chamber, which we have fitted up quite cosily for sitting-room and study. Carpet, chairs, pictures, bookcases, etc., give it quite a homelike air. But it isn't the old nest, and wouldn't be if every straw were brought here and laid over again ; for the birds have flown. Sweet nestlings, how much comfort we have taken in feeling them under our wings! But they are fledged now, and it is the ordering of the great Providence, without which 'not one sparrow falleth,' that they should spread their wings. May the dear God guard and feed them, and shelter with his love the boughs on which they build! "

Here, the pen was laid aside for more pressing duties, and the Autobiography was never resumed.

Another hand has tried to tell the story, as much as possible in his own words, by extracts from journals, private letters, and *Register* letters, newspaper cuttings, etc.

XV

EXTRACTS FROM JOURNAL.

1866.

EXTRACTS FROM FAREWELL SERMON AT CHURCH GREEN.—
MINISTRY AT LARGE.

His journal of 1866 says : " My salary, at first only fifteen hundred dollars, was afterwards increased to eighteen hundred, and subsequently to twenty-five hundred. A few friends have been disturbed by my preaching on national affairs, but the great majority have been good, warm-hearted friends. I fondly hoped that interest enough in the society might be awakened to induce the proprietors to sell the present church, and with the funds build another in a more favorable location ; but that hope was blasted by a vote of the proprietors, early in the spring, to ask leave of the Supreme Judicial Court to dissolve the corporation and divide the property."

May 15 " I started on a tour to the 'Far West.' My dear friend, George A. Blanchard, residing in Dubuque, Ia., not only gave me the most cordial invitation to make his house my home, but offered me generous facilities for travel. It was a delightful journey. The immense extent of our country, its untold richness, its inexhaustible resources, its beauty, the kindness of friends and the goodness of God, were all abundantly manifest."

July 1, 1866, "Being the close of my ministry at Church Green, and the closing of the church for religious purposes, I preached from the text, 'A voice from the temple,' — Isaiah lxvi. 6."

A few extracts from this sermon tell the story of the three years' ministry : —

"It is not strange that the old church where for long years, in sorrow and joy, we have come up to keep holy time with those we love, should have been very sacred in our thoughts and to our religious affections, and that, when its portals are opened for the last time, it should be filled with voices for the heart, which, though silent, may be far deeper and more impressive than any which come from choir or pulpit. . . .

"You are carried back again to those early days when the church was thronged and every seat was filled. Again you see the old familiar faces and forms. They crowd the porch, they walk up the aisles, each with his familiar step and air. They take their seats, some at your side, some yonder, each in his place. You stand again at the baptismal font with your children. You remember how fervently your heart prayed for a blessing upon the little ones on whose brows the pure waters of baptism were sprinkled. You come again to your first communion, and are reminded of the freshness of your vows, the fervor of your prayers, the entireness of your consecration, the fulness of your love, the sacredness of your purpose. You recall seasons of special religious interest, when gospel truth was bread for your hungry souls, and when 'your hearts burned within you' with a new love, as he whom you honored and trusted 'opened to you the Scripture.' You remember that season of deep sorrow, when you came up here with an overburdened heart and went away with the burden lifted, and a comforting assurance that 'He doeth all things well.' . . .

"There is only one really sad thought connected with the giving up of this old church of sacred memories, only one. Changes are inevitable, they are good, they are divinely ordered. They help on the soul and the world, painful as they sometimes are. The one really sad thought of the hour is that this religious society is to become extinct, to die,— to die, with all the means of living at its command; to die of its own free choice, voluntarily, suicidally.

" It has been plain for a long time to those who have watched the rapid changes in the city, and the inevitable drifts of commerce, that this church edifice must be given up. No efforts in the ordinary line of pulpit ministrations could prevent the slow but sure decline of the congregations. Even the eloquence and prestige of Dr. Dewey were as unavailing as the faithful and able labors of Dr. Young to change the ebbing tide. When I first preached here, four years ago this summer, it seemed about dead-low water, but, small as was the hope of any permanent increase in numbers or interest here, yet large and well grounded, as I thought, was the hope that in due time this church would be removed to a locality where it might look for a revival of its old prosperity. . . .

" I seized upon that hope, and held it fast ; and, the more I learned of the real condition of things among

you, the more clearly I saw that this was the only reasonable hope of continued life. You had already lost
the elements of continued growth. The Sunday-school
had been given up for sheer lack of pupils. Most of the
young people had left the church to go where they
could feel the breath of young life and worship with
their companions. Few remained save the aged and
those in middle life. . . .

"This perpetuation of the society by removal seemed
in itself so simply and plainly right, so in harmony with
all the hallowed and reverential associations of the
church from the beginning of its history, so accordant
with the natural promptings of a faith that feels its own
worth,— in short, so many 'voices from the temple'
all conspired in urging it,— that I was unwilling to believe, till constrained by painful facts, that it would not,
in some way, be done. . . .

"But a large majority of the proprietors of this religious society have voted to ask leave of the Supreme
Court *to die*, to dissolve the corporation and divide the
property. I rejoice to know that this contemplated dis-
solution is not by the general consent of all its members. Indeed, had it not been for the votes and influence of the pew-holders who have ceased to worship
with us, it is doubtful if the measure could have been
carried.

"But my ministry here, though failing in this, its leading hope, has not, I trust, in all respects been a failure.
It certainly has not failed to bring to me, notwithstand-
ing its many discouragements, a large share of real
pleasure. I have enjoyed my pastorate from the first
hour I stood in this pulpit till the last. I well remem-

ber the peculiar feelings of that first hour. There was something in the place, its venerableness, its fitness for worship, that impressed me. There seemed to be mysterious influences around me, making me feel that it was good to be here, and giving me the impression that I was here for a special purpose ; and, though no fruit of my ministry may seem to justify the feeling, it has cheered me through all my labors, and even now, at their close, gives me the hope that, little as I have accomplished, my coming may have been a necessary step to some other field of labor I may more worthily fill.''

His journal of that date says : —

"Some time previous, knowing that our society would probably close its house before long, I had received an earnest invitation to accept of a ministry at large at the South End. My heart was strongly drawn to it, but, after serious and prayerful deliberation, I declined, and accepted instead the duties of a missionary of the American Unitarian Association.

" I commenced this work Saturday, July 6, 1866. In some respects, my Boston ministry has been the pleasantest part of my ministerial life. I have enjoyed being in the city greatly. My health has been exceptionally good. My opportunities for fellowship with the most cultivated ministers of our denomination unusually large. I have enjoyed the meetings of the Boston Association and the Ministerial Union, and they have been profitable to me. I have found many good friends, and I am cheered with the hope that my ministry in its higher aspects has not been in vain. Eighteen have been added to the church, among them my own dear

boys, William and George.   This was a joy to my heart.
May God bless them, and keep them faithful to the end !
And may he bless with his love and guidance all the
members of that ancient church and society, no more to
worship together in the dear old temple made sacred by
so many hallowed associations ! "

Thanksgiving, Nov. 29, 1866.   " We spent the day
with Aunt Tempie.   Laura and James with their two
children, Joseph and George, were here.   Will also with
his Anna was with us at tea and in the evening, but
George was at Fitchburg.   Laura's babe is a beautiful
boy, but I fear he is not long for earth : his eyes are too
bright.   The little soul seems just ready to come out of
them.   Perhaps he is in search of his baby sister Mary,
whom the angels took more than a year ago."

It was this little Mary whose birth anniversary was
always commemorated, and of whom the grandfather
wrote to the mother nineteen years afterwards : " I am
glad you continue that most touching custom.   It was
sweet when you gathered the children of her age to keep
the advent.   It is fitting, now that she is neither child
nor maiden longer, to have ripe womanhood represented.   It helps to bridge the way between the two
worlds, so that the sweet intercourse can be continued
to heart and inward vision."

The fatigues attendant upon the constant travel and
the necessary absence from his family which the missionary work entailed induced him to accept the invitation which was *again* proffered him by the Benevolent
Fraternity of Churches to a " ministry at large," at the
South End, Boston.   He says : " The work has its attractions for me.   I have long felt that there is a large

class of persons in the city whose wants are not met by the ordinary ministrations of religion. We need more *free chapels.* If this be the work for me, may the Holy Spirit make it plain!"

December 15. "To-day handed in my acceptance of the call named above. I am to enter on my work the first Sunday in January. I feel happy in my decision. I trust it has been wisely made. But I shall need strength and guidance from above. O Father, grant it for thine own love's sake. Amen."

XVI

EXTRACTS FROM JOURNAL.

1867-1876.

New South Free Church. — Extracts from Journals, Annual Reports, etc. — Death of Mrs. Tilden. — Death of Little Laura.

Jan. 6, 1867. "Yesterday I preached in Concord Hall, Concord Street, Boston. Subject, 'The Necessity of Free Churches.' It was a severe storm in the forenoon. In the afternoon it brightened and stopped snowing, though the walking was bad. I walked from Charlestown Neck to the hall after dinner. Got there in time to see how the little Sunday-school was conducted, after which we held a service, some twenty or thirty present. This is the beginning of the pastorate which I have accepted of a free church.

"We commence with the remnant of the South End Mission. It is a small remnant, very small. I judge there are scarcely a dozen adults who may be relied upon. But it is plain that a free church is needed, and I have accepted the charge in faith and hope that with God's blessing a church may be established, open alike to rich and poor, where that class especially who first heard Jesus gladly may find a religious home."

January 13. "We had an encouraging number at our service this afternoon. Many of my old friends were present. I think I can count upon some of them for permanent members of the free church."

February 22. Waverly Terrace, Shawmut Avenue, Boston. "We have once more a 'local habitation and a name,' though it is not yet on the front door. We have not waited in vain. We like our house much. It is sunny, cheerful, roomy, and, what is very rare for Boston, it has a pleasant front yard with trees and shrubbery. It is sweet to feel that we have a home once more. Mary is happy as a child in fitting up the house and making it homelike. We hope the boys will soon be with us again. Praise God from whom all blessings flow."

March 7, 1867. "Yesterday the workmen broke ground for the foundation of our new free church. It sent a thrill of pleasure through me as I saw pick and shovel going down to the hard pan, and the teams taking the loose earth away. So with our moral and spiritual picks and shovels may we go down to the hard pan of God's truth, as shown in Jesus, and build our spiritual church on that,— not on the loose earth of alluvial creeds, the deposit of a spent epoch, or on the artificial base prepared by theological pile-drivers, but on the *hard pan* of the everlasting and eternal. A church built on that will stand. No beating storm, or furious wind, or dashing wave can move it."

April 24, 1867. "Our school is growing: our prospects are bright. The Church of the Unity has just contributed ten thousand dollars towards the building of our new free church."

Until about the first of May there had been only afternoon service and Sunday-school. Mr. Tilden wished a morning service. Some of the timorous ones feared that the movement would go down if people could not go elsewhere Sunday mornings. "Let it go down, then," he promptly replied. "We will make a trial next Sunday morning, and then we shall know how many really belong to us." The experiment was tried. There was a larger attendance than usual, and henceforth no Sunday ever failed of a morning service.

June 6, 1867. Anniversary Week. "Having been requested by Mr. Lowe to speak in regard to the missionary work in which I had been engaged, I consented. Felt badly, but, when the time came, was assisted, and succeeded better than I feared. It was my first speech in Music Hall. I probably never addressed so many people before. But, after all, what is an audience of two thousand but one of two hundred multiplied by ten? The material is essentially the same, only more of it. The difference is in size, not in sense."

August of this year (1867) was spent in Marshfield. His journal says: "We have been twice to Scituate. Last Sunday met Mr. May, and heard him preach. It was refreshing to listen to his sweet voice once more. In the afternoon a communion service was held, in which Mr. May presided, Brother Fish and myself participating by each offering a prayer. It was a delightful occasion, a real Whitsuntide in our experience, a day white with the tokens of God's love, bidding the tide of sacred memories flow into heart and soul, a refreshing flood."

Sept. 27, 1867. "I have preached twice without manuscript since I returned from the seashore. I succeeded well, judging from what I heard said of the sermons, though the second attempt was not so satisfactory to myself as the first. I commenced another sermon designed to be given without manuscript, but wrote it out so fully that I concluded it was best to read it. I find it isn't wise to make too elaborate preparation. The preparation needed is of *thought* rather than words. When I have plenty of thought, there is little difficulty in putting it into form. It clothes itself. But, then, we think so much in words that it is difficult to collect thought without clothing it as we think; and just here is the danger of writing too much, so that, when you come to speak, you are fettered, perhaps tripped, by the double effort of memory and original expression. I find I am more easy and free in my utterance when I have only the leading ideas, letting them clothe themselves as they will."

Dec. 30, 1867. "Not a word in my journal for three months. I hope there is some record in my heart, for those months have been crowned with divine goodness. If all blessings found record in manuscripts, 'the world itself would not contain the books that would be written.' My work progresses hopefully. On Thanksgiving we had our children with us.

"On Christmas we were all invited to Laura's. We had a delightful time, to be remembered with gratitude to God for all his goodness, and especially for such precious children and grandchildren as he has given us. They are a joy to our hearts. May the dear Father fold them all in his loving arms forever!"

The society continued to meet in the hall, up two flights of stairs, for more than a year, while the church, corner of Camden and Tremont Streets, was being built.

Sunday, April 5, 1868, the first service in the vestry was held, the room above being still unfinished.

Of this he writes as follows : —

" It was stormy in the morning, but right in the midst of the sermon the clouds broke, and a flood of sunshine burst into the room. It came like a benediction from the skies, a baptism of light and cheer we were glad to hail as a happy omen." .

A few weeks later, on the evening of April 28, the church was dedicated.

Of this work he says, seventeen years later, in his farewell sermon : " Our numbers had so increased in Concord Hall that we began our worship here with a very encouraging attendance. We were not many, it is true, but we were united and our hope was large. Soon after the dedication the society held a meeting and organized under the title of ' The New South Free Church.'

" I came here to change the mission chapel to a free church, seats free to all and welcoming all, rich and poor alike. It had seemed to me that a church for the poor alone was just as far from the spirit of the gospel as a church for the rich alone, that both were narrow and clannish, and that a true church of Christ should be lifted above all outward distinction, and be a church of humanity, whose doors should swing on hinges of the most cordial welcome to all who would come and worship, and work together for the grand objects of a Christian church.

" On this broad plan the church was organized, on this base we have worshipped and worked. It is not a mission chapel, though we rejoice in our missionary work, and think we can do all the more effectively without the name. It is a free church, and to those who think the free should be dropped we say this is our special glory. It is our crown of rejoicing. For this the church was built, for this it is sustained,— not as a church on the ordinary close corporation plan, but as a free church, absolutely free to all, without regard to outward distinction of wealth, culture, or color,— a church in which all are welcomed by virtue of their simple humanity as the equal children of a common Father.

"Our numbers have never been large. My early hopes in this respect have never been fulfilled. For I was sanguine enough to hope at the beginning that a few years would see our church filled, and I even imagined how, in case of need, we might push out a wing towards Tremont Street, to seat a hundred or two that could not be accommodated in front. But, alas! it was only the wing of a hopeful imagination, and was never spread."

At one time Mr. Tilden could look over the congregation and see one or more parishioners from every parish over which he had ever been settled, who, leaving their country homes for the city, had sought out their old pastor, and gladly placed themselves once more under his guidance and spiritual care.

Mrs. Judge Shaw, Mrs. Ann Gould, Mrs. and Miss Wheelwright, Miss Russel, Messrs. Willis, Taggard, and Taylor were among those who followed the retiring pastor from Church Green, enabling him by their presence and pecuniary assistance to change the character of the work from a mission chapel to a free church.

Others who did not attend the Sunday services made glad his heart by their contributions to the "poor's purse" and their aid in all efforts to meet the necessary expenses of the work.

A few extracts from some of the Annual Reports made to the Executive Committee of the Benevolent Fraternity of Churches may be of interest.

In the Annual Report for 1875 he says :—

"The attendance on our Sunday morning service is encouraging, both in numbers and in manifest interest. As our doors swing both ways, and egress is as easy as access, none stay with us except from choice. So we have no grumblers,— a rare felicity, which we highly appreciate. . . .

"We numbered on our Sunday-school roll at the close of the year, including teachers and officers, two hundred and eighty-three. I regard the Sunday-school as a vitally important branch of our free church work. As we hold our session in the afternoon, I am enabled to take the superintendence of it; and I am accustomed to think that I could better be spared from either of the other Sunday services than this.

"It is said sometimes that our free churches are too much like the other churches. If the other churches are all right, this should be to our praise.

"It is said there are no dirty or ragged children in our Sunday-schools. We are delighted to have visitors notice this, for, not believing in dirt or rags, our effort is to clean and clothe. Again, it is said that well-to-do people attend our free churches. We are very grateful that they do. It is one of the brightest spots in our work. We welcome all such, not merely for the pecuniary aid they render, but as missionaries of the gospel of brotherhood. . . .

"There is a wide difference between giving and ministering. With only money one may give; but only with love and sympathy can one minister. Desiring to make our free church in some humble measure a *ministry*, we have commenced another year in good heart and hope."

One of the special features of this ministry was the Friday evening conference meeting, of which he says : "The various themes of Christian believing and living are treated in a familiar way, inviting questions and free conversation. Many who attend them count very fondly upon this oasis hour coming between the Sundays."

"We cannot report the number of conversions at these or any other of our meetings. We leave all this with Him who 'knoweth the heart,' content to hope that some soul may be comforted in its sorrow, strengthened to bear patiently the heavy burdens of life, and inspired with a brighter hope and a warmer love for God and man, by joining with us in prayer and song and spiritual communion on these occasions."

Who of those who attended these meetings can forget the strength of his conviction of the immortal life, as, with his face illumined and his soul aglow, he seemed to be gazing into the open heavens, and making it as real to us as the world in which we are now living?

No account of this ministry would be complete which did not speak of his faithful co-worker, Mrs. A. L. Mayberry, who was connected with the mission when he first took charge of it, and between whom and himself existed a sweet and strong friendship, lasting not only through the seventeen years of his pastorate, but to the end of his life.

In one of the Annual Reports he says : " I wish to bear testimony to the fidelity of your missionary Mrs. Mayberry, and to the marked ability with which she has performed, and is still performing, her arduous duties, and to her special fitness for her peculiar work, — a work requiring a rare combination of Christian sympathy with sound judgment and practical wisdom. I count it a great favor to have for a co-laborer one so well fitted for the work, and whose interest in the object of the mission is so deep and hearty."

His journal for September, 1869, says : " We spent our vacation at Whitefield, N. H.   While we were there, dear George sailed for Liverpool, on his way to Paris, where he hopes to spend some time in the study of his profession.   It is hard to have him go ; but, still, I am glad he has the ambition to desire it.   May God bless the dear boy, and make his stay abroad fruitful of many blessings."

November 7.   " We hear from our absent boy every week.   It is a cordial to our hearts.   Our boy at home has just started in business.   He is a first-rate fellow. May God prosper him ! "

December 7.   " Had a charming letter from George yesterday.   We are thankful for these words from the dear boy.   They are meat and drink to his mother and me.   We are blessed in our children, the three on earth and the one in heaven, immortal links in our golden chain.   O Father, may the chain that binds us all together draw us all closer to thee ! "

August, 1870. "Dear George returned the latter part of June, enriched by study, travel, and — love. We have such confidence in him we feel sure that the one to whom he has been attracted must be pure and noble, though we have never seen her.

"Dear Will and Anna had a daughter born to them on the 19th of July. They have called her Mary Anna. God bless the little darling with its father and mother!

"We have now four grandchildren, two here on the shores of time and two on the golden shores of eternity. Joseph Tilden, now eight years old, a bright and beautiful boy, Laura's first-born, and the little first-born of Will and Anna, here in the flesh, and Mary Foster and Georgie, children of Laura, now with the angels in the spirit land.

"May the invisible arms of Love Divine, holding the seen and the unseen in their embrace, fold them all safely and lovingly forever!"

May 11, 1872. "Day before yesterday was my sixty-first birthday.

"When I was young, in the early part of my ministry, I thought a minister should retire from pastoral charge at fifty, and preach only now and then as occasion might call. As years went by I ran up the slide to sixty as the period for retiring. But here I am at sixty-one still in the harness, and hoping to hold on some years more, if the good Father should spare my life. I love the work, it is as dear to me as ever. And, although I get tired *in* it, I never get tired *of* it, and, as soon as I am rested, I long to take up again the old staff of ministerial duty. It is a budding rod, and blossoms with many a joy as we clasp it, and climb with it the ever-ascending path of common duties."

In November, 1875, she who had walked by his side
for over forty years

"Passed through glory's morning-gate,
And walked in Paradise."

A brief illness, typhoid fever, ended on this earth a life
always delicate, but a life of untiring devotion to husband and children.   A sermon preached soon after her
going away has the following : —

"What this precious one was to me and to her children my tongue refuses to tell.   I could not speak it
if I would, and, with her native reserve and shrinking
from publicity so freshly before me, I would not if I
could.   But you know how often, as we have prayed
together here, we have thanked God for our homes,
and asked his grace that we might be true to all home
loves and duties.   What my home has been to me and
my children was owing much more than I can tell you
to the loving wife and mother, so faithful, so tender,
so true, who was so largely its light and joy.   Home
was her earthly heaven, and her thoughtful care, her
wise counsel, her sweet and tender affection, made it
heavenly to us all.   Few knew her beyond the circle
of her personal friends.   She was quiet, retiring, inclined more to silence than to speech, but so pure and
chaste in word and thought and life, so transparently
truthful, so simply and naturally good and true, and
loyal always to her own highest convictions, that to
know her was to *love* her."

His journal has the following : "Some weeks after
mother rose, George and Alice kindly left their home
in Brookline to spend the winter with me.   In Decem-

ber, feeling worn, I was advised to go away for a little season, and went to Washington, D.C., for the first time. I found much to interest me, and was benefited by the change. On my return, I stopped in New York, and there heard that little Laura Mary was sick in Boston of scarlet fever. When I returned, which was early in January, 1876, she was very sick, and little Charlie was taken ill the next day. After two weeks of dreadful suffering little Laura became an angel.

" She was a very lovely child. I think that at times she had the most radiant face I ever saw, in one so young. She was full of exultant life, with robust health, rosy cheeks, and sparkling eyes, that flashed through her golden hair as she shook it over her face in glee.

" The very day we followed her dear form to the field of peace little Charlie was so sick that it seemed as if he might not live till we returned, but the next day he was better, and as soon as possible his distressed parents took him and the babe Alice out to their Brookline home, where he rapidly recovered."

" Will and Anna have now two beautiful girls, May and Cora."

June 27, 1878. "I have another little granddaughter,* the child of dear Alice and George. The dear God bless the sweet lamb and its happy parents, and, whatever its name may be, may it be written in the book of life ! "

* Edith Selina.

XVII

EUROPEAN TRAVEL.

1878.

In the summer of 1878 Mr. Tilden went abroad for eleven weeks, his pulpit being supplied by labors of love from brother ministers, Dr. Lothrop in his case calling it "a toil of fondness."

In speaking of the proposed trip, Mr. Tilden says : " I have no excuse for going on the ground of illness or overwork. I am remarkably well, never having had the ministerial sore throat and being in no special need of a sea voyage or change of climate on account of physical prostration. I go because I want to. I take my daughter with me because I want her to help me enjoy what may be enjoyable in the trip, for all pleasures are more than doubled in being shared by those we love."

" We sailed from New York in the steamer 'Devonia' of the Anchor line, June 29. The day was clear and bright, like the hopes of the large party of two hundred and forty odd, about to launch forth together on our Musical and Educational Excursion, as it was rather ambitiously called. The friends who came on board to shake hands and say a parting word were unusually numerous because of the unusual number about to embark, so that the waving of handkerchiefs from the hundreds on the pier, as we hauled out into the stream, was prolonged and enthusiastic. But when we were fairly off, and were conscious that three thousand miles of ocean stretched out between us and the land we were seeking, we did feel — I did, I confess — a little bit, just a little, you know, as you would if you had been one of us.

"But our noble steamer moved off stately and gracefully, till the last waving flash of white from the receding pier and city was lost. Then each wiped the — dust from his eyes, and looked out on the beautiful view which opened as, without a sail spread and scarcely a ripple at the sharp prow, we glided down the harbor, by Staten Island, through the Narrows, and out by Sandy Hook."

Of the celebration of the Fourth of July on shipboard he says: "Some one of our company had written a half-seas-over poem, to be sung to 'America' and 'God save the Queen,' and, as I was the only one to whom the handwriting was familiar, it fell to my lot to read.

"We had few to sing, but, with Carl Zerrahn for a leader, it was bound to go. So, after the gun was fired and the hurrah fitly rendered, I planted my feet far apart, and with a stout man at my back with a hand on each shoulder to keep me steady, the paper snapping in the wind and wet with the spray, I read the verses, the first and last only being sung. As we had only one copy, I had to deacon the lines two at a time, and we pilgrims, 'while the breaking waves dashed high,' sent out our voices on the wings of the grand old national air, with the roar of wind and sea for a chorus."

"We arrived in Glasgow July 9, and our first day's journey was over the principal Scottish lakes and the region known as the Trosachs, to Sterling, the Royal Castle, and thence past the historic Bannockburn to Edinburgh.

"Giving only one day to Edinburgh and its attractions, we took a special train by the North British Railway to Melrose, visiting the ruined abbey and the home of Sir Walter Scott, then through Carlisle, Leeds, Sheffield, Leicester, and Bedford to London.

"I think I never enjoyed a day's ride so painfully as that day, in the little, uncomfortable box cars made in the shape of an old-fashioned stage-coach, with door on the side fast locked for fear of accidents. The only redeeming features were the weather and the views. The scenery was all new to us, and as interesting as it was charming.

"The first thing that struck me was the almost entire absence of forests, groves, and trees generally. But the rich grain-fields were waving with golden harvests, just then being gathered, and the grass on hill-slopes and valleys had the same peculiar light green we had observed on the lawns and domes of Ireland and on the mountain borders of the Scottish lakes. It was curious to an American eye to see how all the houses in Scotland, in country as well as in city and town, were built of stone. We do not remember a single building of wood in all Scotland. Even the shanties on the country hillsides and valleys have their walls of stone with thatched roofs. The scarcity of forest timber is the obvious cause. It gives to all structures, great and small, an appearance of solidity and durability, in singular contrast with our American deal and clapboard method of construction.

"As soon as we strike the line separating Scotland from England, we strike brick. All through England, especially in the country, brick is the prevailing material for building. But the views on either side, as we sweep on in our lightning express, are 'dissolving,' save those at a distance, which did not seem in such earnest haste, and remained longer in the field of vision. These gave us a glimpse of the rural beauty of England and the richness of her highly cultivated soil.

"Here, in the place of the stone walls of Scotland, the eye is rested with the green hedges, which very largely take the place of fences all through England, dividing the fields into parallelograms, rhomboids, and other geometrical figures, creating a landscape quite unlike anything we see in our country districts.

"But the New England eye searches in vain for a barn in all England. This seems odd enough to a Yankee, accustomed to regard the barn of the farmer as quite as essential as his house, generally much larger, and often better-looking and more cared for. But the climate of England, so much milder than ours, obviates the necessity of barns by permitting farmers to stack their hay in the open air. But they do it with great care, thatching the top of each stack like a cottage roof, to shed the rain and keep the hay fresh and sweet. The long rows of sheds, seen here and there, tell of sheltered retreats for feeding flocks and herds in storm and cold.

"But it is growing dark and we are getting tired of looking, when the engine whistles and the brakes go down, and the guard cries out, 'Bedford.' This is only forty-eight miles from London, and, if you have ever read 'Pilgrim's Progress,' you will remember it was in a jail in this old town John Bunyan, about two hundred years ago, wrote his immortal volume. We, too, are pilgrims now, glad enough that we are within two hours of the 'hub' of England, which, however foggy and smoky and dark it may be, we look forward to as a 'celestial city' to our aching bones.

"An hour or two more of reticent nodding, jouncing, and pensive contemplation, quite in contrast with our jubilant spirits earlier in the day, and we are roused by the cry of 'London.' It is eleven o'clock. But the immense platform is crowded with hack-drivers and policemen, and general confusion. In the crowd is the junior member of 'Cook & Sons,' on whose tickets we are travelling. He is there to meet us, and greet us, and assign us to our quarters for the night. The several divisions are called to gather in companies, for the coaches in waiting. We could not all be accommodated at one hotel. Each division had been assigned, so we must guard against getting mixed. My daughter and myself had enlisted in the 'Third Division.' We waited in vain for the call. No Third Division,—what did it mean? We had heard 'Second Swiss' vociferated with unction, but had no knowledge of it,—had never heard of it. We began to feel anxious. The most of our party had gone. It was getting toward midnight. 'Second Swiss' was again shouted, as if by one looking up stragglers. 'That isn't our name!' 'Yes, it is.' Unknown to us, our name had been changed some time on the voyage, and we who left New York as members in good and regular standing of 'Third Division' arrived in this hubbub of England at midnight as 'Second Swiss.'

"We were relieved to find we had a name, though it had been changed by our sponsors without our knowledge. But it was not a pleasant experience. A good night's rest, however, carried off the nameless sensation, and we awoke refreshed for London sight-seeing, promptly responding ever after to our new name of 'Second Swiss.'·

"As we came into the city in the dark, perhaps it will be well first to go out again a little way on one of the elevated railroads and see how the city looks as you approach it in open daylight. The view from the elevated track is peculiar, not in landscape, but in roof-scape. You look out on acres and over square miles of roofs and chimneys spread out like a small Sahara, with here and there a single building rising above the rest. On each of the thousand chimneys standing like grim sentinels on this waste of roofs there are as many chimney-pots as flues. Multiply each stack by two, three, four, five, or six, as the case may be. These pots are of all sorts, sizes, shapes, and colors. There are tall pots and short pots, straight pots and crooked pots, round pots and octagonal pots, pots ornamented and pots plain, pots in groups and pots single, pots black, pots red, pots brown, with all the intermediate shades which London smoke is capable of producing,— all placed there simply to aid the draught, without the slightest idea, probably, of how much they would add to the picturesqueness of the roof-scenery of the great city."

Then follow visits to the Tower of London, the Houses of Parliament and Westminster Abbey, St. Paul Cathedral, the Albert Memorial, statue of Lord Nelson, and many other places of interest. Of the old cathedral he says: "I should not care to worship there save on great occasions. I love life better than death, the living present better than the dead past. Still, the place is full of solemn interest, and I am glad to have trodden its marble floor and looked on its monument of departed glory."

"July 17 we embarked at Harwich for a twelve hours' run over the North Sea. Landing at Flushing, but not stopping, we take train for Antwerp. We pass through only a little strip of Holland, but it is a good sample of the 'hollow country,' for it lies below the sea-level, protected by embankments from the ocean tides. It is a low, level plain, highly cultivated, with very few trees, and these quite diminutive in appearance.

"Streets and avenues are often bordered with small poplars, looking as straight and prim as the toy trees of children and about as large. We did not see a good-sized, respectable tree in this whole region. But what Holland lacks in trees she makes up in windmills. The reason why water doesn't run down hill in Holland is not owing to any perversity of the water, but only because there are no hills for it to run down. So the winds that sweep in from the North Sea are made to do the grinding and flouring of that rich grain country.

"It was the season for harvesting, and the men and women were in the fields, doing their *level* best. Woman's right to do a man's work, wherever she can, seems to be fully allowed all over the continent. Whether she duly appreciates her privilege I don't know, but the fields she joins the man in cultivating give tokens of golden harvests.

"I was surprised to see the extent of the shipping in Antwerp, and the splendid docks she has erected for its accommodation. Its quaint old streets and market-places, the large number of uniformed soldiers, the curiously bonneted peasantry, and the street cafés, converting the sidewalks and half the street into beer saloons, seem very odd to an American eye.

"But its main attractions to an overnight tourist are its cathedral and museum of art. In all the vicissitudes of war to which the city has been subjected, the cathedral, with its spire shooting up four hundred and four feet into the sky, has been deemed too beautiful to be destroyed.

"In the south transept is the great masterpiece of Rubens, 'The Descent from the Cross.' It is wonderful for its delineation of death, bloody, cruel death,— wonderful as a work of art, but to me it is dreadful to look at. It is like looking at the crucifixion itself. I wonder how people can stand and admire the art, the force and vigor of the muscular delineation, the admirable foreshortening of a limb, or the exquisite coloring, when the whole picture — just because it is so masterly — is so ghastly and horrible.

"In the museum one is painfully impressed with the dolorous character of most of the pictures. I did not understand the reason of this till I learned they were mostly collected from suppressed convents. I think a large share of the pictures might have been suppressed, too, without harm. They perpetuated the old idea of appealing to the religious sympathies through various forms of the suffering and dead Christ.

"These painful pictures are so multiplied that at last I walked by them with my hand for a screen to shut them out, glad to find now and then some object of sweet and happy life on which to rest the pained vision.

"Of course there are some beautiful pictures here, but they are mostly of a character to make the bright sunshine and pure air outside a particularly pleasant change.

"Indeed, the air and sunshine, the moon and stars, are about the only things here that seem homelike.

"But we must be off for Brussels, leaving many things of interest unnoticed.

"Brussels is a very beautiful city, combining the old and new, narrow, old-fashioned thoroughfares with broad spacious avenues, old Flemish houses with fine modern structures, in a very charming way.

"Two things everybody must see, however short his stay and whatever else he misses,— the lace manufactory and the cathedral.

"I must tell you a little about our dinner, or '*table d'hôte*,' as it is called. Here in Brussels it consisted of twelve different courses. As there were just fifty of us, it took six hundred clean plates to serve our party. This sounds very luxurious. It gives a suggestion of very high living. But it is anything but that, I assure you. The first course is a few spoonfuls of soup of some sort. Then perhaps a small piece of meat. Then a potato as a special course. Then fifty more clean plates, and a bit of cauliflower is served; another fifty clean plates, and a bit of something, you don't know what, and so on, number eleven being generally a chicken's wing — where they get so many chickens' wings is a mystery — and number twelve being a thin slice of ice-cream, a mere suggestion, just enough to moisten the mouth and make you think how nice it would be if you could only have some to eat as well as taste. And after all this clatter of dishes, called out of courtesy *courses*, you rise faint and hungry, thinking what you would give for one good, old-fashioned square meal.

"We have no time to speak of the museums, the picture galleries, ducal palace, palace of the king, and the like, but, before leaving, I must quote a word or two which I find jotted down in pencil. 'It is funny to see how we are stared at and jabbered about by the people here, as if we were from New Zealand or the interior of Africa. Even a dog harnessed to a milk-cart barked at me this morning, showing that he perceived I was an exotic. He evidently felt himself high above me, though not too high to speak, in his own way, which I understood better than most I heard.'

"After a day's ride, with the thermometer at 80,° we arrive at Cologne, and go at once to see the grand old cathedral, not stopping to wash or sup. I name it as a warning to all travellers never to be guilty of such folly. We were too tired to see and too hungry to appreciate if we could have seen. The next morning, when rested and breakfasted, we went again, and, lo! what we were too tired to see the evening before came out in all its grand old glory."

Then comes a wonderful day on the Rhine, the beauty and grandeur increasing with every mile. His note-book says : "6 P.M. The last hour has exceeded all the rest. I am full. I close my book, and content myself with looking, l'ooking, looking."

Then a night at Wiesbaden, a railroad ride from Frankfort to Heidelberg, which, he says, "was about as beautiful as anything this side paradise could be. Heidelberg, the famous old university town, lies in the charming valley of the Neckar, girt about with everlasting hills. The university, the castle ruins, with their old gardens and winding paths, the magnificent views from the legendary heights, no words can fitly describe."

Baden-Baden, Strasbourg, a Sunday at Schaffhausen, and the journey to Switzerland is entered upon.

"Our course through this wonderful land is zigzag through the elevated plateau, leaving the long Jura range on the right and the broad Alpine belt mainly on the left. Our first stopping-place after leaving Schaffhausen was Zürich, the Boston of Switzerland, the hub of Swiss intelligence and industry.

"The next day's ride was to Lucerne, a queer old town, with its buildings all jumbled together clear down to the lake shore. Its old walls and watch towers, and narrow bridges for foot people only, its church and cathedral, the famous ' Lion of Lucerne ' by Thorwaldsen, cut out of the solid rock,— these, and more things than I have time to name even, are full of interest.

"On the afternoon of the last day of July we were booked for the ascent of the Rigi, and must go then or never, whatever the weather. But we were full of hope, with just doubt enough mixed with it to prevent its intoxicating influence.

"By the help of our kangaroo engine, we first mount up over the little village, getting a balloon view of its house-tops and church spires. And now we mount higher and higher, opening out into a sky view of the beautiful lake below and the valleys spotted with villages and waving with golden harvests. 'Oh! this is charming,' we all say, and keep saying it with emphasis, just as if somebody had doubted our assertions; but there was no one to doubt, and we were all ready to declare that this view alone would richly repay us for a night on the summit, even if we saw nothing more. No sooner said than done. A listening cloud near by took us at our word, and closed in upon us forthwith. The beautiful picture vanished. Our adjectives changed to meet the changed conditions. Our spirits fell with the barometer. Conversation took a more subdued and serious cast. We were resigned,— of course we were; but how could we be jubilant? Our little kangaroo, however, didn't seem to mind it, and kept pushing us still on and up, till he landed us on the summit. Here we alighted. We *could* see the immense hotel, and for that we made our hungry and thirsty way. Having found our rooms and refreshed ourselves, we walked out into the dense cloud. I had often wished myself in the clouds, when a child, looking up as they floated over so gracefully. It didn't seem nearly so nice now as it looked then.

"But we congratulated ourselves on being almost six thousand feet up in the air. True, we could not see anything, but we might if it should break away; and so we strolled round, trying a sort of Swiss contentment and take-it-easy.

"Soon I observed a group gathered on the western brow of the summit, as if looking down at something. Was it a goat on a sheltering precipice, or a gallant young man gone down the perilous cliff to pluck a mountain daisy for his lady-love? I would go and see. I went, and saw! Every now and then the strata of the cloud below us, growing thin, would reveal patches of the landscape below. The whole valley being bathed in sunlight while we were in cloud, these little gleams of beauty we got through the gauzy veil of mist were the most charming I ever saw. There we stood and watched for the openings in the veil. For a long time the clouds would sweep by, so heavily laden that nothing could be seen but the thick, impenetrable leaden gray, extending far down the mountain side. But we buttoned up our coats and hugged our shawls, and waited till by and by another view of the transfigured valley would suddenly break upon us, all the more wonderful in its beauty for being seen in its golden radiance through this veil of mist.

"Watching these dissolving views of Nature's own making, time passed swiftly, and the sunset hour drew nigh. Should we get a view of the mountains? Nobody could tell, but we were mostly Yankees, and could guess. That we didn't guess alike or guess right was of no consequence. There was a satisfaction in exercising our gifts. But the clouds did settle, and wander off, like herds on the mountain side going home. The heavy cloud which the Rigi had worn all the afternoon slipped off his head and wound itself round his stalwart form as a mantle. The valleys were filled with the billowy mist, and away off, where

we knew the snowy peaks must be, a ring of clouds
hung suspended, hiding all. But it was not quite sunset yet, and we waited. Here and there a spot in the
belt of cloud grew thin. Hundreds of eyes were looking ; for ours was not the only party on the summit, and
groups of expectant faces on the knolls and elevated
platforms around were turned mountain-ward with
eager gaze. A shout of joy! Some one has caught
sight of a white peak through an opening in the cloud.
Another blessed rift, and another peak is seen. And
now another in a new direction! And yet another!
The excitement increasing as one after another dis-
covers a new peak in the breaking clouds,—a discovery second only to that of Columbus, when from the
deck of the ' Pinta ' he sighted the longed for Western
shore.

"At last, when all had become discoverers, the excitement abated, and we all settled down into a calmer
enjoyment of the scene, as peak after peak, range after
range, came into view. So clear is the air that they
seemed close to us, though some of them may have
been forty miles away. As the sun declines, the glory
deepens. At last he kisses one after another good-
night with his golden lips, and the gathering darkness,
hiding them from view, gives rest to our weary eyes.

"Congratulating ourselves as the most favored of
mortals, we go to our suppers and our beds with grateful hearts.

"After a short, cold night, we were roused by the
blast of the mountain horn as the dayspring colored
the east, and, half dressing ourselves for fear we should
be late, rushed out into the cold, damp mountain air,

and waited for the dayspring to brighten into dawn. It seemed to be a long time brightening, but at last there was light enough to see the white peaks just beginning to show themselves on the dim horizon. They looked cold and shivery. Perhaps it was the reflection of ourselves. We stamped our feet, circulated in and out among the queer-looking bundles of clothes hastily tied up into a resemblance of men and women, and tried to hurry up old Sol. But it was in vain. He was slow as a Swiss in his movements, but sure; for, see, at last he has kindled a light on the tip of that summit yonder. See it creep down the snowy sides, and then suddenly leap over to another peak, and yet another, and another, until the Bernese Oberland is all ablaze with mountain glory! It was a glorious sight."

Alpnacht, Brienz, and Giessbach were visited, a memorable Sunday at Interlaken, then Freibourg, quaint and curious, was reached. Of this he says: "It is built largely on the steep slopes of a deep ravine, through which runs a small stream, which is spanned by a gossamer-like suspension bridge, nearly a thousand feet long, the longest, it is said, in Europe.

"Across another ravine close by is another suspension bridge nearly as long, and more than three hundred feet above the water. I don't exactly know why it was, but, when I went to the edge of that highest bridge to drop a pebble into the stream three hundred feet below, I stood off a little from the rail, and reached over, so that I didn't see just how long it took for the stone to fall. And, then, as I walked on and over alone, in the rain, I found myself inclining to the centre of the bridge, and walking very quickly. Of course it was only because it rained. These tight rope bridges over yawning chasms may be very safe,— I suppose they are,— but it takes a little time so to adjust one's feelings to them as fully to enjoy the landscape views they give,— especially when a loaded team meets you on the centre, and you feel the whole Swiss wire settle beneath you.

"We were sorry to leave the odd jumble of a city built on slopes so steep that the inmates of one tier of houses look down into the chimneys of the next neighbors below, where you can trace the old city walls of the feudal age, and where the hotels are so accommodating as to let you drive right in through the front door, a whole omnibus load, and alight in the carriage room and stable, which occupy the first floor."

The next day he was in Geneva. He says: "It is the most densely populated of any Swiss town, and since it slipped out of the hands of Napoleon, after that little mishap at Waterloo, and was restored to the Swiss Confederation, it has been one of the foremost cities of Switzerland.

"Here John Calvin, that stern, strong, powerful theological dogmatist, lived and wrought, fighting with Luther, Melanchthon, and Zwingli the battles of the Reformation.

"For every blow he struck for political and ecclesiastical liberty the world will hold him in honor, but his unrelenting persecution of Michael Servetus for a difference in the interpretation of Scriptures he was pleased to call heresy, culminating at last in the burning to death of Servetus by a slow fire of green wood, incited and sanctioned by Calvin and his associates in

Church and State, is a stain upon his character as well
as his name, which no palliating circumstances can
ever wash away.

"While there, I found, though with difficulty, the
spot where the shameful tragedy took place.   My
first inquiries at the hotel were fruitless.   No one
seemed to know anything about it.   All knew about
Calvin ; but who was Servetus ?   I finally went to the
American consul, and even he was obliged to inquire,
so sweetly forgetful the Genevese had become of that
little excitement caused by the burning of a heretic
three hundred years ago.   At last I found the place
where the martyr to free thought was burned.   No
stone, no token of the heroism or the hate there revealed, marked the spot ; and, as I stood there alone,
how could I but thank God for the marvellous change
in human thought and religious toleration ?

"The 'Académie,' a fine building, contains a portrait
of Servetus, under which is written, ' Burned at Geneva
for the honor and glory of God.'

"But we look once more on the charming lake and
its surroundings, spend the last franc we can spare at
the persuasive stores where so many attractions tempt,
and, grateful for our thirteen days of never-to-be-forgotten pleasure in this cloud-land of beauty and grandeur,
take the train for Paris.   We pass out of the station,
catch a glimpse of the women washing their clothes in
the rushing Rhone, shoot out into the open country
and follow the river down the valley, where grandeur
and beauty still follow us, as if reluctant to part, till
twilight comes on, and after a night on wheels that
know no rest, and allow but little, we find ourselves in

the dim morning light in the midst of what is called the finest city in the world."

A few days in Paris, a few days in London, and the homeward bound voyage is embarked upon.

In his own church, September, 1878, he said: "When I last stood in this pulpit, eleven weeks ago to-day, to tell you a little of my proposed trip, I spoke, from the words of a hopeful prophet, of 'going down to the sea with a song.' For, while I was not unmindful of the perils of the great deep, I was sure that, whatever might befall, it was always safest and best, every way, not to anticipate calamity, but to go forth with a song of trusting faith in Him 'who holdeth the waters in the hollow of his hand.'

"And now, as I come again to meet you and greet you, after nearly ten thousand miles of travel by sea and land, without a single accident or an hour's serious sickness in the whole journey, the precious old Scripture, 'If I take the wings of the morning and dwell in the uttermost parts of the sea, even there shall thy hand lead me and thy right hand shall hold me,' comes to me with a new meaning.

"I have been borne on the wings of many mornings and varying winds to the uttermost parts of our Atlantic Sea, and back again with so rich an experience of his protection and blessing that, if I have not felt his invisible hand guarding, the fault must be looked for in myself, and not in that providence of love which overarches us all, and always.

"I have had a good time, have enjoyed much, have seen many things new and foreign; and yet I have seen but a little streak of ocean waters, and only a narrow belt of Scottish, English, and continental scenery and life, just enough to show what travel *would* reveal, of interest and instruction, if one only had the time and means to do it leisurely, reaping, binding, and binning, on the way, all the rich harvests of historic associations waving luxuriantly on every hill and plain.

"But I stayed long enough. I had rather have my bird's-eye view, taken on the wing, and home than a long stay, with a longer separation from the only people that care anything about me on the face of the earth. I have always told you on returning from my short vacations, spent at the mountains or the seashore, that the best part of going away was coming home again; and this becomes more emphatic as the distance increases. So that, as I have been about ten times as far away as ever before, I am ten times as glad to be at home again, to look into your faces, to give and receive the cordial greeting, and to know that the same divine hand which reveals itself in the uttermost parts of the sea is seen and felt, also, in its guidance and protection on the land just as truly."

XVIII.

CHARITY LECTURE.

1879–1880.

REST.— MARRIAGE.— CHARITY LECTURE.

AFTER another year devoted to his chosen work, his journal of Oct. 5, 1879, says: "I preached from the text, 'I am weary.' I told my dear little flock I was too weary to go on with my work, and must rest for a season. It is a great step to take, but it seems the right thing to do. God grant that so it may prove. The Rev. Francis S. Thacher supplies my pulpit for ten Sundays, occupying my rooms and serving the society as its pastor. May the dear God bless him and his labors!"

Sunday, December 22. "Having recovered my strength, I resumed my labors to-day with a Christmas service and communion."

Feb. 19, 1880, he was married to Miss M. Louise Haley, who had been for twenty-five years a parishioner, his dear friend, Rev. Dr. H. W. Bellows, performing the ceremony.

On the first Sunday in December, 1880, he delivered the annual "Charity Lecture" in Hollis Street Church, and the following correspondence ensued: —

BOSTON, Dec. 7, 1880.

Dear Sir,— After the conclusion of the exercises at Hollis Street Church last Sunday evening it was unanimously voted by the representatives of the churches having charge of the Charity Lecture that a copy of your excellent sermon, and of the poem with which it concluded, be asked of you for publication. They thought that in no better way could they endeavor to recall the public attention to this oldest charitable institution in Boston than by giving a general circulation to your most interesting sketch of this charity and to your touching poem. We hope that the same exalted motive which inspired you to write them will prompt you to comply with their request.

Yours sincerely,

G. WASHINGTON WARREN, *Chairman.*

JOHN CAPEN, *Secretary.*

To this Mr. Tilden replied as follows : —

Dear Friends,— Your kind note, transmitting to me the vote of "the representatives of the churches having charge of the Charity Lecture," in which you are pleased to urge so persuasively my compliance with the vote, gives me all the more pleasure that there was not the most distant thought of such a request being made when the hasty sketch of our city charities, beginning with the oldest, was written. But surprised as I was by your request, and inadequate as I know the paper to be, I cheerfully yield it for print, if, on further thought, you may deem it desirable.

The "Christmas Story in Rhyme," with which I closed, was written for another occasion, and printed a few years ago in the *Old and New*. As it suggests a kind of charity that no *organizations* can fully supply, a charity to which all are called by the Holy Spirit of Human Sympathy, I yield that, also, to your wishes.

Yours for all good things, *old and new,*

W. P. TILDEN.

A few extracts from this lecture may be read with interest. The text chosen was from Heb. xiii. 16: " To do good and to communicate forget not ; for with such sacrifices God is well pleased."

He says : "I have been so much interested and edi-
fied in looking over the ancient records that I beg the
privilege of noting some things which may prove of as
much interest to some of you as they have to me.
These records have been kept with remarkable fidelity
and legibility, showing the good penmanship of colonial
days, and making it easy to trace the stream of benefi-
cence which it chronicles, and which has watered the
wastes of poverty in our city for one hundred and
sixty years.

"The head-waters of the stream, like most head-
waters, are lost in obscurity; but the first recorded
spring bubbled up from a little circle of benevolent-
hearted folk who were accustomed to meet quarterly,
on Sunday evenings, for charitable purposes, at the
house of one Elder Brigham.   After the Elder's death
they met with his son Henry, and still later at the
house of Deacon Jonathan Williams, such ministers as
they deemed desirable and could obtain being invited
to preach.

"But there is no record of these meetings up to
1720, when it was decided to request the ministers of
the town to take their turns in regular course. With
this new arrangement the record begins. Cotton
Mather, naturally enough, was the first to preach ; and
he took for his text the words that I have quoted : 'To
do good and to communicate forget not ; for with such
sacrifices God is well pleased.'   Dr. Mather was at this
time about fifty-seven, in the prime of his powers, a
colleague of his father, Increase Mather, in the pastorate of the North Church, the father being in advanced age. The first meeting was held March 6,

1720; and a collection was taken of thirty pounds and ten shillings, distributed among sixty-one persons. At first these quarterly gatherings were known simply as 'Charity Meetings,' but subsequently as 'The Quarterly Charity Lecture.' Under the latter title the organization has come down to us.

"For twenty years after the new departure the meetings were still held in the house of Deacon Williams; but in 1740 they went to the 'Chamber of the Town House, where the Representatives meet.' Two years later is this quaint record: 'March 7, 1742, Mr. Crocker, a young gentleman, preached for Rev. Thomas Prince. Such a thronged assembly of women, boys, &c., that the gentlemen who usually attend could not get in. Collected £75. Lost by ye thronged assembly at least £30.' This is interesting, as showing that in those primitive times they thought more of the amount collected than of the *largeness* of the congregation.

"In 1785 it was thought best to remove to the Old South Meeting-house. Here they continued to hold the lectures until the great fire rendered it unfit for use.

"I find by the record that I am destined to go down to posterity, or up to the top shelves of the Historical Society, as the last preacher of the Quarterly Lecture in the Old South Meeting-house while it was yet a church, and before it became itself an object of public charity. To one whose prospect of posthumous distinction is limited there is some comfort even in this."

"All the Mathers — Increase, Cotton, and Samuel, father, son, and grandson — were on the stage when the record of this charity began. Here we meet with Wadsworth, Foxcroft, Chauncy, Colman, Checkley, Peter Thacher, Joseph Sewall, and Thomas Prince of the Old South, famous as a preacher and a man of letters. This was the Prince whose quaint prayer, when the French fleet was on its way with the intention of laying Boston in ashes, is thus thrown into verse by Longfellow : —

> "'O Lord, we would not advise,
>   But if in thy providence
>   A tempest *should* arise
>   To drive the French fleet hence,
>   And scatter it far and wide,
>   Or sink it in the sea,
>   We would be satisfied ;
>   And thine the glory be.'

" The fleet never arrived.

" Here, too, we meet with Mather Byles, the first minister of Hollis Street Church, ordained as its pastor near a century and a half ago, who during the latter part of his life, in Revolutionary times, was arrested for his sympathy with the Tories, and put under guard, which was changed from time to time, till his final release, leading him to say, with his usual wit, that he had been 'guarded, regarded, and disregarded.'

· " Here, too, we meet with Dr. Belknap, of hymnal notoriety, and Howard, John Eliot, Dr. Cooper, Dr. Kirkland, Channing, Buckminster : here, also, we meet Greenwood, Ware, and Pierpont, and so on to those who are still among us, honored and beloved.

" One of the many things noted in this record is the

fact, very simple in itself, that 'June 7, 1830, *Rev.* Ralph Waldo Emerson preached.' The title sounds queer now. But we can almost hear his low, rich voice repeat rather than read the text he chose for the occasion: 'Let no man seek his own, but every man another's wealth.'

" 'Sept. 2, 1838, Rev. Mr. Bartol preached. This being the first time he was ever called to preach this lecture, he knew not the hour, and came late.' I know of no one who can better bear this record, since in his later youth no one has shown himself more free from the charge of what has been called a '*belated* theologian.'

" This ancient and honorable charity has raised and expended, during its one hundred and sixty years of work, two hundred and eighteen thousand dollars. It must be said, however, that a large part of the annual receipts, of late years, has come from the bequests of a former generation, the interest of these bequests being added each year to the collections.

" The smallest box-collection recorded occurred on Dec. 6, 1863. It was one dollar and sixty cents. But even then the shades of the departed came forward and made up the amount to one thousand four hundred and forty-one dollars and eighty-nine cents. The worthy scribe makes this comment: 'The lecture was very thinly attended, so that a similar occurrence will probably stop the *procession* of the contribution-boxes.' 'One dollar and sixty cents ! !' he adds, with two scornful exclamation points."

Then follows an account of the various charitable and beneficent organizations of Boston ; and the sermon closes with an earnest appeal for "the sweetest and most blessed charities where hand and heart go together, and the soul of the needy one is fed with real sympathy, while the body is supplied with needful food."

XIX.

SEVENTY.

1881.

May 9, 1881, "his generous-hearted parishioners celebrated his seventieth birthday by inviting as many of his old friends outside the parish as the church could accommodate.

We copy from "Seventy," a little book printed, but not published, and which was a record of the services of that evening : —

"An informal meeting was held at which reception and refreshment committees were appointed. Mrs. Maybury, Mr. Tilden's assistant, though her name does not appear, was, virtually, a most active and efficient member of all the committees by her wise counsel and invaluable assistance.

"Mr. Henry C. Whitcomb, who was the first man to greet Mr. Tilden to his new field of labor in Concord Hall, fourteen years ago, was selected to preside ; and Mr. William Parkman, an active member for years, born on the same day as Mr. Tilden, was invited to speak a word of welcome to the assembled friends.

"THE OCCASION." — May 9, 1881.

"The weather was delightful, and the church well filled with parishioners and invited guests. The Boston Association of Ministers, having been invited to meet with Mr. Tilden, was largely represented.

"The pulpit and platform were tastefully decorated with flowers, all gifts of love; and the whole church, in its chaste simplicity, seemed to reflect the smile of the happy people gathered.

"The services opened with a voluntary on the organ, followed by the Lord's Prayer, chanted by the congregation.

"Mr. Whitcomb then rose, and said: 'Dear friends, we have met together to-night, as a loving family and its guests, to congratulate our dear pastor, friend, and brother on this his seventieth birthday. It is not an occasion for sadness, but rather for joy and gladness; and may our hearts go out to God in thankfulness and love that our pastor has been spared to us for so many years, in the fulness of his strength and vigor, to guide and counsel us to a better living and preparation for the life beyond! We can well say the world is better for his living; and may the Lord crown his coming years with glory and strength! Our pastor's twin (in years), brother Parkman, will now give to the friends present our word of welcome.'

"Mr. Parkman, in an off-hand, free-and-easy vein, touched with humor, as is his wont, made a pleasant speech of welcome, which was responded to by Rev. S. K. Lothrop, D.D., in behalf of the Boston Association, as follows:—

"'*Mr. Chairman and Friends,*—It falls to my lot as moderator of the Boston Association of Ministers to thank you for the welcome you have given us to this pleasant occasion,—the celebration of your pastor's seventieth birthday. Let me assure you that all the members of our Association, his brothers and co-workers in the ministry in this city and neighborhood, feel as deep an interest in this gathering and its purpose as you do. We are as ready as you are to hold our brother Tilden in grateful reverence and honor. We dare not say that we know him as well you do, who see him day by day, week in and week out, year after year, as he discharges with singular wisdom, fidelity, devotedness, and success the duties of his ministry among you. But we know him well. We know something of his history and more of his progress, development, power, and usefulness. We know,— at least I know, for brother Tilden told me so many years ago,— and I dare say it is known to all of you; and, if it is not, I am glad to tell it, for it is to his glory and honor. He said to me many years ago, " Brother Lothrop, the first time I ever heard you preach was in 1835 or 1836, in Mr. Stetson's church at Medford; and at that time I was a journeyman ship-carpenter in one of the Medford ship-yards." I have loved and honored Mr. Tilden ever since he told me that. I believe, if I had been a journeyman ship-carpenter at the age of twenty-four or five, I should not have had energy or power enough to work myself out of that ship-yard into the pulpit, much less into an honored and eminent place in the pulpit. Brother Tilden has done this. We know that he has never been called to any duty that he has not discharged thoroughly well to his own honor and the acceptance and satisfaction of those who called him to perform it. We know that in every parish of which he has had charge there the kingdom of God has grown and enlarged ; that everywhere he has left impressions upon hearts and consciences which time has not oblit- erated, but life and character have given testimony to their abiding power. And now, arrived at that ex- cellent age which may be regarded as simply the full maturity of human power, we find him here to-night, surrounded by his loving parishioners and friends, in the vigor of health and strength, with a glory in those full white locks that fill us with reverence (and some of us with a passing shade of covetousness; for why should brother Tilden have such a quantity of those locks, and I, his senior, so few?), and with the fulness of experience, wisdom, and love beaming in his counte- nance, with everything about him giving hope and promise of long years of happiness, honor, and useful- ness yet to come. . . .

" ' " God buries his workmen, but carries on his work." In gratitude and thankfulness, let us remember the fathers who have fallen asleep, and the legacy of hon- orable fame they have left us. Let us imitate their virtues and avoid their faults, if they had any ; and let us all, the elder and the younger, according to our years and our strength, keep our hands at the plough, and see that we cut a clean, deep furrow, straight for the truth and by the truth. Sure I am that brother Til- den will do this in the future as in the past. In the name of the Association and in behalf of his brethren, I congratulate him upon having reached this golden period of life. May it last many years, in all its glory, beauty, and usefulness ; and, when the end comes, may it be like the launch of one of those beautiful ships which he helped to build in his youth,— a slow, grand movement, growing more and more grand and majestic, till at last, like as it floats out upon the water, he may float in peace and safety upon that mighty ocean of spiritual life for which his soul has been so thoroughly prepared.'

"Rev. E. E. Hale, D.D., responded to the call of Mr. Whitcomb as follows : —

"'It will hardly be believed that I am stepping so closely upon our friend's footsteps that I could give to this assembly anecdotes of his early ministry. For when I was breaking the ice myself, in that curious and fascinating experience when a young man begins, one of the cheerful and happy prognostics for my professional life came to me when I first heard his name. I was in the city of Washington, detached thither to take such care as a boy could of the Unitarian pulpit in that city. As I made my first visit in one of the stalwart households of that city, they told me of their regret in leaving Concord, in New Hampshire, because they had to leave our Mr. Tilden. It was to me a charming picture of the tie knit, not in many years, between pastor and people; and I know I did my best to learn from them by what magic that tie was woven. The impression I formed of this young man has never changed, as to-night I need not say. And one of the happinesses of life now is that we are thrown together as two colleagues here, both still young men, and permitted to do our work side by side.'

"The presiding officer called on Rev. C. A. Bartol, D.D., who said : —

"'*My Friends, my Brother, my Brethren, and my Sisters,*— Dr. Lothrop spoke of our comparatively more or less *knowing* Mr. Tilden. I was reminded of the modern positivist, materialistic, utilitarian, experimental, scientific notion of knowledge, as of facts generalized by the understanding from impressions of sense. But, indeed, do we not know persons as well as phenomena, appearances of things? It seems to me we know them even better. Properly speaking, in the strict meaning of the word, we cannot be said to know things at all, but only to know *about* them, to recognize certain properties in them; but persons are really known to us. They are nearer to us, and things are farther off. We go round anything as we go round a mountain. But the person is close to us, and we know him or her more truly, living in our sight or vanished away. The affections know, the heart knoweth. Now, Mr. Tilden is a man we know by our love and trust. I remember, at the ordination of Charles Follen to the ministry, Dr. Channing thanked God for a man in whom we could confide. I have only to say that in Mr. Tilden we can and do confide. We know him, with his radical thought, conservative heart, courageous speech, reverent and spiritual mind, uniting all extremes in a beautiful proportion. May he long still live, and stay here to teach and console!'

"Poems written for the occasion by Mrs. C. A. Mason of Fitchburg, Mrs. T. H. Burgess of Boston, and Miss Elizabeth Thacher, a teacher of the Sunday-school, were then read.

"A few extracts from some of the many letters:—

"*My dear Old Friend and Young Heart,*—Please communicate to your society my inability to join them on the 9th of May in celebrating their pastor's arrival at the canonical goal of human life, and my extreme regret that I can only share in spirit the interest of that occasion. I should so much like to give them in person my testimony to the unchanging devotion of your soul to the highest and purest interests of humanity, the constancy of your friendship, and the enviable power of holding to you forever those you once attached. I should dwell upon my happiness in having been for seven years (when you were by no means so ripe as now) your summer parishioner at Walpole, N.H., and of sharing the universal feeling there,—what a lucky and happy people they were to have so *large* a minister in so *small* a field. . . .

"I know what kind of a slip you have given old Time, and, while allowing him to make his notches in his own record, have carefully prevented his making them in your spirit. I sometimes think you wear his outward livery (a great white head and beard) only to deceive him, and make him think you his humble servant; for I find you very boyish and alert and enterprising when I look beneath the disguise. I should like to take lessons against a remote future, if you are really as young and gay as you behave.

"Affectionately your young friend,

"H. W. BELLOWS.

"*My dear Brother,*—I received the very kind and cordial invitation from your church to join in the observance of your seventieth birthday. The announcement was very startling, and, Thomas-like, I refuse to believe that my friend is a whit older than when we swung the broad-axe together. Do you remember when, laying out frames and hewing heavy timber, we discussed almost fiercely the high themes of 'fore-knowledge, free will, and fate,' 'till, in endless mazes lost,' we ended about where we began? Do you remember how cordially we differed on doctrinal points, and how you would hammer away on the hard side of Calvinism?

Do you remember,— if you do not, I do,— when I was about leav. ing Andover Seminary, your earnest invitation, twice repeated, to preach in your pulpit at Concord, on the Sabbath? It seemed to me then, and does now, that was a liberal thing. But do you remember my reply? If you do not, I do; and a pretty narrow and mean reply it was, I think. I said: ' You must not expect me to return this. I am willing to preach in your pulpit, but not willing that you should preach in mine.' Nobly you accepted the terms, and it has been a shame to me ever since. . . .

" Let me congratulate you at threescore and ten that your large eye is undimmed and your natural strength unabated.

" Lovingly and fraternally yours,

" WM. T. BRIGGS.

"Mr. Tilden, being now called upon, received a warm welcome from the audience, and spoke as follows : —

"' *My kind Parishioners and Friends,*— What a pity a man can never be seventy but once, especially when he comes to "the canonical goal," as Dr. Bellows calls it, with blessings so many and so rich as greet me here to-night !

"' I do thank you all,— my ever thoughtful and generous parishioners for this birthday party, my kind friends for accepting the invitation to share the occasion with us, and for the cordial words and kindly greetings from present and absent ones in prose and verse. I am in a mood to-night to pardon all the extravagance of friendship. I rather like it. I shall make believe it is all true till to-morrow ; and even then let in the light upon it very cautiously, the illusion of being somebody is so sweet. A man's seven-tieth birthday is no time to deny or even distrust anything said in his praise. It is wiser to swallow it all. It is probably his last chance.

"'And, now, what shall I say for myself? It would be safer to hide behind your fragrant screen of compliments and say nothing. But I am *seventy*, the *hero* of the evening; and, though indebted to Father Time for all these honors, I must speak.

"'As nothing is set down to egotism after three-score and ten, and as we are here in a free-and-easy, pleasant-fellowship sort of way, I think I will venture to tell you a little of my early life, and how it was, with so poor an outfit, I squeezed into the pulpit. The strong contrast of my early life with the early lives of most of those who are in the ministry may give some interest to the simple story it would not otherwise have.'"

Then follows the story of his early life and struggles, told substantially as in this Autobiography, and closing as follows: —

"'Dull and commonplace as my ministry may have seemed to others, and little as there is to show for it anywhere, I have nevertheless enjoyed it so completely that, could I live my life over again, I should not hesitate for a moment what profession to choose. It would be the ministry. It would be the Christian ministry. It never seemed grander, more glorious, or more hopeful than now. But I should want to be better prepared for it. As there are no gifts, so there is no culture too rich to be laid on its altars. I wonder that more young men are not drawn to the ever-growing, ever-deepening, ever-widening, ever more and more attractive ministry of redeeming love. I thank God afresh on this my seventieth birthday that I have been permitted to serve even as a drop in this mighty tide of Christian influence, so manifestly lifted by the heavenly orbs which, spite of all the sediment of error and superstition mingling with it, are steadily lifting the world to a higher life, and bearing it on its heaven-appointed destiny.

"'Dear friends, again I thank you for this delightful occasion. You will never know how good a thing it is to be seventy till you get there. And, when you do, may you all have as true friends to congratulate you and as many blessings to move your hearts with gratitude to God as I have to-night!'

"After Mr. Tilden had closed, during a moment's pause in the exercises, Mr. Hale rose and said, 'I think we shall agree that the world has not been wrong for eighteen centuries and a half in thinking that a carpenter's shop and a fishing boat are the best schools for apostleship and ministry.'

"The congregation then united in the hymn,—

"'Press on, press on, ye sons of light,'

which went gloriously to the tune of 'Missionary Chant.'

"All present were then invited to a social tea in the vestry below, which was filled with a happy throng of people, who, as they greeted each other, were borne along by the current to extend their congratulations in person to Mr. Tilden, who received their cordial greetings and good wishes as they passed on.

"The long table was richly decorated with elegant flower-pieces and bouquets,— the tribute of kind friends for the occasion,— and bountifully spread with refreshments from the homes of the parishioners and friends.

Back of the platform where Mr. Tilden stood to welcome his friends was his picture, wreathed with smilax,
and on either side, in figures wrought with flowers,

1811.   1881.

" During the collation the delightful fellowship continued. Friends anchored side by side in snug harbors for happy chat, or sailed round in small fleets, hail-
ing old acquaintances, and signalling some word of
good cheer in keeping with the happy spirit of the
evening.

" At last the time came for saying 'good-night'; and
the large company retired to happy dreams."

The following letter from Dr. H. O. Stone, of Framingham, a former parishioner of Concord, N.H., was received too late to be read at the birthday party : —

Dear Friends of our Beloved Septuagenarian,— I will address
you to the exclusion of the latter, lest his modesty be offended by
the plain, unvarnished tale unfolded.

In the year 1844, not long after Mr. Tilden's settlement over
the Unitarian society in Concord, N.H., I became one of his
parishioners, listening to his sermons, enjoying his society and
friendship, and blessed by his spiritual ministrations. During
the years of his service there anti-slavery and the kindred reforms of peace and temperance were discussed as never before.
Filled with the spirit of Jesus of Nazareth, and yearning with his
whole soul to preach the "glad tidings of deliverance to the cap-
tives" and oneness with the Father, Mr. Tilden faithfully delivered
the message impressed upon his conscience and reason.

One or two incidents of his career there will indicate his spirit
and conduct.

At that time Stephen S. Foster, who, by his fearless and persistent rebukes of Church and State for their complicity with
slavery, had drawn upon himself the hatred and wrath of the

pro-slavery elements of society, was lecturing in New Hampshire. He was feared and denounced by recreant ministers and time-serving politicians. To fellowship him was to incur the displeasure of these classes. This sturdy modern prophet one summer Sunday went to hear our "son of a carpenter" preach. The services were conducted with the serene consciousness of the Father of all, habitual to the preacher; and his convictions of human responsibility and duty were uttered with his usual impressive earnestness. In his sermon, he alluded to slavery in unmistakable terms, and at its close, looking straight at Stephen Foster, said, "I see one in the audience whose zeal and labors in the anti-slavery cause are well known: I should be glad to hear a word from him"; thus vindicating the freedom of the gospel he preached, the freedom of the pulpit he stood in, and contrasting them with the pro-slavery churches who had spurned Stephen and dragged him out of their meeting-houses with violence. He, all unused to having the courtesy of free speech tendered him, rose and expressed the satisfaction he had received in listening to the sermon, and said he had nothing to add.

In those days it required the courage of a hero to speak for the slave, especially when persistency in demanding for him freedom as his birthright and as the duty of slaveholders and their northern accomplices, aroused the fears of the timid, lest the agitation should break in two the organizations which by some persons were considered of more value than human liberty. It was in such a crisis that spiritual wisdom and celestial insight guided our pastor and lifted him to a plane of thought and action where the fear of man is never a snare, but trust in the infinite God enters the soul like a strengthening angel.

Well do I remember the occasion when, after one of his earnest rebukes of the great national sin and stirring appeals to each individual conscience, some who loved the old Unitarian Church trembled as if an earthquake had unsettled its foundations. It was whispered: "Such preaching will not do. We shall go to ruin." Not so thought our preacher. The very next Sunday he discoursed from the text, "Stand fast, in nothing terrified," in which he reviewed the whole ground, in no defiant spirit, but in a lofty strain of moral and religious enthusiasm, reassuring the timid and strengthening the faltering, and so set the old Unitarian Church upon the rock of eternal justice.

When the encroachment of the slave power culminated in the Mexican War waged for the extension of slavery, an impetus was given to the cause of "peace" which resulted in the agitation of that reform all over the North. Here, too, the pupil of May was not behind his teacher. Without waiting for a fast-day privilege, he spoke from the pulpit, in small gatherings outside, and in conventions.

At this period there was the coincidence in Concord on the same day of a Peace Convention and an assembly of New Hampshire volunteers on their way to the seat of war. Mr. Tilden, with Adin Ballou, looked in at the war party. Some of the speakers referred to Mr. Tilden's well-known opinions of war so pointedly and in such scornful terms that he felt called upon to reply. He rose with a countenance pallid with emotion, and in a calm and firm voice spoke to the assembly of the gospel of peace as presented by Jesus in the New Testament. He told them that it was his duty as a Christian minister to preach that gospel, and they knew that the work they were entering upon was directly opposed to the spirit and teaching of Jesus. He was heard in silence. It seemed as if an angel had hushed the air that the sweet tones of peace might enter the ears of that armed multitude. Our preacher had conquered for the time an army with muskets and banners by the sword of the spirit. New Hampshire's quota marched out of the capital with this benison ringing in their ears.

But time will not permit me to dwell further upon the fidelity of our friend in every field of labor during his brief ministry in Concord. He was as true in the temperance movement as in other reforms, enlightening public sentiment and uplifting the downfallen.

The same spiritual graces, social qualities, and tender sympathies, the same ringing laugh, hearty pressure of the hand, and words of cheer, the same trustful prayers uplifting afflicted souls, endeared him then as now to all who came within his influence. Dear friends, you know all this better than any words can express.

Now, my dear brother, come back within the hearing of my voice, while I thank God for all your ministry in Concord did for me, and for all your friendship has done and is still doing. The light which surrounds the Infinite Spirit can alone reveal it in its fulness. In that light may we walk to the end of time, and beyond enlarge and purify the affection which death cannot obliterate!

Very sincerely yours,

HENRY ORNE STONE.

XX.

COMMUNION SERVICE.

MR. TILDEN had long been dissatisfied with the small number of our worshipping congregations who were interested in the communion service.

As one who loved the service and longed to see it lifted out of "the letter which killeth" into "the spirit which giveth life," he was continually asking himself, "What shall be done with our communion service? What *can* be done to awaken a rational and intelligent interest in it? Why is it that some of the best, or, if not the best, just as good and just as Christian men and women as any in the congregation, never partake of the symbols? They believe in Jesus just as truly, thank God for his mission just as deeply, desire his spirit just as earnestly, and have the love of God and man at heart just as sincerely. Why, then, do they never stay to the commemorative rite? or, if they stay, never partake?"

He says: "It is a serious matter, especially with such ministers as believe in the rite, and long to see it observed, not by a select few, but by the whole congregation.

"Possibly, with some other method of administration, the observance may be made to seem more simple and natural, and so win the favor of those who have hitherto stood aloof from it.

" Is there any such method ? We think there is. Dr. Furness, of Philadelphia, was the first, as far as we know, to suggest and adopt it. He proposed to his church that the symbolic bread and wine should not be distributed, but stand on the table to speak through the eye to the heart, of the self-sacrificing love of Him who gave himself for the world's uplifting, the minister interpreting their significance.

" No one who knew Dr. Furness could doubt for a moment his reverence for Jesus, or his love of the wonderful character he had made the study of his life. But it was a change ; and changes, however rational and needful, always come slowly. One who said that, if he wished to *give up* the communion, he thought this a graceful way of doing it, fairly expressed, perhaps, the common feeling with which the new method was received. But to me it seemed a step up out of the letter into the spirit, and I hailed it with joy. I saw in it the solution of many of our difficulties. It settled forever the temperance question, so far as the communion was concerned. We could still use wine as a symbol, if we used it as a symbol only. All could then participate in the service without any misgivings, just as all may look upon the cross, and think their own thoughts of its meaning and of Him who died thereon. Parents and children could now come together, and none would be disturbed by having the symbols offered to him, when he desired only the bread and wine of devout thought. All, absolutely *all*, of every shade of Christian faith, could now together think of Jesus, and thank God afresh for his living and dying love for man.

" Fully believing that this method was simpler, more

natural and rational than the old, we have adopted it, not without some dissenting views, of course ; for old associations are strong, and we seldom pass without a protest of the feelings, at least, from the old to the new, even when reason tells us that the new is better.

"But, having passed, I am more and more gratified with the new method. The expressions of satisfaction that came to me after the first use of the symbols, as symbols only, with the whole congregation as spiritual communicants, filled me with a sweet assurance that I was right in my hopes. I found that many felt as I had often done, that the mere eating and drinking, or rather the making believe eat and drink,— for to that the old method is reduced,— was no aid, but a hindrance, to the spiritual enjoyment of the service. What made the service quickening and helpful was not the unnatural attempt at eating and drinking with no view to physical nourishment, but the thought waked, the aspirations roused, by the contemplation of the matchless One. With tears on his cheek, one man told me after that service that he had never before felt that he had anything to do with the rite or the rite anything to do with him. Now he began to *feel* its meaning.

"It should be said, however, that some of our people would still prefer the old way, with all its disadvantages and limitations. But, as the new method has the many advantages already named, it has been adopted in faith and hope of greater good to a much larger number than was ever reached in the old method.

"The New South Free Church, therefore, instead of having 'given up the communion,' as some have intimated, has made this change in the sincere desire

to make *more* of the service, not less ; to free it from
what to many seems artificial, and open alike to parents
and children, old and young, professors and non-pro-
fessors, even as many as ever think of Jesus with gratitude or feel the shadow of a desire for more of his spirit
of self-sacrificing love.

" Four times in a year — at Christmas, Easter, Whit-
Sunday, All Saints' and All Souls' — we keep our feast
of commemoration. We try to make these occasions
great days for our little church,— days of reverent joy
and gladness, not for a few, but for all, the children's
voices adding a note of gladness to our sacred songs.
We give our own interpretation to these old days, so
long held sacred by the Church, of which, though dis-
owned, we claim to be a part, however small,— a twig,
if not a branch of the living vine,— and would keep
them sacred to the great truths they stand for, and to
the memory of Him whose name we honor, whose spirit
we crave, and in whose blessed work of redeeming love
we would in some humble measure share."

The order of service on the Sundays when the commemorative rite was observed was as follows : —

> Organ Voluntary.
> Sentence and Prayer.
> Hymn.
> Scripture. Prayer.
> Hymn.
> Address (at the table).
> Hymn.
> Scripture and Prayer.
> Responsive Service.

The congregation being seated, the minister, breaking the bread, will say : —

"When Jesus broke the bread in the upper chamber, just before his crucifixion, he said, 'This is my body, broken for you.' And, when he took the cup, 'This is the New Testament in my blood, shed for you.' It is significant that, while the twelve who reclined with him at the table ate and drank, Jesus himself refused the cup, saying : 'I will drink no more of the fruit of the vine until that day when I drink it new with you in the kingdom of God.'

"We use these symbols now as symbols only, as Jesus used the wine, of which he did not drink. This bread is only bread, this wine is only wine ; and, at best, it could only nourish the body. To feed on these literally 'is not to eat the Lord's Supper.' We would discern the real presence in these symbols, and nourish our souls on that. Through this veil of material things we would commune with things eternal. We would feed on that living bread which came down from heaven in Christ, and which our Father is continually giving us. We would drink of the heavenly wine of self-sacrificing love for God and men, and all things true and good, and so remember Jesus as to enter more fully into his spirit, his Sonship, and his great work of Redeeming Love.

"And now, that each one may have an opportunity to think his own thought, pray his own prayer, question his own soul, commune with his own heart, and be still, we will unite in a season of silence." This silence is broken by the minister, when all unite in chanting the Lord's Prayer. Benediction.

Mr. Tilden never lost his love for and his strong interest in this method of observing the commemorative rite. In a lecture to the students of the Meadville Theological School he says : "My counsel is, therefore, to you who are studying for the ministry of our liberal faith, do not attempt this new method unless you *believe in it*,—thoroughly believe in it. And, when you do, you will make your people believe in it ; and you and they, if I may judge from my own experience, will enjoy it as never before.

"Dr. Furness's successor, Joseph May, did not believe in it, and so went back to the old method. My successor in Boston has done the same. This is not at all discouraging to one who is converted to the new method. It is just what every change has to contend with, temporary relapse into the old ways. It is a reflex wave, which recedes for the time, while the ocean tide is all the time rising.

"For one, I believe the new method is destined to rise. I think it is linked with the heavenly orbs. I believe no crowned Canute of ecclesiasticism can order it back. It will roll in by and by and cover our Unitarian flats, and float our grounded barges and refresh us with a new wave from that eternal sea of spiritual life that is ever lifting us out of the bondage of the letter into the freedom of the spirit.

"Whether this method be widely adopted in our day or not, I feel a strong assurance that it will more and more prevail in our liberal Church. It was born of us ! born of the head and heart of one of the truest lovers and most reverential students of Jesus our body has ever produced. It fits our thought. It is spiritual. It shows the rational meaning of the rite, and sweeps away all the old objections to its general observance.

" Whatever a few may say against what they call a destructive innovation, just as the Catholics regarded the restoration of the rite to primitive simplicity by Zwingli as dangerous and destructive, still if we fully believe that the new method is better than the old, should we not, in the spirit of Zwingli, make one more change in this rite of the Church that has passed through so many, and cut it clear of all materialism, making it a purely symbolic and spiritual commemoration ?

" I should be proud to belong to a church that would venture to take this step, and glad and grateful to be an instrument, however humble, in bringing about a consummation so devoutly to be wished."

XXI.

END OF BOSTON MINISTRY.

1883–1884.

RESIGNATION.— FAREWELL SERMON.— CHARGE TO REV.
G. H. YOUNG.

MAY 20, 1883, Mr. Tilden, at the close of his sermon Sunday morning, read the following letter, which
he told his people he had sent to the Executive Committee of the Benevolent Fraternity of Churches : —

BOSTON, May 9, 1883.

Gentlemen,— I am seventy-two years old to-day. I am also in
the seventeenth year of my pastorate of the New South Free
Church. Putting the two together, and remembering that years
tell in more than one sense, I herewith send in my resignation of
the office I have so long held, to take place at the expiration of
the present year, Dec. 31, 1883.

I make this communication thus early that you may have abundant time to select the best man that can be obtained to continue
the work.

I do not propose to withdraw from the ministry, which I love as
well as ever; for, though an old man, I hope to do some further
service in some lighter field of labor. But I am beginning to find
the multiform duties of this position, which are more arduous and
constant than the pastorate of an ordinary church, rather too much
for my strength. And, besides this, I have a growing conviction
that a new voice and a fresh hand, especially the voice and hand
of a younger man, would do more and better service than I am
now able to do. I am happy to say that no lisp from any one of
your committee, or any delegate of the Fraternity, or any member

of our Free Church, has ever come to me with the slightest suggestion of a wish that I should retire. My resignation comes
solely from my own conviction that the time has come.

But I cannot close this note without most cordially thanking
you, gentlemen of the committee, and all who have preceded you
during my pastorate, for the uniform kindness you and they have
extended to me during my long and pleasant ministry.

That God may continue to bless you in the great and good
work you have in charge, and guide you to a wise choice in filling
the vacancy at the close of the year, is the heart's desire of

Yours truly,

W. P. TILDEN.

His last sermon as pastor of the New South Free
Church was given Dec. 30, 1883, in which he says, "I
choose a text that has not a drop of sadness in it,—
that inspiring word of Paul to his church at Philippi,
'Rejoice in the Lord alway, and again I say, Rejoice.'

"We will shelter ourselves this morning under the
brave words. Then, if we are tempted to sadness, we
will let in the gladness as well we may ; for surely a
seventeen years' ministry, with trials so few and blessings so many, must hold in its wide arms abundant
cause for rejoicing in the Lord again, and yet again.

"Seventeen years is a long time when it is front of us,
and we look expectantly along its waving and uncertain
lines. But when we have passed over and through,
and have left them behind, they dwindle into a span,
and seem almost as shadowy as a remembered
dream. . . .

"But we are happy to-day in looking forward as well
as backward,— happy in having with us not only the
angel of memory with the closed volume, but the angel

of hope also, with her open book, pointing her prophetic finger to the new ministry with which the new year will open."

After a retrospective view of the work of these years he says : —

"And now, my dear friends and parishioners, what shall I say in view of all your kindness and forbearance, your lenient judgment and patient listening,— some of you for the whole term of my pastorate and others for a shorter time, but just as kindly? I might as well say nothing, and let your own hearts interpret the gratitude I feel for all your many kindnesses. I shall bear away with me also a sweet assurance of your real friendship and best wishes, given in so many ways, as one of the evidences that my ministry has not been in vain. . . .

"I count it a most felicitous arrangement that my successor, Rev. George H. Young, is to be installed on the evening of this my last Sunday with you, giving me the privilege of joining with you all in his inauguration, not leaving you a single hour without a minister, his work beginning the very moment mine will end, when, at the same stroke of the time, the old year and the old ministry are rung out as the new year and the new ministry are rung in.

"To make this ministry a useful and a happy one, something else will be necessary besides his devotion to his work,— your devotion to your work; for he comes not to do your work for you, but to help you in doing it for yourselves, that you all, working together as a band of Christian believers, may not only continue the work of a broad, free church we have begun, but carry it forward and lift it higher and strike its roots deeper until, through God's blessing, the fruits of Christian life will grow in such sweet clusters that all will know without asking that this is a living branch of the living vine.

" Oh, there is a great work for you to do here, if with united hearts and willing hands you all take hold and help your new minister to do it! He can do nothing alone ; but, with God's grace — never withheld — and your cordial co-working, you and he together can do all things,— all things that Heaven requires,— and that will be a work large enough to make the very angels long to share it with you.

" I hear it whispered that one and another are thinking of leaving when I go. That is the worst compliment you can pay to my preaching. Go away because I go! Why, if you have loved the little church of our liberal faith, where we have worshipped and worked together so long, if you have rejoiced in its Christian hospitality,— rejoiced that here outward and artificial distinctions are cast out, and all invited to come as the equal children of a common Father in a faith as bright as Christ's own, and a spirit of humanity like that which led him to go about doing good,— then my going only because I feel myself not fully equal to all the work required would seem to be a new reason for your staying to strengthen the hands and encourage the heart of him who comes to give to the cause here the freshness of his manliest powers. . . .

" If you let the thought of usefulness as well as pleasure enter into the question, could you do as much good anywhere else ? No : stay, *all of you stay*, cheering the new minister with your hearty and cordial co-operation and cheering also the heart of the old minister, when he is away, with the glad tidings that the church of his love and prayer is rising through your united labors into a higher Christian life and broadening its field of Christian usefulness."

In his charge to the new pastor the same evening he says : " Take a kindly and tender care of my little flock. I have been with them in their joys and sorrows, hopes and fears ; and now I am about to leave them I feel very solicitous for their real religious welfare. · Somehow, my own shortcomings loom up before me in such formidable shape that I feel like charging you to shun all my faults and bring all your own virtues to aid you in taking the tenderest care of them. You are to be their spiritual helper, their religious friend. You are to be a counsellor to the young, a brother to those in the prime of life, a son on whom the aged may lean with confidence and trust.

"But remember that in this *free* church, as in other churches, you must give your best strength to your pulpit sermons. There is no church in Boston where a good, stirring, earnest Christian sermon will be more highly appreciated than here. You come with a large stock of old sermons : I charge you to use them sparingly. A new sermon is better than an old one, if it isn't so good. Somehow, our sermons, like ourselves, bear unmistakable signs of the year of our Lord in which they were born. They may have been good in their day, but the day is past, and to lean on them is fatal. Saul, in his great strait, fell forward on his sword, and committed suicide that way. It was common among

old warriors. But many a minister from middle life on
has committed suicide by falling back on his old sermons. It is an easy death, to be sure ; for the old
sermons have seldom point enough to hurt, but the
result is just as sure as the old method. As you would
live, then, and have your people feel the throbbing of
your fresh life, keep studying, keep thinking, keep
writing.

"And I charge you to do your best every time.
Don't save your great thoughts for great occasions.
Fresh thoughts, like fresh peaches, should be used the
day they drop. Keep them for a great party, and they
spoil. One of the most successful ministers we have
ever had in our liberal faith said to me that he told
his people all he knew every Sunday. He emptied
himself, and left it to the next week to fill up. Of
course, it was playful exaggeration, for it was Dr. Bellows who said it ; but there was a great truth in the
playfulness. The stream must be kept running if the
water is to be kept pure.

"Look aloft, open your soul to the Holy Spirit, follow
the highest light, and so by pureness, by knowledge,
by long-suffering, by kindness, by the Holy Ghost, by
love unfeigned, by the word of truth, by the power of
God, by the armor of righteousness on the right hand
and on the left, do the work of an evangelist, and make
full proof of your ministry !"

XXII.

ROWEN.

1884.

THE book in which he kept the record of his preaching after this date was headed " Rowen."

In a sermon on " Old Age," he said : " I wish to
emphasize the healthiness to mind and heart, too, of
regular work of hand or brain. It does more than we
know to keep the faculties bright and the mind actively
interested in the world of thought and duty in the
midst of which we live. It vitalizes the blood in brain
and limbs. It helps to make old age happy and useful.
Active minds under healthy pressure often shine the
brightest after the mid-day of life, as the sun in the
heavens often pours out its warmest rays after it has
passed the meridian. Illustrations of this are seen
everywhere. Every city and town and neighborhood
boasts its old persons who have kept on ripening till
the angel of the harvest came. . . .

" Every time we meet an old friend, after a few
years of absence, we see the marks left on face and
form by the footfall of time; and how gently and
gradually dear Mother Nature lays her white crown

upon our heads or draws new lines on the face,— so gently and gradually that we never know just when it is done, any more than the oak knows just when its leaves are changed, or the golden grain when the husks are bleached."

He was unconsciously drawing his own portrait in these words, and also giving the key to his perpetual youth.

Mr. Tilden, believing that the people would more readily become attached to the new minister in the absence of the old one, and consequently the best interests of the church promoted, accepted the invitation which had been previously tendered him to preach for two months in Meadville, Pa., and on the next Sunday, Jan. 1, 1884, stood in that pulpit.

He became immediately interested in the church, the people, and the Theological School. The two months grew into four under the hospitable roof of Professor Frederic Huidekoper.

A letter in the *Register*, which he wrote from Meadville, speaks of the School as "beautiful for situation," and says: "If it be not the 'joy of the whole earth' quite yet, it is surely the joy of a zealous group of young prophets, who aspire to be 'a joy to the whole earth,' when they shall have completed their course, and have become the true prophets of the Lord.

"Meadville is a delightful town. True, it is not Cambridge; but it has a college as well as a theological school, and a French creek nearly as large as the Charles River, and subject to overflows such as that little classic and aristocratic stream never experienced. Nevertheless, Cambridge has some advantages, especially for such as graduate from the university. But for the young men out in the country, who in farming, lumbering, or at the carpenter's bench hear a voice calling, 'Come over into Macedonia, and help us,' and who, if they ever respond, must do it at once, without a college preparation,—for such hard-handed but warm-hearted young men, whose eyes are opened to the glory of our liberal faith, and who are not afraid of hard study and hard work in making preparation for a useful life, Meadville is the place. It is quiet, it is healthy, it is central,—in short, just the location for a school of robust prophets who come to study, not the literature of religion merely, but how to do brave service for the kingdom of God. We need more of this class of Christian workers in our liberal Church. There cannot be too much learning if it be all consecrated to the world's uplifting. But, when learning makes a man dainty and fastidious, when it makes him sigh for the flesh-pots of rich societies, and look scornfully on small places with low salaries, however great their need of a spiritual helper, then the learning is a clog, a hindrance, a stone around neck and heels, which has sunk many a man, leaving only a few bubbles on the stagnant waters to tell where he went down. The learning for ministers is the learning which enlarges the heart while it broadens the intellect, which brings one into closer sympathy, not with the refined and the cultivated merely, but with that class who first heard Jesus gladly, — 'the common people.' Religion in white gloves is not the kind for which humanity waits. It is bare-handed, muscular piety that isn't afraid of hard work in hard soil that we most deeply need.

"We have ministers enough for our large and rich congregations, more than enough. A long file of them is always waiting for a vacancy in the delectable places. They would rather wait; for death is always busy, and disaffection, swifter than death, is always dissolving ties and opening doors. They would rather wait till the lottery is drawn, in the forlorn hope of a prize, than accept the call of that little struggling church, where the pay is small, however large the prospect under undismayed and manly labor.

"We have, according to our Year Book, seventy-five parishes without ministers. The most of these, of course, are small and poor. We want ministers for these seventy-five small, poor churches, each one of which may grow into a mighty power for spiritual life under the guidance of a brave soul touched with the spirit of God.

"We want as many more to fill new openings and calls for live, earnest, self-sacrificing men, to break the bread of our liberal faith to those who are hungering for it. Who will come to Meadville or go to Cambridge, to prepare for such a work? The schools are one in spirit and purpose, in aim and end. Each should rejoice in the prosperity of the other, as they both do in every token of deeper religiousness on the part of those they send out to work for God and man in the great field of the world.

"Young men, in city and country, rich or poor, from farm or mechanic's bench or academy, who among you, to whom our liberal faith is dear, will come and enter on this broad field of hard work and poor pay,— a work whose reward is in itself, and whose check only the bank of heaven will honor?"

As Mr. Tilden had no longer a Boston parish, he no longer needed a Boston home, and, besides, he wanted to be nearer the children and grandchildren he so dearly loved, and who filled so large a portion of his heart. His daughter Laura, with her husband and son, lived in Dorchester. His eldest son and family were near, and his youngest son had a home in Milton (the Hawthornes). And these three households were all within little more than a mile of each other.

His heart had already decided the location, even before his son George sent to Meadville the plan of a cottage, with the offer of land in his own garden to build upon. A letter written at this time says: "You see, I can't preach much longer. We must have a home somewhere. That corner of the garden is made on purpose, and George's plan is inspired. Happy man that I am! such children and grandchildren, and a cot for our old age in prospect. The hope is blessed. The fruition with Him who doeth all things well."

This home, the ground for which was broken by his little grandchildren March 13, 1884, was christened the " Red Cottage." It more than realized all his fondest hopes, and was to him the harbor of refuge after all his wanderings, the dearest spot in all the world, the place from which his spirit took its upward flight.

Before leaving Meadville, he received the following letter : —

REV. WM. P. TILDEN :

Dear Sir,— In the name of the congregation of the Independent Congregational Church of Meadville, I take great pleasure in inviting you to return after the summer vacation, and continue the ministrations which have been so acceptable for the coming year.

In sending this invitation, I am especially gratified at being able to accompany it with such a complete list of signatures, which will prove to you the entire unanimity with which your return is desired by the whole congregation.

I do not know that we can offer you any inducement to remain, longer with us, save the very simple one that we *need* you; and, since it is so much more "blessed to give than receive," I can but hope that our very necessities will plead eloquently in our behalf.

Most sincerely yours,

Lucy T. W. Tyler, *Secretary*.

Meadville, Pa., March 27, 1884.

Many things contributed to make the stay in Meadville delightful, not the least of which was the renewal of his old acquaintance with Dr. A. A. Livermore, President of the Theological School, through whose influence, probably, the first invitation to preach in Meadville came, and by whose invitation also he had given a course of lectures to the students. So he consented to come for a part of the next year, from October, 1884, to May, 1885.

On his homeward journey he spent a few days at Old Point Comfort, and was for a short time the guest of Rev. R. R. Shippen, of Washington, preaching for him morning and evening. While in the city, he dined one day with Frederick Douglass, who says in a letter afterwards: "I see the kind-hearted and brave minister of the gospel who had the courage to invite me, an unknown and despised fugitive from slavery, into his new pulpit in Norton, Mass., to plead the then much persecuted cause of the slave. More than forty years have passed since this, to me, important event, and I rejoice that I live to speak of it, and you live to note my grateful mention of it. I like to look over the field of the

past and recall such incidents ; and I rejoice that I
have lived to have your dear white head once under my
roof."

After a summer in the Red Cottage, Milton, he returned to Meadville Oct. 1, 1884.

The hospitality of the Huidekopers was boundless.
Two delightful months were spent with Mr. Alfred
Huidekoper, and four months and a half with Miss
Elizabeth G. Huidekoper, who opened to the pastor and
his wife her large house and larger heart. Saint Elizabeth he ever afterwards called her. In both households everything possible was done for his comfort and
happiness.

In preaching and lecturing and in delightful social
intercourse the winter sped swiftly. At its close the
following letter appeared in the *Register* from the pen
of Dr. A. A. Livermore : —

We have a sad farewell to say to-day to our venerated pastor,
Rev. William P. Tilden. He has for two seasons ministered to
the Unitarian church, out of his rich spiritual experiences, and
from the fountains of a warm, loving heart. These qualities make
him one of the youngest and freshest of our ministers. If the
advanced in years like him because he carries a white head and a
fully stored history of more than forty years of usefulness, the
young love him because he is young as the youngest in cheerful
spirits and fond sympathies. How wonderfully various are the
gifts of men ! How every man is a new world in himself, unlike
any that went before or any that shall come after ! Brother
Tilden is a world in himself ; and the peculiarity of his world is
that it possesses to an unusual degree the attraction of gravita-
tion,— he is one of the drawing kind. In that respect he re-
sembles the great Master himself, who drew all men to him, and
whom the people heard gladly. He has done much to revive our
church, increase the Sunday congregations, add members to the

church, and harmonize and spiritualize conflicting religious views. He takes a sensible, practical outlook of the times, and gives a charitable interpretation to aspects of thought and speculation which some regard as boding no good to the future of our Zion.

Not only in the church have we had beautiful and deeply Christian discourses and services, Sunday after Sunday,— for he has made only one exchange since he has been here,— but in the Theological School, both last year and this year, he has given lectures on the duties and aims of the ministry of the most useful and telling character. To specify no other, that on " Sealed Orders " would make a column in the *Register* that would benefit not only every theological school in the land, but even the lords of the pulpit themselves. Especially in setting the duties of the preacher and those of the pastor in due and true perspective with one another, he has done excellent service. Nor is he the man who says one thing and does another. His ministry here has been distinguished not only for constant industry, fresh new sermons, eager and wide reading, but helpful calls on every possible son or daughter of the parish, the looking up of the stray lambs of the flock, and hearty mingling in social gatherings, both in the society and in other churches. In one word, it has been all along *the renovation of the ministerial office*, in church and parish, brought down to date, filled out in its opportunities of usefulness, and breathing the Christ-like and helpful spirit. It is not the new wine in new bottles so much as the good old wine, mellowed by time and experience, in new bottles. But our blessings brighten as they depart; and now we have to bid farewell to our friends, and to wish them all manner of happiness in their Milton home, which they abundantly deserve.

XXIII.

ROWEN.

1885-1886.

BRIGHTON.—ATLANTA.— MAY MEMORIAL SERMON.—LECTURES AND BACCALAUREATE IN MEADVILLE.—CLOSE OF MINISTRY AT BRIGHTON.

SEPTEMBER, 1885, he took the supply of the Brighton pulpit for a few months, and while there made an exchange of seven Sundays with Rev. George L. Chaney, of Atlanta, Ga. From the latter place he wrote to the *Unity:* " We are not ' marching through Georgia,' only in camp for a time. We are here in this city of roses and balmy air on an exchange with brother Chaney, who is at the North with his sick wife, now happily recovering from a long illness. We find they have together been doing a noble work here, winning the honor and love not only of their own people, but of outsiders, by their earnest work in behalf of a Christianity that is deeper and higher and broader than any ' ism.' Their return to Atlanta will be hailed with joy. The Church of our Father has a fine chapel, with a corner lot in the centre of the city reserved for a church edifice when the time shall come. It must come at no distant time ; for the city is rapidly growing, and minds and hearts are opening to the glory of our growing faith. This pioneer movement inaugurated by the Chaneys is no longer an experiment. It is an established fact. We have one church of the future in Georgia, and may confidently hope that the ten times one will come through hard working and patient waiting. We have spent a most delightful season here with the saints and sinners of our own and other faiths, and shall bear away pleasant memories and bright hopes of our brave little church planted here and planted to grow."

In June of that year, 1886, he went to Meadville and gave a course of eight lectures to the students of the Theological School, and two sermons, the last being the Baccalaureate, in ten consecutive days. On September 12th he gave a sermon in Syracuse, N.Y., on the unveil- ing of a mural tablet to the memory of his dear friend, Samuel J. May.

A brief extract from that sermon is given here : —

"Calm as a June morning, but firm as Gibraltar, he was a moral hero. No wonder a phrenologist, on examining his head, told him he should have been a soldier. Indeed, he was a soldier. He had not missed his calling : only his warfare was of the higher kind, and his weapons

> " ' Those mild arms of Truth and Love,
> Made mighty through the living God.'

"Then he came to you,— fortunate people,— and blessed you for more than a quarter of a century. I say more than a quarter of a century, for he blessed you after he resigned his pastorate just as he did before, until a voice from heaven whispered to him, ' COME UP HIGHER,' and, with a faith in the immortal life scarcely less clear than sight, he rose.

" What he was to you in all those ripest years of his ministry, in the church, in the home, in the schools, in the city, in the nation, what a son of consolation he was in all your sorrows, how sincerely he rejoiced with the rejoicing and wept with the weeping, what a preacher he was of truth and righteousness as he saw it, how loyal to his highest light, how ready to meet danger and death in obedience to the higher voice, how, when the great hour of emancipation struck, his soul leaped forth in joy and gratitude at the glorious consummation of his life-long labors and prayers, and then the growing beauty and glory of his life as the shadows lengthened and the sunset hour drew nigh,— all this, and more, you know so well that I can only hint at what, to you, is open vision.

" It was my privilege to be with you fifteen years ago, — oh, how the years fly ! — when we met in the old church for the last offices of faith and affection. I never witnessed such an occasion. Dearly as I loved him, it did not seem like a funeral. It was rather like a grand and solemn *apotheosis*, the crowning of a noble soul with the highest honor man can ever receive,— the revered love of his fellows, won by noble living.

" Many of those who gathered around the grave, and looked up, not down for him, have since passed on, leaving only a few of the old-time veterans in the moral fight to gather now and then, with ever-narrowing circles, to talk over the 'times that tried men's souls.'

" But still you keep his memory green. In the gratitude of your hearts, you have made this new church of your love and prayer a ' May Memorial,' that his name and memory may still mingle with your best thoughts

and highest aspirations. And now his kindred in flesh
and spirit have asked the privilege of placing on these
walls their memorial of honor and affection, to show
their personal love of the man you have so delighted to
honor.

"'HE WAS A GOOD MAN.' Yes, and a great man,—
great in Christ's idea of greatness, when he said to his
disciples, WHOSOEVER WILL BE GREAT AMONG YOU,
LET HIM BE YOUR MINISTER,— the greatness of service.

"That he fought not with carnal, but spiritual weapons required not less courage, but more, as it calls for
more heroism to be stoned for truth than to stone
him who assails it. His courage was tempered with
the Christ spirit. With no cry of 'Lord, Lord!' he
followed closely in the Master's steps. With what a
mighty 'Amen' in our hearts we heard those words of
his dear friend, President White, spoken at his grave :—

"'Here lies before us all that was mortal of the best
man, the most truly Christian, I have ever known,—
the purest, the sweetest, the fullest of faith and hope
and charity, the most like the Master. Had our Lord
come upon this earth again, and into these streets, any
time in these thirty years, he was sure of one follower.
Came he as black man or red man or the most
wretched of white men, came he in rags or sores, this
one dear friend would have followed him, no matter
what weapons, carnal or spiritual, were hurled at the
procession.'

"Golden words ! History and epitaph in one. We
cannot add to them if we would. We can only repeat
the text,— 'HE WAS A GOOD MAN.'"

On the last Sunday in December, 1886, Mr. Tilden

closed his engagement in Brighton, feeling that the society had been long enough without a resident pastor.

It was a pleasant year of ministerial service, though a good deal broken into by the Southern trip and the Meadville lectures.

The drive of one hour from Milton to Brighton was through a delightful part of country and city, and was most enjoyable. A choir of young girls and boys was organized while he was there, in which he took great interest, calling them always " my choir."

XXIV.

ROWEN.

1887–1889.

THE first Sunday of the new year 1887 he was invited to preach in Plymouth, Mass. This was followed
by eight delightful Sundays in the same parish, the
people wishing him to supply their pulpit for a time
after his return from another Southern trip.

In March he writes from Atlanta to the *Register:*
"Forty-eight hours apart, as the cars fly; but the cli-
matic change, as we experienced it, was from winter
to summer. Sunday, 6th inst., we waded, knee-deep,
through driven snow to the Church of the Disciples,
Boston, to speak a word to the lonely flock who missed
the voice of their good shepherd. Soon may they hear
it again! Sunday, 13th, we are here at Atlanta, in a
perfect spring garden, peach-blossoms in all their glory,
crab-apple and pear-trees just putting on their deli-
cately tinted robes, the blue-green grass carpeting the
lawns, and the young wheat almost tall enough to

wave. The change seems magical as well as delightful. Atlanta is really a very beautiful city. We thought so last year. We think so this year still more vigorously. It is constantly growing, not only in population and business enterprise, but in that architectural finish and beauty which one hardly expects to see in a city so young.

"Mr. Chaney is just now holding services in Chattanooga, another rapidly growing city, four hours away, where he hopes that the corner-stone of a new liberal church may be laid. He thinks that the time has fully come for 'church extension' in these new fields."

A few weeks later Mr. Tilden writes from Chattanooga as follows : "This rapidly growing city is known as 'The Southern Gateway of the Alleghanies'; and, although it sounds slightly ambitious, there are solid *terra firma* reasons for so regarding it, since the Tennessee River, on a graceful curve of which the city is built, pushes its way between the mountains, marking the only natural path to the region beyond. The Indians called it Chattanooga, or 'crow's nest,' because, doubtless, of its being such a cosey retreat, hemmed in by the surrounding heights. But its natural advantages as a landing near the 'Gate' for receiving and shipping the primitive products of the surrounding country led to its settlement by the whites, who obtained a charter in 1852.

"The war, sweeping away everything in the settlement, slaves and all, left the soil clean for a fresh beginning. Since then the growth of the place in commerce, in manufactures, in numbers, and in wealth, has been wonderfully rapid, and is still rising in a perfect freshet of prosperity.

"During the last few months there has been a boom in real estate here, which has made some small land-owners comfortable and large ones corpulent. But the freshet is subsiding, and those caught on the bars will have to wait for another boom to take them off. But our chief interest in the city just now is not in its commerce or its corner lots, but in its religious needs. We are here, by advice and counsel of Bishop Chaney, to see if there be any call for Unitarian church extension. Of course, everybody else is here before us, Catholic and Protestant. 'If you had only come last year,' it is said, 'you could easily have started a church; but now the liberals have joined the other churches, and really,' etc. But, remembering who gave the cheering promise, 'The last shall be first,' which fits our tardy habits as if made for our special benefit, we went to work. The bishop came here for three Sundays, while we supplied his pulpit in Atlanta; and then we came for three Sundays more. Our place of meeting is an 'upper room,' up two flights, not 'large' or 'furnished' like that at Jerusalem, but with numbers most encouragingly akin to that early Christian gathering. But, if numbers were few, opinions were many, ranging all the way from old-fashioned Unitarianism to new-fashioned nothingarianism, with a freedom of expression that was sublime in its transparent honesty. One would have hardly deemed it possible to get so many opinions from so few persons. It was a unique company. It was plain that the creed must be very simple and general that could unite them. But, fortunately, we had no creed to offer, only a purpose of getting good and doing good; and on this broad ground we found a cordial response.

"Here is a grand chance for some young Eliot or Chaney to give himself, soul and body, to founding and building up a liberal church — a church of the spirit, a church of humanity — in this charming 'Gateway of the Alleghanies.' "

April 24 he preached in New Orleans for Rev. C. A. Allen, in whose charming home and in that of Mr. C. Holloway a week was spent,— the week of the Southern Conference. This in itself was a great delight; and both gentlemen were unwearied in their kindness to the strangers, showing them the attractions of their lovely city, its homes, its typical gardens, its cathedral, market, old French and Spanish houses, its many present beauties, and the traces of its historic past.

The next Sunday was spent in Nashville, Tenn. A letter to his daughter at this time says: "We have been here nearly two days, and have found but *one* Unitarian, and he doesn't know whether he is one or not. But I have engaged the Olympic Theatre for next Sunday morning and evening, and then and there hope to make my début as an apostle of our blessed faith. Should there be only that one present, who doesn't quite know where he stands, I shall hope to drive him from the fence, and make him see where he is before I get through. But I guess there will be two, possibly three, so that we may claim the blessing promised to that number. That we are homesick goes without saying; but we bear it, promising to each other, if we ever do get home, we 'won't do so again.' "

The next Sunday was spent in Birmingham, where he preached only in the evening, as he was unable to procure any place for morning service. He returned to Atlanta the next day, May 9 (his birthday).   He writes home as follows : —

Dear Children and Grandchildren,—Thanks, thanks, thanks, for telegram and letters. Oh, how refreshing they were, when I reached Atlanta after a seven hours' ride from Birmingham, in a hot sultry, dusty day! I could sit and think of you all, and of what you were thinking and doing, for I knew we poor estrays would mingle with your thoughts.

I was all alone, so I jolted, and mused, and thought, and loved, and longed amid a crowd of tired travellers, comforted with the sweet thought that we were pointing homeward, though fifteen hundred miles away, and that every jolt and lurch brought me a little nearer to the "little Red" and all it stands for.

So far we have had, on the whole, a good time, though fatiguing. But you may be assured, my dear ones, that after this we shall be as glad to stay at the "little Red" as you will be to have us.

If we didn't love you all so well, we could stand this being away better, but love is a great *pull-back* to the missionary zeal of an old man.

After two more Sundays in Atlanta he went to Charleston, S.C., where a warm welcome awaited him from Rev. and Mrs. E. C. L. Browne, whose two hearts he had made one some twenty-five years before.   He supplied the pulpit for Mr. Browne one Sunday, and was introduced by him to the congregation as the "good gray head which all men knew."

A letter from Mr. Browne at this time in the *Register* says : "Father Tilden, the loved bishop of souls, has touched our south country with his episcopal benignity, a spirit more genial than our breezes, and a smile, not prostrating like our sun, but carrying the strength of faith.   After establishing several churches (potential) *in partibus infidelium*, strengthening the faith and

zeal of the congregations in Atlanta and New Orleans,
cheering the Southern Conference with the optimism of
his experience, giving his hearty benediction and charge,
as well as example, to the young evangelist, now working alone in the far South-west, last of all he brought the
treasure of his presence to Charleston, lingering with us
in a whole restful week of communion before his final
ascension to Boston. We can still hear his voice,
though his presence is gone. What a peculiar thrill
is in it, vibrating with a mingle of human sympathy
and divine hope. He came as we have known him
of old,— as when, twenty-three years ago, in the April
freshness of a New England town, he preached in the
old church on the hill my ordination sermon. He came
the same, unless one is reminded of Jones Very's
thought,—

> "'Father, there is no change to live with thee,
> Save that in thee I grow from day to day.'

But he goes in another character. He will hereafter
be Rabbi Ben Ezra to us; for no one ever more persuasively said, in obedience to this law of fulfilment,—

> "'Grow old along with me!
> The best is yet to be,—
> The end of life, for which the first was made.
> Youth shows but half. See all. Trust God, nor be afraid!'

But, whether bishop or rabbi, or brother or father,
whether growing old or in perpetual youth, his good
works follow him, and our love must crown him."

Mr. Tilden's letter from Savannah, June 2, 1887,
says: "We had a delightful stay with the Brownes.

Preached for him Sunday. Came here Tuesday. Did the city yesterday, and it surprised us with its beauty. Sail to-day at about three in the 'Gate City' for dear old Boston and the dearer children, grandchildren, and friends.

" We hope to arrive at the Hub some time Sunday afternoon, if all goes well. And all *will* go well, whatever comes, for 'Our Father's at the helm.' Oh, shall we not be glad to see Boston Light, and the light in so many heart windows ashore waiting for us ! "

After his return he accepted an invitation to supply the Plymouth pulpit for six months ; but, before that engagement was quite concluded, he had a serious illness (bronchitis) which kept him in bed many weeks, and from which, though he apparently recovered entirely, he never regained his former vigor. But he still loved his chosen work just as well as ever, and said after every service, " I thank God that I have been able to preach once more."

About this time the following statement appeared in the *Watchman :* —

Every now and then somebody gives us a moving picture of a happily settled pastor, sexagenarian, who is the idol of his congregation and "doing his best work," as a living refutation of the nonsense about "the dead line of fifty," which limits the usefulness of ministers. This, however, is raising a false issue. Nobody charges upon churches that they summarily dismiss or get rid of their pastors as soon as they are fifty years old. No doubt a man who is well preserved physically, and able for his work, may often live on with the same people for years after that date. But suppose a man on the shady side of fifty to be (from no cause that is to his discredit) without pastoral charge : what are his chances of receiving a call, or even of being asked so much as to supply a pulpit for a Sabbath or two ? When somebody will instance such a man whose services are in brisk demand, we will admit an exception to a very general rule. When two are named, we will reconsider the question."

The *Register* says,—

" If the *Watchman* is willing to count Unitarians, we will move a reconsideration, and mention two men past seventy in constant demand among us,— Dr. A. P. Peabody and Rev. W. P. Tilden."

Oct. 8, 1888, he commenced a six months' pastorate in Wilmington, Del.

A *Register* letter says : " There is a large Quaker element in the society here, which is very interesting. The Hicksite Friends are essentially Unitarians, and easily and naturally affiliate with us, especially the rising generation. They bring what Matthew Arnold called 'sweetness and light.' We welcome both.

"Our little vine-clad brick church is delightfully situated on a street abounding in churches. We have a Sunday attendance of near a hundred, sometimes more.

" Wilmington is a rapidly growing city. Its rolling surface gives picturesqueness to its billowy streets, and limits horse-cars to the more level lines. The quaint old houses of a former generation, sprinkled in here and there among the new ones, are very interesting. But in the prominent streets and out on the hills are some elegant structures of the modern style, showing how wealth and taste are united in making the city beautiful. The bird's-eye view from high points of the Brandywine and Christiana Rivers, that encircle the city in their liquid arms, and pour their united waters into the broad Delaware as it sweeps on to the capes, is very grand. As a seaport, Wilmington has great advantages. Its shipbuilding interest in wood and iron is most refreshingly prosperous. One vessel is no sooner launched than another keel is stretched upon the blocks. The yards are so full of men as to remind me of Medford fifty years ago. Wilmington is sure to grow, and the first Unitarian society to grow with it."

His home letter for December 25th says: "Hail! and a merry Christmas to you all,— Laura and the doctor, Will and Anna, George and Alice, Joseph, and May, and Cora, and Charlie, and Elsie, and Edith,— thrice merry, merry, merry Christmas to you all. Well, it is good for the inward eyes to see you. You look as if you had had a good dinner. The turkey and pudding shine through. How did we come? Not on the wires or through the telephone, but in the good old way of thought and affection by which Adam and Eve held intercourse the first time they lost sight of each other among the trees of the garden. We talk of abolishing time and space with electricity and tin tubes: bungling inventions they are in comparison with the electrical battery of the brain and heart by which we can girdle the globe in less than thirty minutes, and dine with our loved ones whenever we please, however far away. But we didn't come to talk philosophy or eat dinner, though we should like a bite, — it looks so nice and smells so Christmasy,— but just to take your hands and look into your eyes and tell you all that we don't get over loving you a bit, and don't want to, though, if we only could ease up a little, it would be more comfortable when we are away down in Delaware."

At the end of six months the *Register* contained the following notice : —

Wilmington, Del.— This society has been enjoying the ministrations of Rev. William P. Tilden for the past six months; and
during that time the attendance upon the Sunday services has
steadily increased. Mr. Tilden has won the hearts of all alike,
young and old, conservative and radical. His eloquent preaching,
his gentle and manly spirit, his fatherly interest and tender sympathy, have so attracted to himself and to the religion he so
thoroughly represents in his walk and conversation, that the action
of the society at its meeting on Sunday, March 10, was both
natural and logical. The following preamble and resolutions
were on that occasion unanimously adopted : —

Whereas this society has enjoyed for the last six months the ministrations of Rev. William P. Tilden, and during that time it has learned
to love and respect his character, and appreciate his high spiritual and
intellectual qualities ; and
Whereas we feel that our spiritual perceptions have been quickened
and our intellectual faculties enlarged and strengthened by his eloquent
and impressive teachings,— therefore,
Resolved, That this society extends to Rev. William P. Tilden a
unanimous call to become its pastor.
Resolved, That the trustees be requested and authorized to make such
arrangements with Mr. Tilden as may be necessary to secure his services
to the society, pledging themselves to sustain and support him in his
pastoral work.
Resolved, That a committee of three be appointed to wait upon Mr.
Tilden, and present to him this call, and urge upon him its acceptance.

Mr. Tilden's decision has not yet been ascertained, but every
member of the society and congregation awaits it with undis-
guised anxiety. It is, perhaps, unusual for a call to be extended
to a minister seventy-seven years of age ; but this society asks no
better service than he can render. And it will be their greatest
pleasure to sustain him with their love and sympathy during the
remaining years of his ministerial work. If he should remain, the
future prosperity of this society will be assured.

Gratifying as this call was, Mr. Tilden, feeling that
the society misjudged his strength, and knowing his inability for continuous work, felt obliged to decline,
which he did in the following letter : —

MESSRS. GEORGE W. STONE, DANIEL W. TAYLOR, AND HEY-
WOOD CONANT, Committee of the First Unitarian Society of
Wilmington, Del.:

Gentlemen and Brethren,— Your kind invitation to the pastorate
of your church is before me. It is remarkable for its cordiality
and for the largeness and entire unanimity of the vote. I feel sure
that such a call to one of my age, who came not as a candidate,
must have warm hearts behind it, and that I may confidently rely
on its pledges of support and co-operation. It demands most
serious consideration. This I have tried to give it. I sincerely
hope I have been guided wisely, and that you will all see, on due
reflection, that my decision is best for you as well as for myself.

When I left my church in Boston five years ago, it was with
the fixed and, as I think, wise purpose of not taking another
pastorate. I left for rest and change, intending still to preach as
long as strength and opportunity continued. Both have been
granted to a remarkable degree, so that these years of here and
there preaching have proved the happiest of my long ministerial
life. Three of the churches to which I have ministered for a
longer or shorter period are now rejoicing in acceptable pastors
and going on prospering and to prosper. When I came to
Wilmington, although an entire stranger to you all, I hoped that
here also I might pave the way for some good man in whom you
could all unite; but, lo! in the abounding kindness of your hearts
you wish me to stay as your permanent pastor. This is as gratifying as it is unexpected, for we all love to be loved. Were I not
remarkably wise, I might yield to my feelings rather than to my
judgment, and accede to your generous proposals. But I know
my inability for prolonged and continuous service too well to take
such an advantage of your kindness. I owe my present health
and strength very largely, I think, to my migratory habits. I do
not stay long enough in a place to get tired or for the people to
get tired of me. I seem to thrive best on the wing, and should
not dare to light for any length of time, lest I should not be able
to rise. Should I stay longer with you, you might love me less
and think less of my preaching. I prize your good opinion too
highly to run the risk. Be assured, therefore, that I am doing
you as well as myself the greatest kindness in declining your persuasive call.

We shall bear away with us delightful memories of your pleasant city and our many kind friends here. We shall ever feel a deep interest in the welfare of your church, which henceforth will be our church, too; and it is our hearts' desire and prayer that in fulness of time one may be sent to you who will prove himself a true helper in the divine life.

Your six months' minister and all-time friend,

W. P. TILDEN.

A letter to his daughter from Wilmington, March 29th, says : —

We hope to come right through on Monday as I wrote you, in spite of George's powerful persuasives to stay over night in New York. What do we care about the little village of New York? A night in the little Red will be more restful than Fifth Avenue Hotel.

Lovingly to all,

FATHER.

A few days later he writes to his dear friend, Rev. C. G. Ames, as follows : —

MAY 9TH, 1889.

Dear Ames,— You guessed right. I write from the culm of my seventy-eighth birthday. I like the altitude : the air is pure and the prospect glorious. I wouldn't go down into the valley of youth or the hillsides of toil, where you youngsters are digging, if I could. I like to be up here, away from the crowd, where I can take life easy, work when I feel like it and then play,— "kiss my hand to the stars," look out on the peaks still higher up, glistening in the sunshine, and the peaks still beyond, that we see only with the inward eye. No! I wouldn't go back if I could, not even to pick up dropped stitches : I should be sure to drop more, and make the hole larger and more difficult to mend. "Only once this way" is the mysterious fiat. The shortcomings we mourn lift us by keeping us humble. My only regret away up here is that I have done so little in a long life, but I try not to let that over-trouble me. The dear God knows it all, and loves me still, as he does all his wayward children.

My life has been so free from crosses that I look for no crown. I have been overpaid, cash down, every day; and, if there were a strict accountant up there, I should be bankrupt and in hopeless debt. But "he delighteth in mercy." It is good to be in debt to him so rich in forgetting love. . . .

I am always, in ever enduring love and immortal hope,

Your own brother,

TILDEN.

In June, of this year he went again to Meadville to repeat the course of lectures which were given to the Theological School in 1886. Again he gave eight lectures and two sermons (the last being the Baccalaureate) in ten consecutive days.

A letter to his daughter at this time says : " Here we are, safe and sound, well homed with Dr. and Mrs. Livermore, who take the best possible care of us. Your hot beef tea was charming. My last cup was in the car, heated nicely by the porter. Meadville is looking gloriously. The old friends seem glad to see us. The school is full and flourishing, and the students listen to my lectures with apparent interest. I have given two lectures, and bear it very well. Tell the doctor I do not forget his wise counsel, and think I have been benefited by it, even if I do not toe the mark exactly. . . . This is a brilliant letter ! The doctor will see that I am not overtaxing my mind. He prescribed *mental rest*, and this note shows how faithful I am to his prescription. My stupidity is most encouraging. I must be convalescing."

His journal of June 30 says : "Was obliged to give up an engagement to preach on account of illness. The wise Dr. Green says I must not preach again until September. So I have cancelled two other engagements, and have gone into the dry dock for repairs, hoping to be seaworthy again in September."

September 1st he occupied the Newton pulpit, and the journal says: "I have not preached before since my Baccalaureate at Meadville. Have been too ill. Thanks to the dear Father for strength restored."

XXV.

ROWEN.

1889.

LATER in the month, September, 1889, Mr. Tilden went to Plainfield, N.J., to preach for seven Sundays to the little society just started there.

He says, in a letter to the *Register:* "There are twelve Plainfields in the United States, showing that it is a favorite name. But we doubt if any one of them equals in rural beauty and general attractiveness this growing city of New Jersey. Situated on the New Jersey Central Railroad, only an hour from New York, less by express, it furnishes not only a summer retreat for New Yorkers, but an all-the-year-round home for many who do business in the great city. With a dry, sandy soil, and good, pure water, it has long been noted for its general healthiness.

"One of its great charms consists in its being a country city. There are no 'blocks,' save in the business streets. Separate houses with generous grounds are the general rule ; and, while it is mainly a plain field as to the surface, it is so picturesquely laid out, with so many curved and diagonal streets, that the usual checker board monotony of cities with a plain surface is largely obviated. The soil, though light, is rich; and the shade-trees, with which the streets are abundantly fringed, have a heavy foliage, which is just now in its golden glory. The population is estimated at ten thousand, and is constantly increasing. Many new buildings, some very beautiful, are going up.

"The city had fourteen churches, representing the leading denominations, when Rev. D. W. Morehouse, Secretary of the New York Conference of Unitarian Churches, came here a few months ago, to see if there were any demand for a church of our liberal faith. He found a few earnest Unitarians waiting for him. After holding a few Sunday evening services, the little band of brave men and women felt they were ready for action; and on the 17th of July, 1889, they organized the First Unitarian Society of Plainfield. Now there are fifteen churches in this city; and the last, though the youngest and smallest, is yet destined, as we fondly hope, to do good and noble service for a progressive Christian faith.

"We are fortunate in having the mayor of the city, Hon. Job Male, an interested member of the society. He is a Unitarian to the 'manner born,' being a member of All Souls', New York, in the early ministry of Dr. Bellows. He came to Plainfield years ago, and is one of the city fathers, widely honored and beloved. As the young society found it difficult to obtain a suitable place of worship, Mr. Male opened one of his private houses, fitting the lower part for Sunday services, and offering it free to the society till they could do better. This has been simply but conveniently furnished by the society. We held our first meeting in the

'Home Church' last Sunday, and the rooms were so well filled as to suggest the necessity of early enlargement. Everything looks very hopeful, and we may confidently count on a prosperous and self-sustaining church as the ultimate and sure result."

At the end of his seven weeks' engagement he returned to Milton to spend the month of November, in order that he might attend the dedication of the new church at Concord, N.H., and also that he might gather about him, as was his wont, his children and grandchildren for a Thanksgiving party.

After preaching in Concord, N.H., before his old parishioners Sunday evening, November 10th, and assisting at the dedicatory services on Monday afternoon, he gave an address at a social gathering in the evening, in which he said : "The three years I was with you, from 1844 to 1847, were years of great excitement. The devil's trinity, as we used to call it,—war, intemperance, slavery,—some of us fought against with all the non-resistant fight there was in us. The two first remain, wounded, but still vigorous, while what seemed then the master evil has been swept away forever. But the opposition to any word spoken against the divine institution at this time, on the part of many, was intense. One of my parishioners told me he thought that nothing of a worldly character should ever be let into a Christian pulpit. As sin is supposed to be somewhat worldly, this was a decided narrowing down of the sphere of the pulpit.

"One good woman on whom I called with brother Thomas, who kindly went round with me to get acquainted with his people, was inclined to be very plain-spoken in her ideas of preaching. Brother Thomas said in his mild way, ' Sister, I think brother Tilden preaches the gospel.' She turned upon him, and said, ' Well, if Mr. Tilden preaches the gospel, you didn't.' ' I think there are some parts of the gospel that I did not emphasize as I should,' said brother Thomas.

"On the other hand there were those who were loyal to the true and the right, who held up my hands and encouraged my heart to speak without fear or favor what I believed to be the truth of God. Could your fathers and mothers only have known that in twenty years from that time 'liberty would be proclaimed throughout all the land to all the inhabitants thereof,' I think they would have kept me another year. But it was all right, for, if I had not gone, you would not have had the blessed ministries of Woodbury, Beane, Gilman, and all the rest, to lead you on to the higher life.

" Dear old friends, and new ones, too, the few who remain and the many who have come in, I rejoice with you in this your glad and hopeful hour. Both the church I preached in and the new one that followed went up, prophet-like, in flame, and now another, fairest of the three, has risen on the spot. Here the fathers worshipped, and here the children and the children's children shall gather for the worship and work of the church. Hopeful outlook. Theory is giving place to life, and theology is blossoming into the fruit of pure religion. It remains only that you dedicate yourselves, the only true temple of the Holy Spirit, to God and man."

After a happy Thanksgiving in the Red Cottage,— never a happier or merrier,— he returned to Plainfield for the winter, the following letters having been re-ceived : —

Rev. W. P. Tilden, Milton, Mass.:

Dear Sir,— Our Board of Trustees, having satisfied themselves as to their financial resources, now authorize and intrust me to tender to you on their behalf an invitation to take the regular pastoral charge of our society for as *long a time as you can stay with us*. . . . The Board desires me to state that the unanimous voice of the society expresses the hope that you will accept,— in which hope earnestly joins,

Yours very sincerely,

Charles W. Opdyke,

Sec'y of the First Unitarian Society of Plainfield, N.J.

Nov. 3, 1889.

A letter of Nov. 6, 1889, from Rev. D. W. More-house, Secretary of the New York Conference of Uni-tarian Churches, says : —

Dear Mr. Tilden,— I went over and preached for the little flock in their cosey new home last Sunday. If you could have wit-nessed the eagerness with which the people gathered around me at the close of the service, inquiring if I thought "it would be possible to induce Mr. Tilden to come back," you would have no doubt about the earnestness of the call to minister to these people. They look to you with a tenderness of attachment which it is very pleasant to witness, and which is to me the assurance that they will so heartily respond to your leadership that a few months more of your ministry with them will put them on a foun-dation so sure that their growth and prosperity will be entirely assured. I do not hesitate, therefore, to beg you to come back and be their minister a little longer; and, in making this request of you, I here renew the promise I made several weeks ago,—that, if at any time you desire a labor of love, you shall have such relief as you need. We do not want to overtax you, but rather it is our desire to make the work as light as possible for you.

We want your presence in Plainfield. All that the loving care
of thoughtful and considerate people can do to make your stay in
Plainfield agreeable will most cheerfully be done. If you can,
under these conditions, see your way clear to accept the invitation
which the trustees, in obedience to the unanimous wish of the
society, will send you, you will confer a great favor and blessing
upon them and me.   Affectionately yours,

D. W. MOREHOUSE.

His record book says : " December 1. Having come
to Plainfield to take the pastorate of the First Unitarian Society for the winter, I preached my inaugural
from the words, 'Greet Priscilla and Aquila, my helpers
in Christ Jesus, . . . likewise the church which is in
their house.' "

In this month he went to Wilmington to help the
dear friends whom he was permitted to call his parishioners the year before, in installing their new minister.

December 27 he writes home : " We don't intend to
be absent another Christmas, if we are this side the
river. We see you can't have a real old-fashioned
Christmas without us. George writes that he thinks
he will take Charlie with him to New York next week.
I have written him to come out and spend a night
with us. 'Oh, that will be joyful.' "

A letter of Jan. 16, 1890, to his daughter, says, in
speaking of the death of a friend : " So the great wheel
of life keeps turning, and we never know whose turn
comes next. That is just as it should be. To *trust* is
better than to *know*. . . . Oh, how we did enjoy George's
and Charlie's Sunday visit to us ! We grew a cubit
and a span while they stayed. Had they remained,
we should have become 'giants in Gath.' "

After the delivery of his last course of lectures in

Meadville, in the summer of 1889, the following resolutions were presented to him : —

Resolved, That we, the students of Meadville Theological School, tender our thanks to the Rev. Mr. Tilden, of Milton, Mass., for his instructive course of lectures upon the ministerial offices, so beautiful in their spirit and so valuable in material.

Resolved, That we feel that the course of lectures just closed, to which we have listened with so much pleasure and profit, would be still more valuable to us if we possessed them in a form more enduring and complete than that contained in the insufficient mental record and the incomplete note-book.

We therefore take this opportunity to express the hope — if we may do so without trespass upon plans otherwise determined upon — that the Rev. Mr. Tilden may find it convenient to put in the enduring form of print these wise counsels to his younger brethren, these words so full of the spirit of manly Christianity, and which surely have proceeded from the experiences of a long and useful life, devoted to disinterested and noble service of the Christian ideals. For many years to come, before we ourselves possess the experience of long Christian service, we are sure that these true words of our venerable adviser will do much to guide us safely upon our way.

In response to which Mr. Tilden made this reply : —

In complying with the foregoing request, I yield the distrust of age to the sanguine judgment of youth, and dedicate these familiar lectures to the students of the Meadville Theological School, past, present, and future, and to all earnest students of "the faith that makes faithful." W. P. T.

While in Plainfield, he prepared the lectures for publication ; and, as it was a great pleasure to give them to the students, so also was it a great pleasure to revise them for publication.

They were issued in book form in March, 1890, under the title of "The Work of the Ministry."

Many appreciative notices of the volume appeared in the various Unitarian periodicals and in the daily papers, and many friends bore loving testimony to its value.

Dr. A. A. Livermore, President of Meadville Theological School, said : " If service to God and man is, as I believe it is, the great end of human life, how nobly to the falling of the last sands in the hour-glass has he fulfilled his part in the great life-drama ! I am more happy than I can tell that he was enabled to print that beautiful book on the ministry,— the best, I believe, on the whole, to be found in the world. It will stand as a monument to his memòry and genius long after we and ours are passed away."

Dr. A. P. Peabody says : " Thanks for your admirable book, which is of unspeakable value as a testimony of what the ministry has been and ought to be, yet in some quarters has almost ceased to be. Nothing could be better."

Dr. John H. Morison writes : " It gives me very great pleasure to say that I have seldom, if ever, read a book with more entire satisfaction than your lectures to the Meadville students. I know of no book of the kind that I think so entirely what it should be, and that I shall be so glad to put into the hands of any young minister whom I know to be very earnest to do all that can be done to fill with fidelity and success the great duties of his office."

From Rev. William T. Briggs, Congregational minister of East Douglass : " I thank you hugely for those Meadville Lectures. I opened the little book, saying to myself, ' I have only time to peep into them ' ; but I was half through before I really took a long breath.

As I read, I kept saying, 'What next! what next!'
When a book holds me in that way, I say there is
something in it. I have praised you so much that it
rather mortifies me to say much more in that line;
but, as to these lectures, 'No man shall stop my boast-
ing in all the region of Achaia!' Your suggestions and
advice chime in most happily with what my experience
and observation of more than forty years have taught
me. I have read a good deal about ministers' advice
to students preparing for the ministry, etc., but have
met with nothing more sensible, practical, and really
inspiring than your lectures."

From Mrs. Thomas G. Wells, a loved parishioner of
early days, and an old friend of many years : —

My dear Friend,— I cannot resist sending you this beautiful
letter of cousin Samuel May's. You can believe it *all:* —

"*Dear Cousin Elizabeth Wells,*— Mr. Tilden's book is so
naturally, simply, and heartily written that it was easy reading, and
I have read a very large part of it already; and I can now express
my thanks to you, not only on general principles, but because I
know how sensible, sweet, and good the little book is. How
happily he steers clear of rocks and quicksands all through the
book as well as in the closing chapter, 'Sealed Orders'! Every
young minister at least might be glad of such a book. He has
rounded out his fifty years of the ministry most fittingly with the
little volume, which will carry along his image and likeness long
after he has passed from earth. To think of his doing such good
work, and so much of it,— for the little volume is brimming over
with thoughtful and sensible ideas and suggestions,— when verg-
ing so closely to his eightieth year!"

I think we all who have any kinship with Samuel J. May may
be glad and, humanly speaking, thoroughly satisfied at the kind of
men he induced to take up the ministry,— witness Frederick T.
Gray, Thomas J. Mumford, and W. P. Tilden, to speak of no
other.

XXVI.

LAST DAYS.

1890.

ILLNESS.— DEATH.— FUNERAL SERVICES.

EARLY in the winter he began to be afflicted with rheumatism, but paid little attention to it for some time. Finally, as it grew no better, but rather seemed to be gaining, his doctor advised rest ; and he very reluctantly left Plainfield for a few weeks' stay in Lakewood, N.J. And his last sermon before the Plainfield society, on the " Passion Week of Human Life," April 30, 1890 (the Sunday preceding Easter), proved to be the last he would ever give.

While in Lakewood, he wrote to the *Register* as follows : —

" Having been compelled by stress of 'under the weather' to leave with great regret the temporary pastorate of this young church, I want to say a further word of its condition and prospects, that sister churches all around, knowing something about it, may extend the hand of Christian fellowship now in its day of small things.

" Paul sent his greeting in one of his Epistles to the 'church in the house.' That is just what the church is at present. It is emphatically a 'church in the house,' a home church, with home accommodations for worship and work.

"The society, though small, contains good stock, 'seasoned timber that never gives,' such as George Herbert set to church music.* Those constituting the society are men and women so thoroughly respected in the community that there is little serious opposition to the new movement. When a minister introduced us to his congregation as 'glow-worms,' intending to indicate the feebleness of our light, we accepted the epithet with pleasure as happily suggestive of our mission,—'a light shining in a dark place.' But, on the whole, there is a very kindly feeling shown by the other churches, which, I am sure, will increase as they know us better, and see that our sole aim is the upbuilding of the kingdom of truth, righteousness, and love."

About this time the following letter was received from Rev. D. W. Morehouse : —

My dear blessed young Friend,—I say *young*, for it is impossible for me to regard you as old. Old in heart and spirit it is impossible for any one to be who is filled, as you are, with the enthusiasm of a faith that makes for everlasting youth.

I can never sufficiently thank you for the splendid work you did for our cause in Plainfield. The society under your charge has become thoroughly homogeneous, and, best of all, has had its religious character distinctly formed. In all this you have made your successor's success comparatively easy. I wish every new society that I organize could be so fortunate as to come under your shaping influence for a few months. And I shall hope that it may be so in many cases yet, for I refuse to believe that rheu-

---

* How well we remember his ringing laugh, when a witty friend remarked, "That was a singular reason why other people should give to the Plainfield Church,—the fact that the society is composed of 'seasoned timber that never gives'! I know that all the societies have more or less of that kind of timber, but it took you to utilize it in the way of reaching other people's pockets."

matism is to be permitted to deprive us of the active co-operation of one who is still one of our most vigorous as well as our wisest preachers.

Yes, you will do "lots of preaching yet" with your lips as well as your life. We cannot let you off. There are so few of us who can make the preaching of our daily life match the preaching of our lips that we cannot spare the eloquent persuasions of the one preacher among us who can beat us all in that respect. So you must not think of retiring from the good work yet.

But the sanguine hopes of his friends were not realized; and after a six weeks' stay in Lakewood, during which he grew worse instead of better, his son George came out to bring him back to the Red Cottage, Milton.

By the doctor's advice he took his bed for a few weeks of absolute rest, hoping that this means, which had brought him effectually through what seemed a more serious illness, would prove equally successful this time. But it was of no avail. His strength steadily declined, his suffering becoming more and more intense.

July 19 he writes: "I have had a long life, enjoyed many blessings, and now, dear Father, thy will, not mine, be done. May none of the dear ones mourn greatly for my going! We don't mourn over sunset, however pleasant the day. Most of the time, as I lie half dozing on my bed, I am amid the old play-grounds of my childhood, on the river or on the sea. Time and again I find myself sailing out of Scituate harbor, which I did so often for seven consecutive years. But I seem always to be bound out, headed toward the sea, never coming in. The water is smooth, and the weather serene and beautiful. I do not have to take any pains to steer. The boat glides serenely in the channel, and there seems to be some unseen hand at the helm. The sea breeze is fresh, and the prospect is beautiful. And so I sail on, but never seeming to get out of the harbor. It is well. Why should I wish to come back, when I never sail 'beyond his love and care,' and when there are loved ones beyond the golden shore who wait?"

But many long weeks of pain were before him ere his feet should stand on the other shore.

As evening drew nigh, he frequently repeated Dr. Furness's beautiful hymn, commencing,—

> "Slowly by God's hand unfurled,
> Down around the weary world
> Falls the darkness. Oh, how still
> Is the working of his will!"

The last time, only a few hours before his going away, it was with feeble and faltering lips, and with many mistakes, but he went on bravely to the end.

He was released from his sufferings on the morning of Oct. 3, 1890. His earthly life was over, but there remained in the hearts of parishioners and friends affectionate and grateful memories, which found expression in loving words from churches and from homes.

Memorial services were held in Norton, the first church over which he was settled, in Plainfield, by the society to which he ministered the last few months and who had his latest word, in Meadville, in Atlanta, in Walpole, in Wilmington, and in Plymouth.

On Sunday, October 5th, after services at his own

home and at the First Parish Church, Milton, in the clear, bright sunshine of a perfect day, the worn-out body was borne to the field of peace.

The service at the Red Cottage was attended only by the family and nearest relatives. The casket was placed in the study so long hallowed by his presence. No one who looked upon his face will ever forget its perfect beauty,— the beauty of a completed life, the beauty of one who already walked in the light of the immortal day.

The silence was broken by Rev. W. I. Lawrance, who repeated the twenty-third psalm and offered prayer.

Rev. Roderick Stebbins made a brief address, and read the following lines from Longfellow's "Bayard Taylor" : —

> " Dead he lay among his books !
> The peace of God was in his looks.

> " As the statues in the gloom
> Watch o'er Maximilian's tomb,

> " So those volumes from their shelves
> Watched him silent as themselves.

> " Ah ! his hand will nevermore
> Turn their storied pages o'er;

> " Nevermore his lips repeat
> Songs of theirs, however sweet.

> " Let the lifeless body rest !
> He is gone who was its guest;

> " Gone, as travellers haste to leave
> An inn, nor tarry until eve.

" Traveller ! in what realms afar,
In what planet, in what star,

" In what vast, aërial space
Shines the light upon thy face ?

" In what gardens of delight
Rest thy weary feet to-night?

.   .   .   .   .   .

" Lying dead among thy books,
The peace of God in all thy looks."

At the conclusion Rev. W. H. Fish spoke substantially as follows : —

" As I rise, my friends, to say a few words, I do so with the feeling that this has ever been a most sacred and consecrated home, an earthly paradise, so near to heaven that there is only a thin veil between. Not alone in precious memories and sweeter affections will he still live, but as a translated spirit, ever living and loving on, a ministering spirit of consolation and peace.

" Dr. Channing used to say that, if we had a new sense, a new eye, we might perhaps see that the spiritual world encompassed us on every side, and then quote Milton's saying, that

" ' Millions of spiritual creatures walk the earth,
. . . both when we wake and when we sleep.'

And I shall love to think of this home henceforth as one to which the angels come with their messages of consolation and joy,— consolation to the dear ones who remain and joy to those who went before.

"This is, of course, not the time and place for eulogy. Fitting words will, no doubt, be spoken at the church to-day, but they will, I am sure, fall below the excellence and the merit of our brother; and, after all shall be said, his character and life will rise to our view as the best eulogy he can possibly receive.

"When Andrew D. White stood by the open grave of the sainted Samuel J. May, he looked down and said, with affectionate and tender emphasis, 'There lies the best Christian that I ever knew'; and Samuel J. May and Mr. Tilden were one in spirit,— indeed, as spiritual father and son in the gospel; and I can say of the blessed one whose outward form now lies in the casket before me, as beautiful in death as in life, there lies one of the best Christians I have ever known. And may the rich consolations which the dear, ascended one has given to others through his long and blessed ministry now be theirs from whom this loving husband, father, grandfather, has been taken! Still may this home continue to open to the heavens and the heavens to it; and may all the members of this family, from the oldest to the youngest, rejoice in the hope of the glorious immortality which this loving and faithful follower of Christ so long preached in the unction and love of the Spirit!"

Another service was then held in the First Parish Church, a few rods away, the body being borne up the aisle by the sons, grandsons, and the physicians who attended him in his long illness. The church was filled with former parishioners and friends from Boston and elsewhere. Many beautiful flowers, the loving gifts of dear friends, covered the pulpit and casket.

Rev. Roderick Stebbins, the pastor of the church, read passages from the Bible, and Rev. Dr. Briggs offered prayer, tender, touching, and comforting.

The congregation then sang one verse of " Rise, my soul, and stretch thy wings," a favorite hymn with Mr. Tilden.

Rev. Dr. E. E. Hale then rose, and said, " All who ever saw this man saw one who walked with God." He spoke of his long fellowship and acquaintance with the risen one, the influence he exerted during a few months' sojourn in Plainfield, and the uplifting influence of his whole life. He said: " He was a lover of nature and of the Word; a great reader, always abreast of the times. He entered into the deepest subjects ; he had an exquisite sense of humor; he was tender as a woman ; he rejoiced with those who rejoiced, and wept with those who wept ; his face was a benediction. Truly, the presence of God was with him,— not as a servant of God, but as a child of God."

Rev. Charles G. Ames said : —

" A beautiful thing has happened. When God's light shines in a man's mind, it makes him wise. When God's love enters the man's heart, it makes him good. When the gift of expression is added, it makes the man a leader and a prophet. Then through his life and through his lips God is revealed. Such a life we have seen, to such lips we have listened. The voice that has fallen into silence was a voice of faith, hope, and love, bringing us a message from the heavens.

" We can hardly be mourners, for this occasion is more like a coronation than a funeral. We can hardly speak of loss, so thankful are we for the gift of such

a life and such service. We have *had* him, we have
had all he could give, his long, full, well-rounded term,
—a noble day's work.

> "'Twelve long, sunny hours, bright to the edge of darkness,
> Then the short repose of twilight and a crown of stars.'

"He was a great believer, and that made him a great
worker, like that early missionary whose motto was,
'Expect great things from God : attempt great things
for God.'

"He lived in an eventful period, a period of much
transition in religious thought, and shared the changes,
yet held fast his trust and his consecrated purpose.
'It is not an enlightened age,' said Lessing, 'but it is
an age becoming enlightened.' Our ascended brother
had served his generation by welcoming the growing
light, and by giving it to mankind. And the beauty of
it all is that he was as good as his word. He taught
with his persuasive lips the truth which had first been
made the law of his own life. He preached righteousness, not as a theory only, but a vital principle, the
very kingdom of God set up in the soul of man.

"No, I will not speak of *loss*, but of richest *gain*,
now and forever secure. In closing a letter, he once
wrote, 'I am fraternally and eternally yours.' Yes,
he is eternally ours. Say this for your comfort : 'He
is eternally ours.' And we who were his fellow-
workers, and all who have shared his inspiring service,
will join with you in saying from tender, grateful
hearts, 'He is eternally ours.'"

The congregation then sang "My God, I thank
thee," this hymn being also a favorite.

Dr. Peabody was the next to add a word of appreciation and remembrance, saying: " I knew him as a student,— perhaps earlier than any one present,— when he was preaching for a year in Dover, N.H, and I was settled in Portsmouth ; and I noticed even then his fervor. No man loved souls more than he, and he won souls. He loved humanity under any form. He spent his life serving and imitating his divine Master, going about doing good.

" His course of lectures to the students at Meadville on the ' Work of the Ministry ' was one of the most important services of his life. I should be unwilling for any young man to enter the ministry without first mastering the spirit of these lectures."

Dr. Peabody closed the services with a brief prayer.

The assembled friends looked once more upon the face so loved and venerated in life, so beautiful in death, and the body was carried to the family lot in Milton Cemetery, where, after a ringing word from Dr. Hale and a hand-clasp from Mr. Ames to the nearest friends, bidding them look " not into the open grave, but into the open heavens," it was laid to rest.

He expressed the wish that his only epitaph might be, " A minister who loved his work."

APPENDIX.

TRIBUTES.

EXTRACTS FROM SERMONS BY REV. H. H. BARBER AND REV. GEORGE L. CHANEY.— PORTRAIT.— MR. TILDEN AS PREACHER BY DR. A. A. LIVERMORE.

WE append a few of the many tributes which were paid to the memory of the risen one.

The *Christian Register* of Oct. 9, 1890, contained the following notice : —

A CROWN OF GLORY.

" The hoary head is a crown of glory if it be found in the way of righteousness." What a crown of glory it was on the head of William P. Tilden ! To one who saw him rise in the pulpit it seemed as if he had just come out of the transfiguring cloud, and that some of the white mist hung about his radiant face ; for his face shone as did that of Moses when he came down from the mount.

There was no William among the twelve apostles ; but William P. Tilden was a man whom Jesus would have chosen if he had met him by the seaside. Indeed, the story of his life and entrance in the ministry has a New Testament, Galilean picturesqueness. It was the story of a young man born on the Massachusetts coast, where he could hear the roar of the sea. He was the son of a ship-carpenter, and there was no pulpit for him in his early vision. His book education was wrought in the district school ; but there was another education which he was wont to call his academical course. It was such an education as Peter got on the lake of Galilee, or such an education as he would have got in the nineteenth century if he had joined a mackerel fleet, like young Tilden at the age of thirteen. "Many a boy," he said, "goes to Exeter to prepare for Cambridge with less pride and joy, I have no doubt, than I started off on my grand expedition, dressed in my fisherman's suit, every article of which, from my red flannel shirt to my pea-jacket and tarpaulin, was made by my precious mother's own hands.

"For six or seven consecutive summers I continued in this academy, learning some things — as is the case, I suppose, in other seminaries — which had better be forgotten, but many other things of a highly useful nature, not taught in other institutions of learning. I really think I was a good fisherman; for the summer I was sixteen I was 'high line,' as it is called, beating even the skipper, packing one hundred and thirty-four barrels, I think it was, caught by my own hands."

"About this time I began with my father in the ship-yard, still fishing during the summer months while I was learning my trade. I wish I had time to tell you a little about this part of my education. The daily recitations in this my university course needed no offset or balance of foot-ball, base-ball, boat-race, or other gymnastics. We took all that the natural way. Our broad axes and mauls were our dumb-bells, whip-saws and cross-cuts our vaulting bars, and deck beams borne up the creaking stage on our shoulders were our patent lifts. We worked from sun to sun in those days, often having a steaming forehood to bend after sunset to use up the summer twilight. But you 'literary fellers,' whose education has been so sadly neglected in these directions, probably don't know what a forehood means. And, even if I should tell you it is a plank to be bent round the bow, set home, buckled to, reined in, wedged hard down, clamped to the timbers, butted and spiked, ready for boring and treenailing, I doubt even then if I should give you a perfectly clear idea, so difficult it is for scholars trained in different schools to understand each other's terms."

Such was the apostolic school in which he was reared. Nor was the Jesus call wanting. It came to him when he was twenty-three years of age, through the faithful preaching of Rev. Caleb Stetson, who ministered in the old parish church of Medford. " My soul was awake now, hungry for the bread of heaven ; and I found it. It seemed to me I had never heard such preaching before. And I think I never had. He was in his prime. And as he unfolded, Sunday after Sunday, the great central principles of the Unitarian faith,— the fatherhood of God, the brotherhood of man, sin its own sorrow, goodness its own reward,— it seemed like a revelation from heaven, as if I had never heard them before. I saw them from a new standpoint. They fed my hungry soul. They gave me back the heavenly Father of my childhood, transfigured and glorified. Oh, how those truths sunned and warmed and quickened my soul ! They arched a new heaven over me, and put a new earth beneath my feet."

Like Paul, he was not disobedient to the heavenly vision. The call came to him with an authority which could not be resisted. His lack of advantage stood in his way. At twenty-five he had to turn back to his simple school studies, and fit himself for the duties of the ministry in a denomination with a high and exacting standard of culture. He tells us how he struggled with Latin and with Greek, how he chalked the Greek letters on a beam over his work-bench, and how he struggled in translating Virgil, to the merriment of his teacher. But at last he concluded to give up a scholastic course. He came under the influence of that noble man, Rev. Samuel J. May, of whom we may say, as Garfield said of Mark Hopkins, that to know him was a liberal education. He guided him into the precincts of the ministry, and he never had occasion to regret the kindly, helpful counsel he gave to the young ship-carpenter.

There are few lives which furnish a stronger contrast to the ordinary traditions of preparation for a Unitarian minister than the life of Mr. Tilden. His preparation was not of books, but of men. His education was wrought in the school of life, and it was there that his ministry was to be exercised. In the course of time the ship-carpenter completely disappeared in the minister; and few of those who heard Mr. Tilden in later years could imagine the disadvantages under which he labored in entering the ministry, at the age of twenty-five, with so slight a literary preparation.

As in the case of the early disciples of Jesus, Mr. Tilden's career showed that the scholastic door is not the only door to the Christian ministry. Unitarianism would have lost not a little, and the Christian ministry still more, if it had not ignored tradition and opened the way to one whom God had called. Many of those who most enjoyed his preaching were men who had received every advantage of a college training. It was a part of the triumph of his life, after preaching in various parishes in New England, to come to Boston and minister there for many years. It was a ministry rich, devoted, benedictory. It was not confined to the pulpit : it radiated in the home ; it was a constant influence in the community. Mr. Tilden preached not only by the power of his words, but by the power of his life. He was of a refined, poetic temperament, a natural idealist ; and if, instead of working at the ship-carpenter's bench, he had passed through college halls, no man would better have appreciated the spirit of Greek literature or life than would he. Some of his hymns written for special occasions reveal his clear poetic vision. He early felt the force of the Transcendental movement. He never lost the glow of his early joy in God or the ardor of his faith in the brotherhood of man. These great truths which inspired him at the first continued to inspire him to the last. They were the essential truths of his gospel.

His life was long and beautiful. He worked almost to the last. It was his delightful mission in later years, after giving up his Boston church, to go out and reanimate feeble societies in other cities.

His last important public work was the course of lectures he delivered at the Meadville Theological School, which were noticed at length in these columns. This book is a beautiful memorial of his own rich and fruitful ministry. His hoary head was a crown of glory, and he did not wait to enter another life to wear a crown of righteousness woven from his own noble character.

From *Unity :* —

Father Tilden — blessed be his memory! — will go in and out among his brother ministers no more. On the morning of

October 3 he breathed his last at his home in Milton, near Boston. From the ship-yard where he toiled as a carpenter, he won his way as one of the sweet poets and gentle prophets of the Unitarian fellowship, growing to the last, fraternal and open as was his spirit. Beautiful was his life, beautiful was the memory of the same. All who ever knew him will find it a little easier to live in the spirit for having touched his genial nature and basked in the sunshine of his countenance.

The *Unitarian Review* had the following : —

Some dim association recurring in connection with the recent illness and death of our beloved brother Tilden led us to turn to the files of an old correspondence, and we came upon the letter from which the following extract is taken. The letter was written during a visit to Samuel Joseph May at Syracuse, N.Y.,— about the time that we had heard, regarding Mr. Tilden, of the very unconventional and bold act of inviting out of the audience into his pulpit one of the people known as "Abolitionists" under exactly the feeling expressed in the words, "I have need to be baptized of thee, and comest thou to me?" The passage in the letter reads as follows : —

"Mr. May gave me a very interesting account of Mr. Tilden, of Concord, N.H. It seems that the New Year's Sermon he sent me was prophetic, and that he is going to leave the place. About a third of the people there resist his independence of speech, though he is a man of real genius, and has the most charming spirit and character in the world, and though these same persons say he is altogether the best Christian in the place. He has been so much with the Abolitionists that some persons are prejudiced against him. But (like Mr. May) he has such beauty of temper and breadth of view and so sweet a moral earnestness that he stands quite apart from the ferocious and uncompromising technical people.*

"He was a ship-carpenter in Scituate, had been in Medford, and joined Mr. Stetson's church; and Mr. May was first inter-

*That is, apparently, those who wore that name like a badge.— ED.

ested in him by finding that he was the writer of some very beautiful lines of welcome, when he preached his first sermon in Scituate. He was an admirable teacher; and, after coming to know
him more thoroughly, Mr. May said to him, 'I do not like to
speak slightingly of any man's calling or occupation, but I am
sorry to see you where you are. You ought to be a teacher of
men. Why will you not devote yourself to it, and preach?' At
this he was much affected, and confessed that it had been a secret
and haunting desire with him, which he never dared once to
speak of. But Mr. May encouraged him to cherish it, and come
to him for instruction and help. So for three or four years, while
working six hours a day at his trade, he went on reading, studying, and conversing. Being a man of great humor and fun withal,
their conversations took a cheerful and jovial turn; and many a
time Mrs. May would put her head into the study to inquire what
particular point of theology was the origin of that last burst!

"At length Mr. May's place was unexpectedly left vacant
while he went over to help Mr. Sewall, and he called on Mr.
Tilden to fill it for him. He was startled, and begged off; but
Mr. May had been insidiously preparing his mind by leading him
to assert first very strongly the wrong and harm of societies depending wholly on the minister, and the duty of other men to do
just such things: so he went. Mrs. May was very distrustful and
uneasy, not having half her husband's cheerful confidence in him;
but she was altogether charmed and delighted, first with the modest and beautiful apology with which he began, and then with the
exceeding fervor and beauty of his service. [The sermon was
one of Dr. N. Parker's or Channing's.] And soon after, when he
consented to preach his own sermons, his reputation spread at
once all over the country, and it was not long before he was regu-
larly employed to preach. Isn't that a beautiful way for a man's
vocation to come to him?"

All the qualities which this letter describes will be recognized
as highly characteristic of the temper of the man, and of the long
ministry, covering just fifty years, which has made him affectionately known to so wide a public. He filled his place always with
a certain modesty and reticence which have kept him, in a degree,
in the shade compared with some more shining reputations.

And, indeed, there was no trait in him more marked than the humility of spirit, touched with a kindly and cheery temper, that made him eager always to see and own the best there was in other men, whom he was alike ready to honor as his teachers and to love as his brethren. Those lives are very few in which through so long a record there is so little to recall not in entire harmony with the first and best impression.

The *Unitarian* printed in full the address "From Ship-yard to Pulpit," prefacing it with these words : —

The following is one of the most charming autobiographical sketches we have ever seen. As it deals with the life of one greatly beloved throughout our Unitarian ranks and far beyond, and one whose recent death touches all hearts with unusually tender sorrow, we are sure we shall do our readers a favor by reprinting it. It was given as an address by Mr. Tilden at a reception tendered to him by the New South Free Church, Boston, on his seventieth birthday, May 9, 1881. The address deals mainly with the earlier part of Mr. Tilden's life. It is a story particularly inspiring to the young,— quite as inspiring as anything in the early life of Franklin or Lincoln or Channing or Theodore Parker. And the story could not be more delightfully told.

The Boston *Post* said : —

Mr. Tilden was beloved by his parishioners for his kindly ways, and his thoughtful care of their welfare; and the good that he accomplished was of no small order. A forcible and interesting speaker, he impressed all his hearers by a remarkable combination of vigor of thought with simple colloquial and yet impressive style of expression. Whatever he said came from the heart, and that feeling won the belief as well as the attention of the listener. . . . It has always seemed somewhat remarkable that, having pursued his studies while at the mechanic's bench, and never having had the advantages of a liberal education, he should have ministered so acceptably to a congregation accustomed to accomplished scholars in the pulpit. At the church -on Church Green, Summer Street, he was the successor of Orville Dewey, one of the lights of the Unitarian denomination, who was himself the successor of Alexander Young, F. W. P. Greenwood, Samuel Cooper Thacher, President John T. Kirkland, and Oliver Everett; and to have ended the succession of able preachers in that church was of itself no small distinction.

The Boston *Transcript* says,—

Possibly no other Boston clergyman has had more close, inti- mate, and appreciative friends than fell to the lot of this recently deceased pastor.

At a meeting of the Boston Association of Congre- gational Ministers held Nov. 10, 1890, the following record was unanimously adopted and ordered to be placed upon the records, and a copy sent to the family of the late Rev. W. P. Tilden: —

The Boston Association of Congregational Ministers, with a deep sense of the loss it has sustained in the death of the Rev. William Phillips Tilden, for a quarter of a century one of its honored and beloved members, desires to put upon its records an expression of its affectionate appreciation of one whom to know was to love, who proved by his life the power of his faith, who illustrated the worth of character, and has left behind him that memory of the just which is blessed.

A minister of Christ because of the necessity laid upon him to preach the gospel, he loved and magnified his office. Impressive and reverential in manner, his word was with power. He never sought notoriety by sensational effects, nor by levity "to woo a smile when he should win a soul." It could never be said of him that

"The hungry sheep looked up
And were not fed."

He did not bring great truths down to the popular level, but he led his hearers' thought to the highest themes, by his own faith strengthened theirs, and lifted them from what is low to what is ennobling.

He preached a living faith. He moved in no settled grooves ; he laid up in and brought forth from his treasury things new and old ; and, while his locks were white with age, his heart retained the freshness of youth, and his mind was ever open to whatever of new truth it might please God to reveal. Therefore, his preaching was with power and unction from above.

His education and training made him familiar with men, and gave him a knowledge of human nature that adapted him to touch the inmost springs of the human heart.

Sensible of his loss in not having acquired a knowledge of books in early life, he labored zealously to supply his deficiencies in that regard, read carefully, and familiarized himself with the best of the best literature, and so imbued himself with the fruits of the best scholarship that, while the common people heard him gladly, the learned and the teachers none the less willingly and profitably sat at his feet and listened to his words.

For fourscore years he walked with God, and to many souls was a ministering spirit, for he not only

" Allured to brighter worlds, but led the way."

In the many parishes where he was called to minister his memory will be tenderly cherished. Those upon whose heads his hands have laid the waters of baptism, those who have sealed before him the vows which have brought to them life's happiest companionships, those who have tasted his sympathy in the hours of their most crushing bereavements, know that he was indeed a son of consolation, and all those who were by him consecrated to the work of the ministry will ever associate him with the most sacred recollection of their lives.

He was a man of strong convictions, and could be a son of thunder for truth and righteousness. He could fearlessly rebuke sin in high places. He was an ardent defender of whatever cause he espoused. He was a zealous defender of the doctrines he believed. But so honest and sincere was he that even those who differed from him respected him, and, though his frankness often created opponents, it never lost him friends.

He possessed great friendliness of manner and cheerfulness of disposition. The sunshine of his smile diffused light and happiness. He loved men as God's children. He was one of those

> " Who God doth late and early pray
> More of his grace than gifts to lend,
> And walked with man from day to day
> As with a father and a friend."

It was no wonder, then, that in death his face shone, as if he had talked with God, and had already received a revelation of things unspeakable.

To his sorrowing family we tender our sincere sympathy in their bereavement. The end of the upright man has been peace. They have the comfort and assurance of faith that their loss is his gain. While we sorrow with them that we are no more to see his face, we rejoice that Unitarianism in Boston has had so noble a representation, the Christian ministry so faithful a member, and we ourselves so loving a friend.

We shall treasure his memory, and find in it an incentive to greater fidelity to our own trust, an encouragement to renewed endeavor, a rebuke to our faint-heartedness, a condemnation of our self-seeking. Being dead, he shall yet speak to us of love and truth, of God and duty, of Christ and faithfulness.

S. H. WINKLEY, *Moderator.*

BROOKE HERFORD, *Scribe.*

Rev. Dr. G. W. Briggs, of Cambridge, said : —

A little while since a true preacher was carried to his grave,— a man whose face was a benediction, whose words were inspiration. When I stood in the pulpit at Milton and looked down upon him, this text kept coming to my mind, " The beauty of holiness." I bid farewell to a life-long friend and brother, whose tongue will speak no more with its sweet persuasiveness, whose pen will no longer write hymns of bright and triumphant faith. But, although dead, he is speaking still with a deathless voice in the hearts that have been gladdened by his presence and inspired by his ministry.

Dr. H. A. Miles, of Hingham, writes : —

I count it among my precious blessings that I have known and appreciated Mr. Tilden. I shall never forget how our acquaintance began. It was during his brief ministry in Concord, N.H. I found on his study table all the then recent books on *every* sub ject at that time interesting the public mind; and I remember saying to myself, This man will inquire widely, and will give the vigor of his nature to the cause which seems to him to be good. Dear man, how he fulfilled that prophecy, and rounded his life accordingly !

He had a merit as a preacher which distinguished him among our ministers who deal so much in ethical, dogmatic, and logical sermons, through the influences of our training, which we can no more escape than we can escape our atmosphere. He addressed the affections, with no extravagance and cant, but with winning directness and manly earnestness. How welcome he was in all the pulpits ! and the loving aureole which enveloped his person drew strangers to him out of the pulpit. I was once in a railway train with him, but he occupied a seat in the forward end, and I in the rear of the car. I observed how every passenger was looking at him, and those leaving or entering the train fixed their eyes on him. Evidently, they did not know him personally, but they were attracted by a genial humanity conspicuous at a glance.

Spared the infirmities of old age, he lived long enough to gather to himself the affections of thousands.

From Horatio Stebbins, D.D., of San Francisco : —

After all the earthly scene is closed, it is grateful to look back, as a traveller, weary a little with the day, stops to look at the glory of the setting sun. What an inheritance do we all succeed to

who outlive such a one as Mr. Tilden! We all feel that the
strength of the world is more solid, and the heavens more pure,
for such a one's having lived. He always seemed to me one of
the happiest men, though he bore the sorrows and wrongs of all.
He had such reliance on truth, virtue, and God that his joy to be
full needed only the sympathies of his fellow-men. Though I
have known him these many years, but not intimately, I have es-
teemed it a great privilege to see him as I have in the two
summers in which I have visited Milton. His fine spiritual insight, his religious sensibility, the ease and strength of his moral
sense impressed me, and I thought that he had about as much
character as any man I ever saw. I know of nothing finer for
any human creature than to leave such an impression on those
who come after him.

Extract from a sermon by Rev. W. I. Lawrance : —

One such, so dear to many of us, and so recently translated
that he seems even more than before a constant presence among
us, is doubtless in all your minds.

Nature did much for that face to make it beautiful, but the love
of God did more, and made it beam with a celestial light which
not even death could dim. Nature did much for the mind and
character, giving natural delicacy, courtesy, affection, for all; but
the grace of God did more, and made every act, every word,
every influence, full of heavenly beauty. No idle words seemed
fitting, no coarse or critical words possible, in his presence.
Sitting, talking with him, the thoughts were drawn upward, and
only the higher things seemed worth speaking of.

From Mrs. D. C. Nash, of Wellesley Hills, Mass. : —

My first acquaintance with dear Mr. Tilden was when I was a
child and went to the public school in South Scituate, thence to
his private school for young ladies. He won the hearts of all his
pupils, manifesting the same Christian spirit then as always
through his whole life.

From Mrs. M. J. Thomas, of Newton, formerly of Concord, N.H. : —

I talked with him of my many cares and burdens. It was selfishness on my part, for he was such a burden-bearer for every one in trouble that, when it got too heavy to bear alone, I was always sure of being comforted by his strong and helpful and loving counsel.

Mr. John Capen, of Boston, wrote : —

I gratefully recall his ready compliance with my request that he should furnish a hymn for the Unitarian Festival. The first was so fine and so cheerfully given that I had the hardihood to — I won't say trouble him — but to apply to him several times afterwards, and always with success.

All of these hymns I keep, and prize as among the best ever furnished for that Festival.

Rev. N. S. Hoagland, of Olympia, Wash., formerly a Meadville student, writes : —

I suppose many theological students really feel less ardor for the ministry during the third year than they do during the first. They have had so much to do with books and so little to do with people that their affections and interests are apt to be for books rather than for people : hence the ministry loses for them her first charms. Mr. Tilden came into my school life at an opportune moment. He renewed my first love. Whether in the pulpit or the lecture-room, he revealed the power and grace of the minister's calling. He himself was an object lesson of what he taught. He won us not so much to himself as to a trustful, loving, consecrated service of humanity.

At a memorial service held in Norton a paper was read by Mrs. E. T. Witherell. She referred to the last sermon he gave in that church on "Beautiful Gates." She says : —

We could all assent to the beautiful in passing in at the gates of childhood, youth, and manhood: but, when one said to him after the service, "I cannot call old age and death beautiful gates," he replied: "Well, when you are as old as I am, you will see it. You haven't got there yet: that is all."

April 21, 1891, was to have been a happy day for us; for on that day Mr. Tilden, had he lived, would have celebrated the fiftieth anniversary of his ordination.

A letter of June 30 says: "I am counting fondly upon being with you, if I am able. At my age all is uncertain; but, if health permits, it would be a great joy to me to keep the anniversary of my ordination with the dear old flock of my first love."

Expressions of sorrow for his death, thankfulness for his life, and of sympathy for his family, were received from Norton, Walpole, Brighton, Atlanta, Wilmington, and Plainfield societies. The latter voted to place a tablet to his memory in the wall of their new church and hang his portrait in the room of their Bible class.

At the memorial service held in Plainfield the pastor, Rev. Hobart Clark, said : —

Whatever creed he might have held, with whatever Christian fellowship he might have worshipped, men who had once known him would say without a doubt, "He has eternal life." And why? Because they have seen it in his face and heard it in his voice. Not to-day only would men say this, as his outworn body is borne to its last resting-place by tender hands to mingle with the dust from whence it came, while he himself has sought a better habitation. They would have said so at any time within these many years. Meeting him upon the street, taking him by the hand, looking into his untroubled eyes, and hearing him speak with equal interest and equal confidence of things earthly and things heavenly, they would have said, they have said: Here is a man who already has eternal life. Here is one who knows God and who lives with him from day to day. Here is one who is already of Christ's fellowship, and who has, not a different life from other men, but more life than ordinary men possess, even though his pulse beat more feebly and his step be slow with the weight of many years. Here is a man whose life is given freely to all mankind, and yet hidden with Christ in God. The ordinary questions regarding what is sometimes called Christian salvation seem to mean very little in the presence of such a man as Mr. Tilden ; and those other questions concerning immortality are still more out of place. Long ago his life had burst the boundaries of space and time. It retained its mortality,— it was proud and glad to do so,— but was already taking on its immortality. He knew no more about the future than other men, but he knew God and was already living in eternity.

Extracts from a sermon preached at Meadville, Pa., Oct. 12, 1890, by Rev. H. H. Barber : —

" He was a good man, and full of the Holy Ghost and of faith." ACTS xi. 24.

The remembrance of a good man's life is a perpetual lesson of virtue, and the influence of a genial and consecrated spirit a perennial cheer and benediction. There is no instruction in faith and morals like the instruction of holy character, and no testimony to the reality of religion like a man in whom it visibly lives and rules. The good man is a " living epistle " of the Spirit, sealed and sent by God for witness and counsel to all who know him. He is an embodied gospel, to charm and cheer us on to new conviction of the beauty and the possibility of the righteous life. Some portion of the Divine Word is made flesh in him anew, for us to behold there the glory of God full of grace and truth.

We have the completed lesson of such a life to study and be grateful for to-day. A week ago news came that our friend Rev. William P. Tilden, after a long summer's illness, had passed out of pain into peace.

To most of you he had been known but a few years; but here and in your homes, as a minister and friend, you felt his rare quality and the cheer and lift of his genial and devout spirit. I have known him near thirty years, since his hand was laid on my head in the ordination prayer. Those who know his history remember that he bore his witness for his convictions and met his rebuffs and hardships for it, none more loyally, as none more uncomplainingly and sweetly. He became a minister near the spring-tide of that zeal for moral and social reforms in which Channing led. It was a good school for courage in the young prophet, as also for wisdom and endurance; and Mr. Tilden was one of those who learned all these lessons well, and witnessed a good confession in loyalty of utterance, as also in accepting the rebukes and penalties of his loyalty. It is well to remember that the qualities that were so pleasing, and the address that had such a fine charm in its open frankness, were not formed in the atmosphere of mere conformity, or the effort to please, but by commending itself first to every man's conscience in the sight of God. But it was his wish to serve; and this desire made him thoughtful and painstaking in his work and in all his intercourse, and developed in him that readiness of sympathy and frankness of address which gave him so much power. He cared for the welfare of men, and knew how largely it lay in the friendly aspect, the kindly word, the encouraging tone.

Beginning as a fisherman and carpenter, he never came to take the scholar's view chiefly or use mainly the scholar's methods. The necessity that made him a preacher without much regular preparation was largely overcome by the freshness and alertness of his mind, which seized the vital points of knowledge, and went straight for the substance of truth. He made up for the early lack of training by a long process of self-training, which lasted his whole life long. He kept his mind young and his zeal for knowledge fresh, and few men came to be more intelligent as to current thought and the great problems of life than he.

He believed that the minister should have spiritual experience of that he was set to teach; or, rather, he sought to be a religious teacher because he had experience of the worth and the reality of the religious life. And, then, he tried to grow in spiritual truth, that he might have more to give. And so power grew with seeking.

He did not care much for analysis in the things of the spirit. Or, if he analyzed, he preferred the touchstone of moral feeling to the measuring-rod of the logical understanding. Religious speculation had his sympathy and even admiration; but he warmed its chilliest and brightened its cloudiest regions with the sun of his devout imagination. He believed in the future of religion and the future of the world, and held all to be secure in the hands of God. He was a son of consolation, a guide to better faith and cheer, a ray of the divine sunshine wherever he went.

"God buries his workman, but carries on his work." When Mr. Tilden was seventy years old, a venerable brother wished for him that his age might be like the launching of one of the ships he had helped to build. And it was so. Almost to the last he was permitted to rejoice and to help others rejoice in the work he loved. No more welcome and helpful service could have been rendered than that with which he repeatedly blessed our church and school here. "Sealed Orders" he called the last lecture he gave us, to emphasize the Divine leading and unfolding that come in the minister's work and life. When his sealed orders came, his life passed quietly down the ways of pain and peace, and out into the unknown waters, to meet his Pilot face to face.

His life has been successful, even as the world counts success, in the warm affection and growing honor and appreciation of men. And that has been because it has also been a success in the truer and everlasting sense of pure aspiration, hearty helpfulness, growing insight of truth, enlarging trust. So, while it kept its early loyalty, it grew, as was fit, more and more into the sunshine.

Extracts from a sermon preached in Atlanta, Ga., by Rev. George L. Chaney, October, 1890 : —

The Christian minister whose recent death invites us this morning to thankful recollection of his life, if not the carpenter's son, was himself, at first, a carpenter. The Spirit found him where it had found his Master, in a carpenter's shop. There, in the wholesome nurture of hand industry, he was hewing out the sturdy frame which was to stand so well the attack and shock of Time. There,

in the society of workingmen, he was learning their way of thinking, as well as their handiwork, and laying the foundation for that
respect for labor and laboring men which made him through
life an intelligent and warm advocate of their just claims upon the
fruits of their labor.

I like to picture him as he must have looked then, if his youth
were any promise of his beautiful, strong manhood — a russet-
haired hewer of wood, with clear, blue-gray eyes, and strong, incisive nose and chin, a mouth with purpose in its close, and with
sweet persuation in its loosened lines when speech or laughter set
it free. A hand and arm that could drive a wedge or shield and
pet a kitten, so strong so tender. A sort of Adam Bede in his
resolute, stanch manhood, his rage at all villany, his love of
beauty, and reverence for good.

And this is the man, hammering and chopping at his trade,
whom a wiser than man chose and called to be a minister of life
and spirit to his age. I do not mean that any audible voice out of
heaven summoned him or any unusual apparition ordained him.
He was called by his own spirit brooding over the sign of spirit
in the amazing world into which he had been born. Among the
causes which made this calling articulate and sensible to the ear
was that of Rev. Samuel J. May.

If spirits out of the body are suffered to attend and second the
labors of kindred spirits on earth, I can believe that something of
the gracious power and sweetness of Tilden was due to the continuing ministry of May.

Dear hearts! true souls! emancipated themselves because devoted to the emancipation of all who were bound by sin, by preju-
dice, by ignorance or misfortune. How like a double star they
shine now in their heavenly Father's home! ...

A manly sturdiness upheld all the gracious sweetness of his
customary speech, as solid masonry upholds the vine that runs
over it. He lived so near the heart of Truth that I think he
sometimes wearied of the slow, painstaking groping after Truth
with which religious manuals and commentaries are filled. I
doubt if his mind ever knew the processes which make the first
principles of religion problematic. He enjoyed God too much
ever to doubt him. Scepticism makes no headway when the

heart-way has been with God. So this child of the Father who is in heaven lived among us full of grace and truth. . . .

I know, from personal observation, how beneficent his ministry in the New South Free Church was. He only gave it up when the burden of years made him unequal to the work. Then, with that readiness to go wherever he was most needed, and to do whatever he could do best, which distinguished his whole life-work, he entered upon a ministry at large which extended from Meadville in the West to Brighton in the East, and from Atlanta in the South to Wilmington and Plainfield in the Middle States.

No longer a candidate for settlement in any parish, he never assumed the temporary charge of a church that did not want him to stay with them. Old churches usually have a weakness for young men, but the older parishes of Meadville and Brighton vied with young Wilmington and Plainfield for this aged minister. There was nothing strange in it, for he was young in heart, a man-child. That old rendering of that older Hebrew name describes him. All ages found in him their delightful companion. With the sober he could show himself sober, and with the gay he could be gay. His laugh was as whole-hearted as his sympathy. It had all the freedom and abandonment of childhood, yoked with manly good sense. It cleared the air into which it volleyed like a joyous burst of thunder. If the sun could laugh, I think it would laugh like that. Reverberating sunshine only could describe it. It was the hilarity of the soul. Such laughter as that dispels disease, banishes sorrow, uplifts depression, rebukes melancholy, delights friends, and reconciles enemies. It is the oil of gladness.

Again and again, when he was blessing us with his benignant word and look, I have wished that he might have his physical youth restored to him,— his soul was always young,— and that he might take us for his colleague in the surely successful work of reconciliation and good will to which he seemed called by nature and consecrated by God. I wonder if in his youth he could have been as winning and converting as he was in ripe old age. I suspect that, like the earlier John, he was a son of thunder in the days when indignation at earth's wrongs prompts the cry, "Shall we command fire to come down from heaven and consume them?" There are flashes of moral electricity, soul lightning, in the record of his earlier pastorates which show that Love had her chariot of wrath as well as her preparation of the gospel of peace. This man was no preacher of smooth things, when the heart of his people needed the cruel kindness of the surgeon's knife. But he dipped his whip of small cords into oil and wine, and offered healing even when he wounded.

He was a singer as well as a prophet in Israel. His hymns had singular concinnity with the times for which he wrote them. They chimed. He poured himself, as it were, so melting was his sympathy, into the mould of the tune and, lo! the musical poem. Occasions of church reunion especially awoke his Muse. He was never more happy in heart or pen than when he was giving expression to brotherly love. He was equally liberal in heart and mind. Nature made him large-hearted: culture made him large-minded. And by culture I do not mean the greenhouse variety. An oak in a conservatory were not more out of place than he would have been among the exotics of merely fashionable society. Always a gracious and dignified presence wherever he might be, he would have soared above the roof of any little establishment that sought to confine him, even as I have seen in the valley of the Yosemite a tree whose foot was in the centre of the house, while its head, two hundred feet aloft, was conversing with the Cloudy Rest and El Capitan.

He died untitled by the theologian's consummate degree; but few were better entitled to it, if Doctor of Divinity means, as it should, an able teacher of divine things. He knew God. The theologians only know about him. I find in him a first-hand dealing with the Spirit. He witnesses the things whereof he was a witness. He dignified all he touched. When he had said grace, the baker's loaf became "bread which cometh down from heaven." His benediction at the close of the service was as the good wine kept till the last. Worshippers who worshipped with him in the Church of our Father will remember how, on Easter Sunday, "in the beauty of the lilies," his prophecy of immortality floated to them across the sea of doubts and sorrows on which their faith goes voyaging in this half-lighted world. Nor will they ever root from their memories the expressions of his face, the fathomless intonations of his voice, the cheer and pleasantness of his society, the delightful encouragement of his listening silence, and the cordial of his speech. He had the pastor's every gift and calling. Whatever his theme, the effect was religion; and the homes he visited felt as if the church had come to them and laid its hand in blessing on them.

Crayon portraits of Mr. Tilden had been hung in three of the churches where he had ministered for a longer or shorter time.

On the Sunday he preached his farewell sermon at the New South Free Church, Dec. 30, 1883, the society placed upon its walls his portrait, the work of Mr. F. E. Wright.

In 1886 Alfred Huidekoper, Esq., of Meadville, Pa., presented to the Independent Congregational Church of that town a crayon by a local artist.

Early in the winter of 1891 Mrs. C. L. Heywood executed for the Plainfield society another crayon, to be hung in the new church soon to be erected.

It was the earnest wish of many old friends and parishioners that his portrait in oil might be placed in the building of the American Unitarian Association, 25 Beacon Street, Boston. A movement for this object was made under the direction of Mrs. A. L. Mayberry and Mr. H. C. Whitcomb, and Mr. E. H. Billings was the artist chosen. The large number of people who wished to share in this testimony of love and appreciation did so with the understanding that any sum in excess of what was needed for the portrait should be given to the endowment fund of the Meadville Theological School, and the committee were enabled to make a handsome contribution to that institution in which Mr. Tilden was so much interested.

On the 29th of April, 1891, the formal presentation took place in Channing Hall, which was filled with loving friends. Dr. A. P. Peabody opened the service with prayer, and paid a tender and eloquent tribute to the early friend, the worker in every good cause, the Christian minister.

We subjoin the following report from the Boston *Transcript*, though it very inadequately represents the beauty of the service and the spirit of the occasion:—

Dr. Peabody said: "Mr. Tilden was identified with the anti-slavery movement and other great reforms, for he felt that to be a Christian was to take to his heart everything that Jesus would take to his heart. Strength and beauty were the great traits of his character. He combined the strength of the Christian with the beauty of holiness which might have belonged to a contented life, but was never marred by the severe work which was his work at a time when the public, to their shame, did not recognize the claims of humanity which he recognized from the very first. But he never rebuked sin with a spirit that did not manifest a love for the sinner as well as for those sinned against. As for his private life and character, all of you who knew him know how kind and sweet and domestic it was. We may well be thankful that his life was prolonged as it was. In behalf of the committee who have had the matter in charge, and who have found their work earnestly seconded by the artist, I present to the Unitarian Association the beautiful portrait before you. I present it not as to a Unitarian Association, but as to a portion of the one universal Church; for his was a name we do not want to confine within the limits of a denomination. He was one of the kind of men that Christ makes,— one of the men who would recognize as a Christian every Christ-like man and woman, one who, when needing a definition of a Christian, only inquired if a man was a follower of Christ."

Rev. Grindall Reynolds received the portrait on behalf of the Unitarian Association, and said: " It gives us the deepest pleasure on the part of the Association to accept this portrait. Our walls are hung with the portraits of a great number of the saints and heroes of the Christian faith, and yet I question whether the portrait of any man more winning, more useful as a Christian preacher and pastor, can be found on our walls than the portrait we gaze upon to-day. I receive it with all the more pleasure because it is a real portrait, because it gives not only the face and form, but the best expression of the man we respect and the man we love." Mr. Reynolds described the work accomplished by Mr. Tilden, and, continuing, said: "He threw into his power as a preacher the power of a deep conviction and a great heart. I can only say in conclusion that it will be a real joy to every one who comes into this room to see this speaking portrait that reminds us of the sweet, loving, devoted, strong man that our friend was."

The exercises closed with the benediction.

The following notice of Mr. Tilden as a preacher is from the pen of Dr. A. A. Livermore, ex-President of the Meadville Theological School, who says, "To a stranger it might seem too laudatory, but to those who knew and loved him it would appear to fall short of the truth": —

REV. WILLIAM P. TILDEN AS PREACHER.

There are three factors involved in the problem of Preaching: 1. Natural Powers; 2. Education; 3. Religious Faith. In all these respects Mr. Tilden was favored with superior advantages in reality, whatever might be a superficial judgment to the contrary.

He was endowed by nature with a fine constitution; built on a large scale, sound, manly, and finely attuned. His physique was cast in a generous mould. By hard labor as a ship-carpenter, in his youth and early manhood, his frame was well developed, so that he passed a hard working life in the ministry beyond the allotted threescore years and ten. Tall, straight, and stately, with a most benignant countenance, haloed in old age by silver locks, he had a right royal mien and dignified address, which would make him a man of mark in any company.

Nor was his intellectual and moral manhood inferior to his physical endowments. He had a large talent of native good sense, the faculty of seeing and judging of things as they were, and a quick susceptibility to discern the true, the beautiful, and the good,— the heritage of an unspoiled nature. While dignified in bearing, his warm heart brought him in sympathetic relations with others, and he wore no stiff professional garb to break the charm.

It was said of one who was self-taught that he had a very poor teacher, but Mr. Tilden was favored in this respect. He had a good instructor, though not from school or university. He drew from pure fountains within, and the aid he derived from his pastor, Rev. Samuel J. May, was of the happiest kind. He had none of the technical bias of learning to warp the native integrity of his soul.

His bright and genial trust in the Fatherhood of God, and the beliefs flowing from the central sun of theology, made him a cheering preacher. His sympathy and fine tone of brotherly love were something better than eloquence, and captivated all hearts. His liberalism had no savor of indifferentism, nor did it fossilize with age.

He grew in power as he grew in age, and his last days were his best days. He kept his mind ever open to whatever new truth, or old truth with new effulgence, was ready to break forth from God, man, nature, or the Bible. One of his characteristic sermons was, " The Word of God is not bound." Few young men were as young and fresh as he was in his faith, which sprang from his heart like a fountain in the sunlight.

The pulpit was his " joy," if not his throne. He was in his native element when he entered it. He loved to preach, and he brought forth fruit in his old age. He never preached with more interest and power than in his last years in Meadville, Plymouth, Brighton, and Plainfield, where he drew most sympathetic hearers.

His whole service was characteristic. That single, arrowy Scripture phrase that began the service and went straight to the heart, and pitched the note of worship, the brief, tender invocation, the reading of the Scriptures, hymns, prayers, sermon, benediction, constituted one harmonious whole, each part helping the others. It was a beautiful idyl, pure in taste, but strong in appeal and persuasion.

He was, as he said of another, a born minister. His good genius found him out in the ship-yard.

Then his new faith was no capricious feeling or holiday sentiment, but deep as life, close as color to the leaf, vital as blood, a gospel that was indispensable to the recovery of man and society, or, in his favorite phrase, "to the uplifting of humanity to a higher plane of action." Hence he was first and always a reformer, and his pulpit a tribune to try and judge the questions of society and the church,— anti-slavery, temperance, peace, purity, politics, and every religious cause of human welfare. But he advocated his most incisive views with such a bland and lovable spirit that none could justly take umbrage, in this respect following the footsteps of his teacher, Mr. May. He never, as the custom of some is, put a stinging snapper on the whip with which he chastised the sins of the day. He took no offensive airs of *I am holier than thou* in his strong appeals. Though his opponents might hate his principles, they could not, as was said of another, but love the man.

In the volume of lectures on the ministry to the students of Meadville, one of the best we have, Mr. Tilden gathered up the wisdom of his long and devoted service in the pulpit, for the help of his younger brethren. He gave little heed to barren speculations, foreign to his own taste and useless to the needs of the plain people. He took the truth which he had already tested and found to be good, and applied it to the service of his hearers. Many preachers are overstocked with pedantic and undigested learning and given to unproved speculations. It is the old scholastic habit brought down to the present day.

In illustrations he was refined and apposite, and mixed his discourses with touches of a delicate and juicy humor, for he had a poetical imagination.

While Mr. Tilden was open-minded to the unfoldings of new truths or the fresh applications of old ones, he was no iconoclast, but kept the even tenor of historical continuity, and respected the

Christian perspective of the chief commandments. He built on Christ, and made his all-persuasive appeal from that "coigne of vantage." As was said of another of our lately translated brethren, he was better fitted to preach to the righteous than to sinners. He could hardly believe men were as bad as they really are. The atmosphere of his church was cheery, bracing, and hopeful. The common people heard him gladly, as they did his Master. "The bright heavens" was a phrase on his lips not seldom. He was our Saint John to take the eagle flight into the heaven, and proclaim the glories of love.

His last years were rich with the ripe fruit and full harvest of Christian experience and a long and loving walk with God. His sermons were bright sparks struck from the anvil of truth and righteousness. His prayers were "foregleams of immortality." His theology was summed up in God as the heavenly Father, Jesus as our leader, sin its own punishment, goodness its own reward, Christianity the divine instrument, life the school, character the end, and heaven our home.

Peace be to his beautiful memory!

www.ingramcontent.com/pod-product-compliance
Lightning Source LLC
Chambersburg PA
CBHW030617030726
47497CB00006B/1535